HARVEST MOON

A RAVEN AND THE CROW ROMANCE

MICHAEL K FALCIANI

Harvest Moon: A Raven and the Crow Romance
A Tanglewood Press Romance

All rights reserved.
Copyright © 2023 by Michael K. Falciani

No part of this book may be reproduced or transmitted in any form or by any means without the permission in writing from the publisher.
For information contact Tanglewood Press at
tanglewoodromance@gmail.com

For Monica. To blue skies and evergreens, this book is for you.

ACKNOWLEDGMENTS

First, to my publisher Christopher Woods and Tanglewood Press. Thank you for your work and commitment to me and this book. To Scott Tackett at Three Ravens Publishing. Thank you for putting up with me and my numerous texts, messages, and phone calls. I continue to be your padawan, (the unruly kind, but whatever.) To Andy who remains my first and foremost alpha reader and to my wonderful editor Cheyenne who I am sure will go though this page and correct it (as she should!)

BOOKS BY MICHAEL K. FALCIANI

The Raven and the Crow Series:

Dark Storm Rising

The Gray Throne

The Dwarves of Rahm Series:

Omens of War

The Raven and the Crow Romance Series:

Harvest Moon

Anthologies:

It Came from the Trailer Park: Volume I

Misfits of Magic

CHAPTER 1

"here's not much employment to be had here in Caldor," Mayor Tamalin stated, looking suspiciously at the barrel-chested man in front of him. "It's late autumn. Nearly every farm has collected its harvest. Had you come a month ago, well, that'd be a different story. As it stands, there's little work left to be had."

A tall stranger dressed in the brown tunic and pants of a peasant dismounted from his chestnut mare and pulled a half-full waterskin from his saddle bag. "I rode past a field north of here on my way in," he stated, drinking deeply as droplets of sweat beaded at the temple of his handsome face. "It wasn't close to being harvested. I saw someone at a distance working diligently in the cornfields."

The mayor's face soured. "That's the Billerton widow," he said, shaking his head. "Her husband already owed the baron a huge debt . . . and that was before he died. Even if she gets the crop in by snowfall, which she won't, there is no way she will be able to afford your services." The mayor leaned his cherubic face in close, and he spoke in a conspirator's hushed whisper. "Word is, she has a fortnight to pay, else the baron will take back that land . . . *and* the widow along with it."

The stranger grunted, took another drink, and stoppered the flask before putting it away.

With his hazel eyes, Tamalin appraised the barrel-chested man in front of him. "You're lucky to have arrived in one piece," he said. "There's been word of bandits waylaying travelers on the road in from Rathstone."

"I had a bit of a run-in with some a few miles back," the stranger stated, scratching absently at the black goatee growing on top of his olive skin.

"What happened?" the mayor asked, intrigued.

The stranger gave a shrug. "They didn't find what they were looking for."

Tamalin's face creased in a smile. "So, despite owning your own horse, you didn't have any coin with you?" he surmised, looking like a man quite taken with himself.

The stranger raised an eyebrow. "Like I said, I'm looking for work."

"Well, you could try down at the Bad Apple Inn," the mayor suggested, looking up at the tall stranger. "The innkeeper has a soft spot for travelers such as yourself. He often has menial chores you could do in exchange for a meal." The mayor paused, studying the stranger like a horse trader examining a prize stallion. "I could put in a good word for you, Sir . . . what did you say your name was?" Tamalin asked.

"I didn't," the stranger said with a grunt, looking past the mayor toward the two-story building near the center of the village. "Thank you for your time."

With a nod, the tall stranger walked past with his horse trailing behind him.

Tamalin's gaze followed the black-eyed stranger,

watching the way he moved. He may have worn the guise of a simple traveler, but something about him was out of place. As the man sauntered along, the mayor observed that he moved with an easy, almost predatory grace. Tamalin lifted one side of his lips, ready to dismiss the stranger from his mind, when he caught sight of a longsword neatly tucked away inside one of the man's packs.

"Son of a bitch," Tamalin swore under his breath, knowing what he had to do. Walking across the mud of the road to his office, he spoke softly to a young man of no more than seventeen winters dressed in the white robes of a scribe.

"Pen a letter to Baron Turner," the mayor ordered. "Tell him we may have a problem."

"What kind of problem?" the scribe asked.

The mayor paused before ducking into his office. "The kind that carries the weapon of a soldier," he growled.

GHERIC WAS MORE TIRED THAN HE LOOKED. BRUSHING THE dust from his tunic, he tethered his mare to the hitching post outside the inn. Looking up, the dark-eyed warrior saw a white sign with a faded green apple swaying in the wind. The words "Bad Apple" were carved underneath the picture and lined in red.

"Stay here, Kat," he whispered to his chestnut-colored mount, patting her fondly on the nose.

The horse nickered softly in protest.

Gheric gave his mare a sideways grin. "By the gods, I've spoiled you rotten," he teased, slipping his horse a carrot from his saddle bags. "I'll get you fed and watered in a bit."

Leaving his horse happily munching on its treat, he stepped onto the inn's landing and opened the door.

He was greeted by the sound of dozens of patrons laughing, cursing, and speaking to one another. The aroma of stewed meat and stale body odor inundated the common room, reminding him of how long it had been since he had last eaten. At two hours shy of dusk, most of the patrons had come to the Bad Apple for a drink and a hearty supper. Striding forward, he moved to the counter and sat down on a well-worn barstool of white pine.

"What can I get you?" asked the server, a slender woman with iron-gray hair.

"What's good tonight?" Gheric asked affably.

The serving woman gave him a once over. "Vegetable stew with bits of bacon, and whatever's left of this morning's bread . . . if you can pay."

Gheric gave the server a friendly grin. "I was told I could work for food."

The serving girl gave him a flat look. "I knew it," she muttered. Turning around, she shouted over her shoulder with irritation in her voice, "Gyles, there's another freeloader here!"

Turning back to Gheric, the serving woman shook her head. "If it were up to me, I'd put you out on the street, but my husband has a soft spot for wandering rogues . . . and you, sir, have the look of a scoundrel."

"Must be the goatee," Gheric joked wryly, tossing her a smile.

Her eyes softened for the briefest of moments. "You're more handsome than the regular miscreants who breeze through town, I'll give you that."

"Kind of you to say," Gheric remarked, leaning forward on his stool.

The serving woman rolled her eyes toward the heavens. "I'd have fallen for that charming smile in my youth, but not anymore. Found myself a good man, far better than the likes of you."

"So, it's not just the goatee?" Gheric queried, an impish grin on his face.

The serving woman snorted in laughter. "No, it isn't," she commented, shaking her head.

The shuffling of feet behind her caused the serving woman to turn back around. "Gyles will see to you," she said in parting as she moved out into the crowded common room.

Gheric chuckled to himself as she walked away. Turning his eyes back to the bar, he got his first glimpse of the inn's proprietor.

"What's this about needing to find some work?" asked the portly innkeeper. His circular head was cocked to the side, and he had jagged red bangs hanging over his eyes.

"You've gained a bit of weight," Gheric appraised, softly enough that only the innkeeper could hear.

The innkeeper furrowed his face in disapproval, looking more closely at the younger man in front of him. "By Jora . . . Gheric, is that you?"

"The same," the tall warrior answered, keeping his voice low. "I just met your wife. Comely woman, though she didn't take much of a shine to me."

"Probably thought you were a scoundrel." Gyles chuckled, looking into the common room as his wife plunked a tray of drinks on a table nearby.

"That's not far from the truth," Gheric replied with a mischievous grin. He gave a furtive glance to his side, and the grin faded from his face. "I received your letter."

Gyles moved his gaze slowly around the room. "We need to talk," he whispered, "someplace private."

"Lead the way," Gheric stood, "but let's keep up the pretense, shall we?"

Gyles nodded and raised his voice, saying, "Well, you're not the first beggar to come knocking at my door. Follow me to the stables; there's always fresh manure to be cleaned. After that, we will see about getting you a meal."

The innkeeper beckoned for Gheric to follow him, and the pair made their way out the back of the inn.

"I DID NOT THINK TO SEE YOU HERE," GYLES SAID, ONCE they were inside the confines of the barn. He moved close, giving the broad-shouldered Gheric a warm embrace. "What happened? Did Khaine release you?"

"Only for the winter," Gheric answered, easing himself onto a rick of hay. "Though he is slowing down—I heard him say he's thinking of retiring soon."

The innkeeper gave his friend an appraising look. "What's this? *You're* sitting down? Getting old, are we?"

"I am a bit saddle sore," Gheric admitted with a wave. "None of us are getting any younger."

"That's true," Gyles good-naturedly agreed. He slapped himself on the paunch of his stomach with the open palm of his hand. "I haven't been to a practice yard in months. Still," he continued, looking at his friend, "you look to be in good form. How old are you now? Twenty-four? Twenty-five?"

"You know perfectly well that I turned twenty-eight this past summer," the warrior replied with a frown.

"Twenty-eight?" Gyles scoffed, feigning surprise. "I've got you by a good fifteen years, lad. Soon, you'll be in your dotage. And what, in the name of the gods, is that *thing* growing on your face?" he continued, pointing at Gheric's scraggly goatee.

"I got here as fast as I could," Gheric said with a laugh. "I didn't think to groom myself on the way."

The innkeeper beamed at his old friend. "For a moment, I thought a rabid squirrel was nesting on your chin," Gyles teased, reaching out and touching Gheric's whiskers.

Both men laughed, though the younger man did so ruefully. "The company misses your humor, Gyles, and your skills as a cook."

"I miss it too, sometimes," the innkeeper admitted, his laughter fading. "Truth to tell, I wish the company had come south weeks ago."

"Aye, we were surprised to get your message," Gheric noted, glancing at the barn's surroundings. "Unfortunately, most of the company had already been granted their leave. Tell me, old friend, what is happening in Caldor that you would request aid from your former employer?"

The innkeeper looked at the door and leaned in close, his voice dropping to a whisper, "Caldor might be a small village deep in southern Rhone, but the baron who rules here is a sadistic bastard bent on gathering power. If the rumors are true, he's had one of his guards put to death only a few weeks back. All because the man refused to put fire to the Willet Farm down the road."

A frown marred Gheric's chiseled face. "He killed his own man for refusing an order? One that goes against the rules of war?"

"Aye," Gyles affirmed. "We heard the guard had a kind spot for the Willets and defied the baron, one Niles Turner. I'm not sure you've ever heard of him, but he made a name for himself at the Great Games last year."

"What event?" Gheric asked.

The innkeeper let out a slow breath. "Quarterfinalist with the sword," he answered. "I've seen him in action once. He'd give even you a run for your money, and I don't say that lightly."

Gheric felt his fighting spirit rise. "Quarterfinals . . . That complicates things a bit if it comes to a fight . . . but tell me, what's the problem? Surely, you did not summon me here because of one man?"

The innkeeper sighed. "Baron Turner controls the influx of all the crops in the area. He already owns a stake in nearly half the farms in Caldor. Should he gain a majority of them, it will only be a matter of time before he has a monopoly on the southern market."

Gheric frowned. "Well, that happens sometimes. I'm sure the baron in Rathstone will alert—"

"No," Gyles said, cutting him off. "The baron of Rathstone is Malhallow Turner, uncle to Niles. Malhallow has sent a platoon of soldiers—some fifty strong—to reinforce the thirty that are already here. Those fifty are completely loyal to him and will safeguard his nephew at all costs."

"What about the duke in Kath?" Gheric asked. "Surely, Mays is aware of the issue?"

Gyles shook his head. "Do you know the last time Duke Mays sent a royal steward here? From what I've been told, it's been a decade at least. Caldor is located on the far end of his baronies."

The innkeeper rubbed his hands together, warming them against the cool air of the barn. "You remember what a lecher he can be. I'm sure Mays is busy chasing skirts on Wales Street. He won't bother checking on the minor lords who govern underneath him as long as he gets what he's owed."

Gheric was quiet for a moment, thinking on his friend's words. "I still don't see the problem," he said at last. "So, this

Baron Turner is a bad ruler—it happens sometimes. I can't just go into the keep and cut his throat on a whim."

Gyles put his hands to his mouth and blew absently on his fingers. "Baron Turner is not just a poor ruler. Last winter, the farmers who lost their lands became indentured to him. Now, they get by on scraps. Once proud farmers of Caldor are eking out a living because of their debt. Hell, I've seen refugees driven from their homelands who have better lives."

"They don't have to be indentured," Gheric pointed out. "They could leave, start over someplace else."

The innkeeper's shoulders sagged. "Those who refuse to be indentured to Niles are killed. Their bodies hang in the market square for days as a reminder of what noncompliance brings."

Gheric let out a deep breath. "Why don't the people here revolt?" he asked. "Rise up against this oppressor?"

Gyles ran a hand absently through his red hair. "Caldor is farm country. These folks are not warriors. They are farmers, both ill-trained and ill-equipped. Most of them cannot read or write—I doubt there is a single swordsman among them. I was a lowly cook for the Battle Mage, and even *I* have more experience in warfare than they do. There's not a lot of fight in most of them—and Turner commands more than eighty trained soldiers."

"Then why am I here?" Gheric asked, annoyed. "If these people won't fight for themselves, what am I supposed to do? I'm a bonny fighter, but even I can't defeat eighty men!"

Gyles sighed, suddenly looking tired. "There is one in Caldor who has resisted the baron. Not with weapons perhaps, but she has defied Niles up until this point."

"She?" Gheric asked, his eyes widening in surprise.

The innkeeper nodded his head. "Aye, a solitary woman with more fire than the rest of them put together."

Gheric frowned in confusion. "Who is it?"

"The Billerton widow, Sabra Billerton," Gyles said. "She alone has defied the baron for the last year."

Gheric was silent for the length of a heartbeat. "Why hasn't she tried sending a message to the duke in Kath?" he queried. "Why haven't any of them?"

The red-headed innkeeper shook his head. "Don't you think they've tried?" he asked in exasperation. "Even if anyone were able to win their way past the baron's guards, they'd *still* have the bandits that surround Caldor to contend with. There are scores of them out in the woods, each itching to swarm any traveler they find."

"I had a run-in with a few on the road earlier this afternoon," Gheric said ruefully. "They were . . . not easily dissuaded."

"Yes, well, there you go," Gyles agreed. "If they harassed you, what do you think they would do to these farmers?"

The portly innkeeper sighed. "Please, Gheric, these people need you. I need you. Can't you send for aid?"

Gheric shook his head. "Winter snows will fly within the month. Even if I could gather help, it would take weeks for anyone to arrive."

"What about Morrigan?"

"She headed north, sailing across the Crystalline Sea."

"Where are Pace and Innara?"

"They are wintering in the old country," Gheric answered with a shake of his head.

"Voe'kune?"

The younger man snorted. "Gladiator Pits in Bagidon. I am sorry, old friend, but we are alone, and I'm not sure what I can do to help."

Gyles hung his head in defeat. "I understand," he said softly. "I'm sorry to have wasted your time."

Just then, a bell began to ring outside in the marketplace. The innkeeper looked up and locked eyes with his old friend.

"I'll put you up for the night," Gyles offered. "It is the least I can do after you've traveled all this way. You can head out at dawn on the morrow, if you like."

Gheric stared at the innkeeper's calculating green eyes in suspicion. "What are you up to?"

"I'm not up to anything," Gyles answered innocently. "I would ask that you accompany me to the marketplace. There is something there you should see."

"Fine," Gheric consented. "I'll go with you to the marketplace. After that, it's a warm meal and a good night's sleep. Is that clear?"

"Whatever you want," Gyles answered mildly. "We must hurry though; I wouldn't want you to miss it."

"Miss what?"

"You will see."

CHAPTER 2

Sabra's feet were sore, and her back ached more than she cared to admit. The side of her left forearm was bruised and bleeding from where she had fallen on a loose stone only minutes ago as she'd loaded the last bushel of corn on her rickety wagon. She did not have time to attend to the throbbing wound, as she needed to get her harvest to the market before it closed. She'd hastily wrapped a bit of cloth around it and pressed forward.

Wiping sweat from her brow with a dust-covered handkerchief, Sabra shook the reins of her wagon, clicking at the massive oxen that pulled it. She'd picked sixty-eight bushels of corn that day, enough to fetch the silver she needed to make a payment on what her former husband owed Baron Turner. There might even be enough left over to purchase a new trough for the irrigation ditch that had been broken by the bandits who raided her farm the previous week.

Sabra squinted her sea-blue eyes from underneath the wide-brimmed straw hat on her head. The sun was still an hour from setting, more than enough time for her to cover the mile she needed to travel into town.

SABRA HEARD THE NOISE OF THE MARKETPLACE BEFORE SHE saw it. Dozens of merchants were selling any number of goods, hawking their wares with the villagers of Caldor up and down the market square. Easing her wagon next to the corn merchant's stand, Sabra pulled firmly on the reins, drawing her oxen to a halt. She leaped down from the seat and walked around the draft animal, patting the massive beast softly on the head.

"Evening, Mrs. Billerton," a tall farmer in front of her said kindly. He cast a quick look at the young woman's forearm. "You're hurt."

"Chaze," she nodded in return at the lanky man, offering his name in greeting. "I took a bit of a fall while loading my crop. It's nothing."

He glanced back at her wagon. "Nice haul," he said with envy. "Your yield was good this year."

"I try," she replied, giving him a tight smile.

He flicked his gaze at his own pair of wagons. "My last delivery of the season," he explained, jerking a thumb behind him. "How much more do you have left?"

"As much as I can pick before the snow flies," Sabra answered. She glanced around the market square and leaned in close to the lanky farmer. "My offer stands, Chaze. Now that your crop is in, I will pay you a solid wage if you come and work for me as you did in the spring. The opportunity extends to your family as well."

The tanned face of the farmer tightened in fear, his eyes darting around. "I . . . Thank you for the offer, Mrs. Billerton, it's just . . ."—he leaned in, his words barely a whisper—"it isn't safe anymore."

"I don't have all day, Mcmasters, let's get a move on!"

came the sharp voice of the crop merchant, a heavyset man with a salt-and-pepper beard that hung well past his neck.

Chaze grimaced at Sabra and stepped forward.

"How much today?" the merchant asked, sitting behind a table draped in red velvet.

"Seventy-four bushels," Chaze answered, his voice a bit unsteady.

"You're late in the season." The merchant frowned. "A few days more, and you'd have had to pay the new tax."

There was a murmuring of surprise from other villagers that were close enough to hear the merchants words.

"What new tax?" Sabra asked, her voice cutting sharply through the noise of the market square.

The heavyset man looked past Chaze as the crowd began to quiet. "I'm in the middle of a business transaction," the merchant snapped, glaring at Sabra.

"I asked you a question, Varfore," she continued, unfazed. "As the man representing our liege, I expect an answer."

"And I said you can wait," the bearded merchant spat back.

The crowd of onlookers fell silent and stopped what they were doing to listen to the exchange.

"Now, if we can continue," Varfore snapped, turning his attention back to the lanky farmer in front of him. "Seventy-four bushels of corn . . . that comes to fourteen silver eagles. Step up to the table and make your mark."

Chaze moved forward and made a swirling X with the dark colored quill on the parchment located on top of the table. The merchant reached into a large money box and counted out fourteen circular coins cast from silver. Chaze placed the coins in a satchel at his waist, thanked Varfore, and moved toward his wagon as quickly as he could.

"Help him unload that corn," the merchant ordered two of

his men, deliberately taking his time before moving on to Sabra.

"What new tax?" Sabra asked, unwilling to wait any longer.

"It's none of your concern," Varfore answered. "Now, please wait while we get Mcmasters's crop unloaded."

Sabra wanted to scream in frustration. Instead, she bit her tongue and stood in the glow of the late afternoon sun, saying nothing.

"By Dourn, it's warmer than I thought," she muttered, taking off her hat and fanning it across her face as she turned around and watched the baron's hired hands unload the wagons next to hers.

Through the now thinning crowd, she caught a glimpse of a man, a stranger she'd not seen before. He was standing behind the crowd, whispering something to Gyles, the innkeeper at the Bad Apple Inn.

A small group of villagers strode in front of him, and she lost sight of the stranger for a moment, but as the crowd parted and she saw him again more clearly than before, her eyes widened, and she felt her heart skip a beat.

He was an extraordinarily handsome man with broad shoulders and deep-set eyes. Dressed all in brown, he carried himself with a quiet confidence she had not seen before. Most unnerving of all was the fact that he was staring right at her.

For a fleeting moment, their eyes met. His gaze sent a thrill of excitement through her, a feeling she'd not experienced in a long time.

"I am ready for you now," stated Varfore, finally giving her the attention she'd asked for.

Turning back to the merchant, Sabra absently placed the hat on her head and put the stranger in the back of her mind.

Had she looked back, Sabra would have seen him watching her with great interest.

"THAT SPITFIRE IN FRONT OF THE CORN MERCHANT IS WIDOW Billerton," Gyles whispered, nudging Gheric with his elbow.

"She's got spirit," Gheric admitted, listening to her exchange with Varfore.

As a man of war, Gheric's keen eyes took in everything about her. "She's injured her left arm," he noted, quietly enough to where Gyles did not hear.

"Arguments with the merchants are a common occurrence with Widow Billerton, I'm sad to say," the innkeeper remarked. "Every time she comes to the market, there seems to be an issue."

Gheric was not listening. From his vantage point, he could not make out much of the woman through the press of villagers. From underneath the confines of her straw hat, she had a tightly wound blonde braid that spilled down the back of a dusty white dress that hid most of her figure. A passerby stepped in front of him, and he completely lost sight of the woman for a moment.

"Dammit, get out of the way," he uttered, not sure why he suddenly felt impatient.

When his line of sight cleared, he felt his breath catch in his throat. The Billerton widow had turned around and was using her hat to fan her face.

"By the gods," he whispered aloud, unable to look away. She was of medium height, standing a hand-and-a-half under six feet. Her brow was covered in a sheen of perspiration, and there was a smudge of dust on her left cheek. It did nothing, however, to mar the beauty of her countenance.

"I thought you might feel that way," he heard Gyles say from behind him.

Gheric canted his head to the side. "I bet you did."

It was at that moment she looked up, locking her gaze to his.

For the breadth of a heartbeat, time stopped. Gheric was enraptured by the woman's magnificence. Even at this distance, he could see the intensity of her eyes. They were as blue as the waters of the Crystalline Sea. Her face, both bold and fierce, held an ethereal beauty surpassing that of any woman he had ever seen. He noted her trim waistline and the sensuous curve of her breasts underneath the weatherworn dress she'd opened at the neck to combat the heat of the fading sun.

"Damn me," he whispered to himself, unable to look away.

Sadly, the moment could not last, as the merchant with the salt-and-pepper beard drew the woman's attention back to business. Cruelly, she turned away.

"This is the woman who is standing up to the baron?" Gheric asked Gyles, his voice low.

"That's her," the innkeeper confirmed.

Gheric turned a pair of accusing eyes to his friend. "Damn you," he swore. "Is this why you insisted I come with you to the market?"

Gyles gave his friend an innocent look. "I don't know what you are talking about," he answered, feigning ignorance.

"Jora's balls," the swarthy warrior cursed. "It is annoying as bloody hell that you know me this well."

"Beauty and bravery, your two great weaknesses," the innkeeper agreed mildly.

"I hate you sometimes."

"I'll remember you said that," the innkeeper replied softly, giving his companion a knowing grin.

"Oh, I don't doubt it," Gheric snapped. "And you are wrong. Just because she's pretty doesn't mean I'm going to risk my hide for her."

"I would never dream of asking you to do that," Gyles said mildly.

"I mean it," Gheric growled more loudly than he'd intended.

A few of the villagers gave him a curious look.

"As you say. Now, we should go, before you garner too much attention," Gyles warned, taking a step away from the onlookers.

"Wait," Gheric said, listening intently to the sudden heated exchange between the merchant and the young woman.

Gyles moved a step further away from his friend. "Why do I have a feeling you are about to do something rash?"

Gheric ignored the innkeeper as he watched Widow Billerton's proceedings with the merchant unfold.

"How much corn did you gather?" Varfore asked, his tone dripping with boredom.

"What's this new tax you spoke of?" Sabra insisted, her own tone biting.

Varfore leaned forward. "The sun will soon dip beneath the horizon, *woman*," he hissed in annoyance. "I have much to do until then, and time is running short. Either sell me your corn or go away—and stop asking me about the baron's new tax. You will find out soon enough."

Sabra's face flushed red with anger. Knowing Varfore was acting on orders from Baron Turner, she let her question go unanswered for the time being. She could not risk losing today's sale. Getting paid before sunset was more important than satiating her curiosity.

"Sixty-eight bushels," she said, fuming.

"A single person, working alone?" The merchant scoffed. "I highly doubt you picked half as much."

"Sixty-eight-bushel baskets, all filled to the brim," she insisted.

Varfore motioned to one of the men next to him. "Hob, go and count those baskets on her wagon," he stated, crossing his arms in front of him.

"That is not necessary," Sabra argued.

"You dare to question the baron's man?" Varfore snapped.

"You took Farmer Mcmasters at his word!" she shot back. "Why is it you don't believe me?"

The merchant's face twisted in a sneer. "Chaze is a respected farmer, and he's been working in the fields all his life. You have been at it for less than a year."

Varfore looked to his underling a second time. "Go, Hob, count them all. If there is so much as a single basket that is underfilled—"

"I've counted them already," came a booming voice from behind them.

Sabra felt a trill of excitement run down her spine at the surety of the speaker's tone. She spun around as all eyes shifted to the stranger dressed in the brown tunic and peasant pants. It was the same man who had been staring at her earlier. Sabra noted he was now standing a few steps in front of Gyles.

"There are sixty-eight baskets, just as she said," the stranger announced.

Varfore snorted in contempt. "Who are you?" he asked coolly.

The man gave Varfore a friendly smile. "No one. I'm just passing through," the stranger answered, his tone neutral.

"Best you mind your own business," the merchant warned. "My man will calculate the total. I'd be surprised if you could count past the number of fingers on one hand."

"If that's what you wish," the barrel-chested stranger replied, nonplussed at the insult. "But it was *you* who argued time was short. It seems a waste of daylight to have your man validate what the lady reported and I just confirmed."

Varfore leaned forward in his chair. "I will do what I think is best. Now, shut your mouth, or I'll have you beaten from the market square!"

Varfore looked at Hob and pointed at the wagon. "Go, do as I command."

Varfore's lackey walked toward the wagon, drawing close to the dark-haired stranger on his way. As he brushed past the man, Hob paused, locking eyes with him. Sabra could have sworn Hob's face turned white as he continued to the wagons. Sabra looked at the stranger again, wondering what he'd said to Varfore's subordinate.

Hob did not take long. After only a few heartbeats, Varfore's man headed back to the stand.

"Sixty-eight baskets," he confirmed, flicking his gaze toward the stranger. "Every one, filled to the brim."

"Hmmpt." Varfore grunted, turning his attention back to Sabra. "Sixty-eight bushels it is. That comes to . . . four silver eagles."

"Four?" Sabra objected as the crowd began to mutter in surprise. "At the going rate you paid Chaze, it should be eleven silver eagles, at least."

"There is less of a demand now," Varfore explained, his voice cold. "The barony has just purchased seventy-four bushels from another farmer. The going rate has changed. It's four silver eagles . . . and you're lucky to get that."

Sabra was stunned. The prices in Caldor rarely fluctuated, as much of what the locals harvested was sent north to sell in the larger, more urban cities on the coast. Varfore was changing the price out of spite. Sabra nearly cried out in frustration.

Turning around, she looked to the crowd. "How can you let this vile behavior stand?" she asked. "You think *I* will be the only one to suffer? If we don't collectively stand up to Niles Turner—"

"*Baron* Turner," Varfore barked, cutting her off. "I am warning you, Widow Billerton, I'll not hear any more seditious outbursts. Do it again, and I'll summon the guards."

Sabra ignored him, casting her eyes to the crowd of onlookers, imploring them to intercede. "Is there no one here who will stand against this tyranny?"

She was met with an uncomfortable silence, fear permeating throughout the crowd.

"Sheep, the lot of you," she spat in disgust.

Varfore snorted in contempt. "Don't mistake the good sense of your fellow villagers as cowardice. They have their own families to care for. You, however, are alone, slag. Now, move forward and sign over your crop. Do it before I—"

"I'll pay twenty silver eagles for your corn," came a voice from behind them.

Sabra whirled around. She saw the handsome stranger in the brown tunic looking at her with a broad smile on his face.

"Stay out of this!" Varfore barked, rising from his seat.

"No," the man answered, his voice cool.

"You are not a licensed merchant," Varfore challenged.

"You are right, good sir, but my backer is," the stranger responded.

Varfore narrowed his eyes. "Who is your backer?"

"That's really none of your concern," the stranger said with a sniff and a wave. "Mrs. . . . Billerton is it? If you'll follow me, I'll have your money for you shortly."

"Damn you!" Varfore bellowed. "The baron has tasked *me* with buying all the corn in the village!"

"Did he?" the stranger replied. "Well, unless you are willing to match my offer, I see no reason that Mrs. Billerton should sell her sixty-eight bushels of corn to you."

"The offer is four!" Varfore snarled.

"I do not accept!" Sabra snapped, stepping toward the stranger.

"Wait, I—" The bearded merchant licked his lips nervously, his eyes darting throughout the crowd. "I will buy your corn for eleven silver eagles. That's the same rate I gave Chaze."

Sabra came to a halt and turned around, her manner slow, deliberate. She shot Varfore an icy look. "I'm sorry, merchant, but there is more of a demand now," she growled, her voice dripping with sarcasm. "The rate you offer is no longer acceptable. It's twenty silver eagles, or I sell to the other bidder. Afterward, you can explain to Baron Turner how you failed to heed his instructions."

A bead of sweat made its way down the side of Varfore's face. "I'll summon the guards," he threatened.

"You do that," the stranger good-naturedly cut in. "I'll need some help unloading the goods. Mrs. Billerton, please. The day is wasting away. Join me, if you would."

Sabra nodded and started toward the stranger once more.

"Wait!" Varfore shouted, perspiration dripping from his brow. "Fifteen," he whispered, sending the crowd into a surprised muttering.

"I'm sorry, what was that?" Sabra asked, looking over her shoulder.

"Eighteen silver eagles," he pleaded, his cruel eyes narrowed in desperation.

"Too late," Sabra replied.

"Jora's balls . . . Twenty it is," Varfore conceded in defeat.

Sabra stopped and turned back, looking spitefully at the merchant. "Write it down on your ledger, now, or I walk."

Varfore, his hands shaking in anger, scribbled their transaction of twenty silver eagles on the parchment. Sabra stepped forward and signed her name next to it. The merchant, sweat now dripping off him, counted out twenty silver coins, nearly throwing them at her.

"Get that corn off the wagon," Varfore ordered to his hired hands.

"Pleasure doing business with you," Sabra couldn't resist saying before she turned away.

"This won't be the end of it," Varfore threatened.

"Goodbye," she replied.

Sabra began to walk away, euphoric at her luck. She knew, however, she had been helped. Looking ahead, her eyes searched the crowd for the man who had spoken on her behalf.

He was nowhere to be found.

CHAPTER 3

Minutes later, Gyles was berating Gheric back in the relative privacy of his stable. "Are you *insane*?" he gaped, his face twisted in disapproval. "I told you to observe the girl, not start a bidding war with the baron's merchant!"

"So, that was her, was it?" Gheric asked, ignoring the innkeeper. "I like her. As I said before, she has spirit. Damn fine looking, too."

Gyles was cursing under his breath. "By the gods, man, you're not listening! Baron Turner will hear of what transpired in the market today! He won't be happy."

Gheric frowned at his friend. "Tell me something, why did you invite me here?"

The innkeeper stared at him wordlessly for the span of a heartbeat. "To help the girl—to help the town! To stop the baron from—"

"That's right," Gheric interjected, cutting Gyles off. "To stop the baron and his evil ways."

The two men stared at one another in a moment of silence.

"Still," the innkeeper dared to venture. "Did you have to provoke him like that?

Gheric shook his head in disapproval. "Why is it that people always think rebellion is a calm, bloodless affair?" he asked. "It's not. It is a grueling, bloody fight, often with casualties on both sides."

"But Gheric, he has guards, more than eighty of them!" Gyles argued. "I thought you'd slip into his keep under the cover and darkness and threaten him into submission. I didn't know you were going to blatantly goad the baron into a killing frenzy by openly defying him in the market square!"

"Yes, well, from what little you've told me of this Niles Turner, I'd wager he is impatient and reckless. More so when he is angry."

Gyles paused, looking at his friend carefully. "You challenged him publicly on purpose?"

"Of course I did. I want him angry. Angry men do stupid things."

The innkeeper sat down on the rick of hay and put his head in his hands. "I don't know . . . it seems risky, both for you and for Sabra."

Gheric moved forward and laid his hand on his friend's shoulder. "It will be risky for us all. In fact, I cannot stay at the Bad Apple Inn. To do so would invite trouble for you and your wife. Besides," he added with a grin, "I need someone in the village I can trust to feed me information. Someone they won't suspect."

"Hmmpt." Gyles grunted. "Half the folks in Caldor have seen you enter my inn. Hell, I was standing right next to you outside the marketplace. I'm sure they already suspect we know each other."

"Not so," Gheric said with a smile. "All any of them

know is that I am a loudmouthed vagrant willing to work for a meal."

"So?" the innkeeper queried.

"So, what if I eat a meal and refuse to work it off?"

"I'd be forced to throw you out!" Gyles said without hesitation.

Gheric's smile widened.

The innkeeper began to laugh ruefully. "Fine, I'll toss you out the door in front of the whole village," Gyles said, shaking his head. "It's been a while since I pitched a vagrant into the street. Might be good for my reputation." Gyles gave his friend a hesitant frown. "If you aren't staying with me, where will you go?"

Gheric did not answer. Instead, he cocked one of his eyebrows.

"I should have guessed," Gyles muttered. "Sabra's far more likely to toss you out on your ear than she would be to let you stay in her home. She's not some rickety old innkeeper either. I bet you'll break something when you land."

Gheric's grin morphed into a smile. "I guess we will find out."

SABRA WAS TIRED BY THE TIME SHE RETURNED TO HER FARM. It had been a hectic day. Up before the sun, she had fed her chickens, pigs, and sheep before cleaning out their pens and collecting more than two dozen eggs. It was almost noon when she was finally able to turn her hand to harvesting corn. Six hours later, she'd gone to town and sold both her crop and the eggs. While she was elated to have gotten such a good price for her corn, Sabra could not help but feel angry. It took a stranger to stand up to Varfore and his men. It sickened her that not a soul in the village had met her eye when she had implored them for help.

To make matters worse, the stranger had disappeared. Something about him had garnered Sabra's interest. He'd been bold and kind . . . not to mention incredibly stupid.

To antagonize Baron Turner's man like that! she thought, shaking her head. If the stranger had any sense at all, he would leave Caldor with the rising sun.

After her stint at the market, Sabra had stopped by the potter's stand to try and put in an order for a new irrigation trench. The potter had rebuked her, saying he wasn't going to go down with a sinking ship, when it was obvious to him her farm would soon be under the control of the baron.

With her heart sinking in her chest, Sabra's final stop had been at the mayor's office, where she made her disbursement to Baron Turner. It may have been a futile effort in the eyes of the village, but with that payment, Sabra had bought herself another two weeks of time.

As Sabra left the mayor's office, she noted there was a loud ruckus in front of the Bad Apple Inn. She could not see what it was, but she decided to head home without investigating, feeling she'd had enough excitement today already.

It was now a half-hour until sunset. Sabra led her oxen into the barn, unhitched the beast from its harness, and brushed him down in the fading light of dusk. Once satisfied, she locked the barn doors and walked into her farmhouse, near exhaustion. Taking only enough time to light a single candle, Sabra collapsed on the thin cushions of her former husband's favorite chair.

Armison, what did you leave me with? she thought bitterly to herself.

After her mother and stepfather had drowned in a tragic accident, she had been left alone with her stepfather's brother. A lecherous man and a violent drunk, her step-uncle had been unable to get what he'd wanted from Sabra. The strong-willed orphan had fought back harder than he'd anticipated after he'd tried to force himself on her. She'd pushed him off her, and he stumbled back in a drunken stupor. Quite by accident, he'd fallen onto the prongs of a pitchfork in the barn. One of the iron prongs had pierced his heart. He had bled out while Sabra had desperately run to town to fetch the local Druid, Temper.

She sighed in remembrance. Sabra had been too late. Despite her testimony that it had been an accident, there was a formal inquiry followed by a trial. At the hearing, the new baron pulled her aside and made the twenty-two-year-old woman an offer that would clear her name of any wrongdoing.

It was an offer she would not accept.

Because of her refusal, Baron Turner gave her a choice. Pay one hundred gold falcons to the crown—an astronomical sum—or be put to death.

As she stood in court stunned at the ruling, a single man had stepped forward from the crowd. Armison Billerton, the richest farmer in Caldor and an old friend of Sabra's mother, agreed to pay the debt. When asked by the baron why he would do such a thing, Armison said it was because Sabra had agreed to be his wife.

Knowing that refusing the old farmer's offer meant a fate worse than death, Sabra had accepted.

Their marriage had been a sham, of course, as Armison

was well past seventy years of age. However, there was little Baron Turner could do, as it was *he* who had set the price of Sabra's freedom.

Unfortunately for Armison, he'd had to mortgage his land against the cost of his new bride. A benevolent man, Farmer Billerton knew it would take him years to pay off the debt, but he did not seem to care in the least. Sabra's freedom, he argued, was far more important.

Sadly, less than six months into their "marriage," Armison had passed in his sleep, leaving Sabra the entire estate . . . and all of its financial obligations.

I'm not sure I was worth it, she thought, looking at the ceiling of the farmhouse and remembering Armison. She shook off her moment of doubt. Even buried under a mountain of debt, this was a better fate than the alternative. She shuddered just thinking about the baron's proposition.

Her thoughts were interrupted by a loud knock at the door.

Sabra's hand slid easily to the knife she kept hidden under her dress. No one had come calling on her in months . . . other than debt collectors sent by the baron. No one of marriageable age had considered courting the doomed widow, leaving her very much alone in Caldor, save for the innkeeper Gyles. The stout proprietor of the Bad Apple Inn was the only person in the village to show her any kindness over the last few months. He had done so on more than one occasion, despite the risk of angering the baron.

"Who is it?" she called out, her muscles screaming in protest as she rose to her feet. "Gyles, is that you?"

"Widow Billerton?" came a muffled voice. "Might I have a word with you?"

The voice sounded vaguely familiar, and she moved

silently to the window. Peeking through the pane of glass, she strained her eyes to catch a glimpse of the figure huddled outside her door. Unfortunately, she could only make out a partial silhouette in the darkness, as her eyes had already adjusted to the light of the candle.

"Whatever it is that you want, I'm not interested," Sabra said, holding the knife firmly in her hand.

There was silence on the other side, and Sabra found herself holding her breath.

"There are twenty silver eagles in your pocket because of me," the voice said at last. "I only ask that you give me a moment of your time."

The man from the market, she thought, and her blood began to race.

"What do you want?" she asked, her heart lurching in her chest. "I'm not giving you any of that money. It's already been spent."

Without warning, the door swung open, and the man took a step inside. "You really should lock this," he advised wryly, giving her a sideways grin. "As I said, all I need is a moment of your—"

"Get out!" she screamed, stunned at his sudden entry. She drew back and swung her knife wildly in front of her.

The man showed remarkable dexterity and swayed out of range, cursing under his breath. "By Jora, stop it!" he hissed, moving inside quickly. "I just want to—"

"Get out of my house!" she screeched a second time, taking another swipe with her knife. "No man will ever force himself on me again!"

More prepared this time, the man blocked her swing with his forearm and spun deftly behind her, clamping his arms to her sides.

"Let go of me!" she howled, struggling like mad to free herself.

"Not while you're flailing about with that pigsticker!" He grunted, bearing her to the ground.

For several seconds, the pair wrestled on the floorboards until she was forced to release her hold on the knife. It spun away across the floor, and he pinned her to the ground, holding her wrists down with his hands and straddling his legs across her torso.

"By Dourn, stay still before you hurt yourself," he hissed. "I'm trying to help you save your farm!"

Sabra stopped struggling at his words and looked up into his dark eyes. "You . . . you want to help me?" she said, panting. "Why?"

"Why indeed?" he muttered sarcastically.

"So, you're not trying to . . .?" She left her statement hanging, hoping he understood.

"Take advantage of you?" He shook his head in surprise. "No, I prefer those who come to me willing—besides, I'm not sure you are my type."

She sourly looked up at him, unconsciously aware of how strong he was. "You're not my type either," she raged. "Arrogant, smug, completely full of himself, and a colossal asshole to boot. You would be the first man I've ever met who did not want something from me."

"Yes, well, call me crazy, but I prefer your *spirit* to your *body*," he said, frowning at her. The man inhaled deeply. "I'm going to let you up. It would be helpful if you took me at my word and assumed I am here to talk only. Do you understand?"

"What did you expect?" she challenged. "You broke into my house!"

"I got tired of waiting," he said. "But you are right. I

should have shown more patience and remained outside. However, in my defense . . . were you *ever* going to open that door for me?"

Sabra stared at him in cold silence.

"I thought as much," he muttered aloud. Gently, he let go of her wrists and stood up, offering her a hand.

"Don't touch me," she snarled, standing without his help. They stood for a moment in the flickering light of the candle, staring at one another. "You wanted to talk to me?" she spat, breaking the silence.

"Might we sit down?" he asked.

"You are not staying," she snapped, looking at him more carefully. "Why are you covered in dirt?"

He looked down and plucked at his tunic. "Oh, this," he said, holding out a pair of sleeves coated in fresh mud. "I got thrown out of the Bad Apple Inn. Didn't want to work for my meal."

She frowned at him. "You mean to say you haven't any money? I thought you said you were going to pay twenty silver eagles for my corn."

"Yes . . . well, I lied. I don't have *any* silver eagles at the moment."

Sabra stared at him, speechless.

"Why is there blood on your forearm?" he asked, frowning at a few spots of red smeared on her sleeve.

"I fell before I came to town," she explained, pulling the bloody garment up past her elbow.

"That doesn't look good," he said, frowning at the abrasion she'd gotten earlier that day.

"It's nothing," Sabra sniffed, turning away from him.

"That needs to be cleaned," he continued, reaching for his waterskin.

"Don't touch me," Sabra hissed, pulling away.

He gave her a withering look. "For the love of the gods, woman, what is wrong with you? I'm not touching you at all; I want to pour clean water on your cut to wash it out."

"I said it's fine," Sabra argued, acutely aware of how much the cut had begun to ache.

"Stop acting like a child. This will only take a moment."

Despite her words, Sabra knew the wound needed to be tended to. "Don't try anything," she warned, moving closer to him.

He let out a slow breath and gave her a sympathetic look. "Someone really did a number on you, didn't they?"

She froze, swallowing the feeling of disgust she always felt when she thought of her step-uncle.

"Whoever it was, I'm not him," the man continued. "I'm asking to pour water on your arm, not for a tumble in the cornfield."

Sabra looked at the man's handsome face, detecting only the truth. Slowly, she extended her arm outward, and the man carefully poured a steady stream of liquid from his waterskin over it. The water was cool to the touch, and the room filled with the spatter of droplets falling to the wooden floorboards.

"Hand me that towel," the man said, nodding at a folded cloth on the table by the washbasin.

Sabra reached over and did as he asked. Their eyes locked for a moment, sending a momentary thrill coursing through her body. She looked away, and he proceeded to gently dab at the cuts, drying the area as best he could.

"Let me wrap it for you," he continued, taking a clean bandage out of one of his pockets.

"Do you always carry wound dressings in your pants?" Sabra asked, in an effort to stem the rising excitement she felt.

He gave her a knowing grin. "I may have noticed your

arm at the market," he said. "I soaked it in wine and honey before I left the inn."

"You mean before you were thrown out!" she snapped, suddenly angry with him. Annoyed that he was having this effect on her, Sabra started to draw her arm away. "Further administrations won't be necessary," she snapped.

"Stop it," he ordered, as though he were chastising a child. "This will keep it from getting infected."

Despite her protests, Sabra ceased her movement. She became intensely aware of how gentle his tough was. His fingers expertly wrapped the bandage, placing a pair of tiny metal fasteners on the fabric to hold it in place.

"There," he breathed. "All done."

The man set the towel back by the washbasin. "Now, let's get down to business."

"You can leave," she snarled, her anger returning.

He gave her a sideways grin. "Don't you want to hear my plan about how we are going to save your farm and keep your independence from the baron?"

Sabra hesitated. "Why would you want to do that?" she asked, after considering his words.

"I have my reasons," he answered, evading the question.

"You want the land for yourself?"

"No, I'm not much of a farmer," he answered honestly.

"You want money?"

The man shook his head.

"Then what?" Sabra demanded. "No one does something for nothing."

The barrel-chested man sighed. "I can see that I bring out the worst in you, and it has been a long day for us both. Clearly, we aren't going to get anywhere tonight. I think it best we get some sleep and start anew in the morning."

Sabra gave him a cold look. "You're not coming back—"

"You'd turn down help harvesting your crop?" he countered, interrupting her.

She made to speak and hesitated, letting out a breath of uncertainty.

"Then I'll see you tomorrow," the stranger said, looking around the house. "Tell me, where do I sleep?"

For a moment, Sabra thought she'd heard him wrong.

"Excuse me?" she asked, recovering quickly.

"My room," he inquired. "Where is it?"

"Are you out of your . . . What makes you think . . . You're not staying here!" she sputtered.

"Well, of course I am," he replied. "I got thrown out of my friend's inn on purpose. I have nowhere else to go now."

Sabra stared at him for a long moment, his words a surprise. "Gyles is your friend?" she asked suspiciously.

"Yes, it is because of him I'm here in Caldor at all," the man explained. "Take a look," he said, reaching into his pocket. Flakes of crusted mud fell to the floor as he handed her a note.

"What is this?" Sabra asked, taking the note from him.

"A letter from Gyles. He asks that you let me stay here until we save your farm."

She looked up at him. "You read it?" she accused.

"I might have peeked," he admitted, shooting a smile at her. "Now, pretty girl, while you are reading over the letter, I'm going to put Kat in your stable, if that meets with your approval."

"Kat?"

"My horse. She prefers to sleep inside, if possible. I just need to unlock the doors of your barn."

Shaking her head, Sabra began to scan the first lines of the letter.

"I can't believe I'm agreeing to this," she remarked,

taking the key from a chain around her neck. "It's a good thing for you that I trust Gyles."

"That is fortunate," he agreed. He extended his hand toward Sabra. "Do we have a deal?"

Sabra looked at his outstretched appendage like it was a venomous viper. "I guess we do," she answered, taking his hand in hers.

The stranger grunted as they shook. "Strong grip," he muttered, noting her calloused hands.

"Make sure you lock the doors before you come back in," she warned, pulling away from him.

The stranger smiled at her and started toward the exit. As he reached for the handle, Sabra stopped him with a question.

"What's your name?" she asked.

"Gheric," the man answered, opening the door.

"You can stay in the spare bedroom," she said.

"I appreciate that," he replied.

"But let's get one thing straight," she continued, ice in her voice, "with the exception of that handshake, you will never lay so much as a finger on me again."

Gheric half turned around and smiled at her. "You've worries aplenty, Widow Billerton; I will abide by your rule."

Without another word, the dark-eyed stranger stepped outside, the darkness of the night swallowing him whole.

Sabra made her way over to the door and closed it firmly behind him.

Dumbly, she sat back down on her former husband's chair and rescanned the letter. It read exactly as Gheric said it would. She placed the parchment on the side table and raised her knees to her chest, encircling her arms around her shins and holding them tightly.

"He will not touch me again," she vowed, thinking of how she'd felt when he'd lain on top of her.

There was a moment when she'd stopped fighting and looked into his eyes. That was when she'd felt it. A feeling, one that had not visited her in a long time—not since her step-uncle had tried to rape her. It was a sensation, both foreign and wonderful.

Desire.

CHAPTER 4

The next day dawned cool and damp. Sabra climbed out of the warm confines of her bed, a dull feeling of fatigue clinging to her eyes like weights cast from lead. The sun was still an hour or more beneath the distant horizon as she dressed in the simple garb of a gray tunic and trousers. Slipping on her work boots, Sabra felt her way into the dining area through the chilled darkness of her home. With any luck, she could breakfast on some leftover cheese and the last of the corn bread she'd baked three days ago.

When she stumbled out of the hallway, Sabra saw a candle burning brightly at the center of her dining table. The smell of cooked food wafted through the air, along with the feeling of warmth radiating from her kitchen stove. As she moved closer, she saw two fried eggs lightly garnished with salt and pepper on a wooden plate. Alongside the eggs was a thick slice of warm corn bread slathered in melting butter. There was a mug filled with spiced cider and a bowl holding a generous portion of black grapes that glistened with the morning's dew.

How did . . . she thought, just before she heard shuffling footsteps from outside the doorway. A moment later, her broad-shouldered houseguest entered, covered in a light sheen of sweat, dust, and horsehair.

"Ahh good, you're finally awake," Gheric drawled, tossing her a smile. "Eat something, but let's not linger. We've much to accomplish today."

The bleary-eyed farmer was momentarily stunned. In her exhaustion, she had forgotten Gheric had stayed the previous night.

"What is all this?" Sabra asked, doubly surprised to see him awake before her.

"It's called 'breakfast,' pretty girl," he answered, furrowing his brow. "Do they have a different name for it here?"

"That's not what I . . ." she began, trying to hide her annoyance. "How did . . . Where did you get these eggs?" she floundered.

"From a wayward owl that fell from the sky," he mocked, shaking his head.

"I'm serious," she snapped, looking at him angrily.

"I went and saw to your chickens," he replied. "I collected more than two dozen eggs—minus four."

"Minus four?" she asked suspiciously.

Gheric raised his eyebrow. "Yes . . . two for you and two for me," he explained, gesturing to her plate. "You do eat eggs, don't you?"

The exchange was getting away from her.

"Of course I do, it's just . . . they're *my* eggs!"

He cocked an eyebrow and looked at her in confusion. "I see," he said at last. "What you're really saying is, *you* can eat them, but *I* can't?" He pointed to the bowl on the table. "How about those grapes? Are they off limits too?"

Her face twisted in frustration. "Don't patronize me," she

growled, sitting down on the chair in front of her meal. "It's my farm. You had no right to help yourself to the food grown here."

"Is that so?" he asked lightly. "In that case, perhaps I should go undo all the work I've done while you were slumbering away."

"I was not 'slumbering away,'" she protested. "It's called sleeping . . ."

He stopped and raised his left eyebrow. "You snore like a grizzly bear, by the way." He snickered, washing his hands in a wooden basin filled with lukewarm water.

"I do *not*!" she snapped, chomping into the bread. "And what were you doing in my bedroom? Did you try to ravish me while I lay unconscious?" she accused, her voice harsh.

"Of course not," he answered in disapproval. "And I wasn't *in* your bedroom; I tiptoed past your door on my way to work *your* farm. Oh, and I forgot, general rules of life don't apply to you," he replied, sarcasm dripping from his tongue. "Widow Billerton can both sleep *and* listen to herself *not* snore, simultaneously."

"That's not what I . . . By Chara, you are the most insufferable man I've ever met," she protested. Chewing absently at the bread, she was surprised at how good it tasted.

"I have some cheese in my bag," Gheric offered, drying his hands on a coarse cotton towel. "Unless, of course, you don't believe in sharing *my* food."

"I do believe in sharing, it's just . . ." She trailed off, completely out of sorts because of his presence. *What is it about him?* she thought, watching Gheric as he rummaged through one of his bags.

"What chores did you manage to finish?" she asked, determined to take control of the conversation.

The dark-haired man sat down, straddling the chair across

from her. "I collected the eggs, cleaned the sheep pen, and fed all the animals in the barn."

"It sounds like you forgot to—"

"I watered the oxen and brushed them down too," Gheric continued, cutting a wedge of cheese with his knife. "By Jora, you should have seen the look Kat gave me. I had to brush her coat twice over until she forgave me."

Sabra blinked at him, trying to think of something he'd left out.

"Would you like some?" he offered, holding the newly cut wedge toward her.

"Thank you," she said automatically, taking the sharp-smelling cheese in her hand. His finger accidently grazed hers, and she felt a momentary thrill at his touch.

Why does he enthrall me so? she thought, placing the cheese on the plate in front of her.

"Since the morning chores are nearly complete, we should be able to harvest a good haul today," she managed to say, trying to hide her excitement at his touch by taking a bite of her eggs.

"Oh, we're not doing any harvesting today," he said. "That can wait till tomorrow."

Sabra stopped chewing her food and looked at him sharply.

"What do you mean we aren't harvesting today? How am I supposed to pay my debt?"

Instead of answering her, Gheric picked up another mug and filled it with cider. "It must have been a fine year for apples," he commented, sniffing at the pitcher. "That aroma is exquisite. I wonder what type of seeds were—"

"Did you hear me?" she demanded, her voice louder than she'd anticipated.

"Yes, I heard you." He frowned. "I think all of Caldor did, at least those who don't have cotton stuffed in their ears."

Sabra drained what was left of her mug, trying to remain calm. "Why don't you want to pick corn today?" she questioned, lifting the pitcher and pouring herself more cider. "I thought you were here to help me save the farm?"

He waved off her question. "Even if we were to harvest all day from now until the first snows fly, there is no way the two of us will get the entire crop in . . ." He trailed off, looking at her curiously as she lifted the pitcher and poured herself another mug of cider. "Arm feeling better?" he asked, pointing at the bandage peeking out from under her sleeve.

"It's fine," she said with a wave, placing the pitcher back on the table.

"I could have sworn—" He began before she cut him off.

"We need to do *something* today," she protested. "The farm isn't going to save itself."

He took his eyes off Sabra's bandage and leaned across the table until he was only inches from her face. She refused to shrink away from him, and she became very aware of his presence. The sight of his handsome features glistening with the sheen of sweat, the scent of him buried under the labors of the morning—even the sound of his breathing echoed in her ears. His quiet confidence filled the room.

Widow Billerton found she was holding her breath.

"There is only *one* thing I want to do with you today," he whispered, his voice serious.

The tension of his words hung between them as Sabra stared into his vibrant dark eyes.

"What is that?" She swallowed, hoping her voice sounded more confident than she felt.

Gheric moved closer until she could feel the warmth of his breath against her skin. Sabra was keenly aware of the heat emanating off his body. He wet his lips and spoke, just loudly enough for Sabra to hear above the pounding echo of her beating heart.

"Together, you and I are going to recruit others to help you," he said, wrinkling his nose playfully.

Sabra exhaled slowly, feeling both relief and disappointment.

Pull yourself together, girl! What is the matter with you? Sabra thought, trying to hold her emotions in check.

"The baron has promised to imprison anyone in the village who steps foot on my lands," Sabra managed to say, leaning back in her chair. "Besides, no one in Caldor will dare step out of line. You saw how they were in the market yesterday."

Gheric gave her a knowing grin. "Good thing we are looking *outside* of Caldor," he replied dryly.

Sabra frowned into her mug. "The only people outside Caldor are the . . ." She stopped, her eyes widening as she understood what Gheric was implying. "You can't be serious." she said with a gasp.

"Oh, I'm deadly serious."

She shook her head in protest. "They will kill you the moment you step foot in their camp."

"If that's the case, you won't have to worry about me 'ravaging you' while you sleep," he quipped, popping a piece of cheese in his mouth.

"But they are bandits!" she argued. "Honorless men, driven from society for crimes committed against the people of Caldor."

"They are also able-bodied men and women who need employment," he countered. "Now, why don't you tell me where we can find the nearest cluster? Then, we can get started."

"You don't understand," she said, shaking her head. "Those bandits, they raid farms all the time. They hit my place last week. A half dozen of them dug out a portion of my potatoes and stole my only horse."

"Let me guess . . ." Gheric said, easing his frame back in his chair. "A powerful bay mare branded with a three-pointed cross on its right flank?"

Sabra stared at him, dumbfounded. "You've seen her?"

"Oh yes. I ran into that group yesterday. We'll go fetch your mare after you eat. Now, finish your breakfast while I get my things."

"What things?" Sabra asked.

In answer, Gheric whipped out a knife from behind the small of his back and brandished it in front of her. Its keen blade flashed in the candlelight.

"These kinds of things," he said, his voice suddenly cold.

Sabra stared at him, shocked at the change in his demeanor. "What did you say to Hob yesterday when he was ordered to count my baskets?" she asked.

"That's none of your concern," he answered.

"How did you escape from the bandits yesterday?" she pressed, unsure if she wanted to know the answer.

Gheric shot Sabra with an icy look. "I gave them something they wanted."

"Your eagles?"

"No," he answered, his voice like ice. "It was something they valued more than money."

"What was that?"

He gave her a predatory smile. "I gave them their lives."

Sabra shivered as fear ran down her spine.

CHAPTER 5

Grada sat quietly in the doorway of her tent, picking through the pile of trash near her mildew covered tent for the third time since sunrise, searching for some overlooked scrap she could eat. Finding nothing, she glanced toward the leader of the bandit group she had joined only a week ago. He was a stocky man who went by the name of Yetter. His sunken sallow face sported an unkempt black beard. Lining his neck were white scars that reached up past his chin on both sides to his ears.

Grada listened as he argued with another member of the bandits in his group.

"If I could have taken him, I would have," she heard Yetter say. "He wasn't like any soldier I'd ever seen. Gave me chills just looking at him."

"It was one man," a tall bandit with pockmarks named Othar exclaimed, his long chin jutting out angrily. "There were three of you. Four, if you count the mouse."

"Drei was with the horse." Yetter snarled, looking at the young waif next to him. "You can't expect a child to fight against a grown man."

"All you had to do was kill him," Othar said with a grunt, his voice cold. "Marn could have used his bow, shot him from a distance."

"Chara's tits," Yetter cursed, narrowing his eyes in anger. "I don't care how hungry we get, we don't go around killing people unless they attack us first. Robbing yes, killing no!"

Othar stood opposite Yetter, glaring at the short stocky man in front of him. "That's the difference between you and me," Othar spat. "I do what it takes to survive. You are a worthless sack of shit!" The taller bandit fingered the woodman's axe at his side, his eyes taking on a wild look. "Maybe it's time for new leadership?"

Yetter returned Othar's glare with one of his own. "You best stand down, boy," the elder man warned, his hand dropping to the hilt of a rusty sword. "Else you'll find you've bitten off more than you can chew."

An evil grin worked its way onto Othar's face. "By all means, let's find out—"

A shout from the east interrupted their quarrel. Grada could hear the dragging gait of their lookout, Marn.

"Riders coming!" Marn shouted, drawing a knife from his belt.

"How many?" Yetter asked, shuffling in front of Drei.

"Two." Marn panted, his left leg dragging behind him— the disastrous aftermath from where a horse had kicked him as a child. "One is the . . . man we tried to . . . rob yesterday. I . . . heard the footfalls. He and one other were . . . headed this way."

"Drei, come with me," Grada ordered, walking over next to the girl.

"Stay hidden," Yetter whispered to Grada, nodding toward the tents. "If things go bad, run north, see if you can find Samson's camp."

Othar spat in their direction. "A pox on you all." He snarled, raising his axe into a fighting position. "I'll gut this bastard myself."

"Go, now!" Yetter ordered Grada, ignoring the wiry bandit and his axe. Yetter moved in front of the four other bandits in his group.

Grada did as she was bid, running as quickly as she could with Drei to duck behind the trees near their tents.

"I'm surprised you didn't scurry away and hide with her," Othar said with a grunt, drawing next to Yetter. "A coward like you . . . Best you leave the talking to me."

"Shut up," spat Yetter, sick of the man's complaints.

"Quiet, both of you," Marn snapped, moving to the northern edge of the clearing. "I'm trying to listen . . . They are close."

The bandits did not have to wait long.

A powerful man wearing a cuirass of boiled leather strode into the camp. At his side was a longsword sheathed in a well-used bronze scabbard. His dark eyes emanated strength and confidence.

Behind him strode a beautiful young woman wearing a wide-brimmed straw hat and a gray goatskin hunting tunic. A cloak of gray wool trailed behind her, billowing slightly in the breeze. She was leading a fierce chestnut mare geared with a worn leather saddle.

"That's Widow Billerton," Grada heard Marn say.

"Who's the arrogant cock with her?" Othar voiced loudly, his contempt evident.

"That's the man from yesterday," Yetter confirmed, sounding troubled.

Othar scoffed, giving the stranger a look of derision. "This is the pissant you ran from? Why, he doesn't look so tough to me. Hell, I could take him myse—"

Faster than her eye could follow, Grada saw the man in the leather cuirass grab something from the back of his belt. A glint of metal flashed in the sunlight as he stepped forward and hurled the object at Othar.

Grada heard a loud *thuck*.

She blinked and saw a knife sticking in the wooden haft of Othar's axe. The pockmarked bandit gave a strangled sound and dropped the weapon, going white with shock.

The stranger brushed past the stunned bandit and stood easily in front of the leader.

"Yetter." He nodded politely in greeting. "You are looking well. Having trouble with your underlings?"

"Nothing I can't handle, Gheric," Yetter answered, glancing sourly at Othar.

The big warrior gave him a friendly smile. "We've come with a proposition for you, if you are interested?"

"That depends," Yetter replied, scratching at his armpits.

"On what?" Gheric asked.

"Who's asking?"

"I am," the woman behind them answered.

"It's Sabra, I believe?" the bandit leader queried.

"That's right," the woman replied, looking past them at the bay mare tied to a tree nearby.

Yetter glanced at the mare and then over to Othar. "What kind of a proposition?" he asked.

"The kind that is profitable to us both," Sabra answered. "I'll make it on one condition. Whichever of you stole my horse, you will return her to me now."

"That's *my* horse," Othar snarled through a row of broken teeth.

"No, it is mine," Sabra insisted.

"I'm not giving it to you," Othar said with a growl.

"If you don't, I'll put my next knife through your foot,"

Gheric said, his voice bored. "I must warn you: it hurts like hell, and good luck walking without pain for the next few months. A wound like that, it might never heal properly, and with winter coming . . .? Well, you might have to take off the whole leg if it were to get infected. But I'll not pressure any man into a hasty decision. You are free to make up your own mind."

Othar turned a light shade of green as Gheric finished his lightly veiled threat.

"You are . . . You're welcome to the bay," he said at last, with a final look at the imposing man in front of them. "She's foul-tempered anyway."

"Good choice," the dark-eyed warrior replied, his hands never straying far from his sword.

"About this proposition," Yetter said, eyeing Sabra thoughtfully. "Does it include food?"

Sabra gave him a slow smile. "Food, pay, and a place to stay, for as long as you like through the winter."

Yetter's eyes widened, and he looked to the rest of his group. "I'm listening," he said.

Sabra walked alongside her bay mare, Dapple, as the sun began to rise toward its zenith. The horse was happy to see her owner again as Sabra slipped the mare a handful of strawberries she'd picked earlier that morning.

Normally, she would have ridden the bay, but Dapple had been left to fend for herself in the week since she'd been taken. The bandits' neglect had sapped her strength, and Sabra did not wish to tire her out needlessly.

Next to Sabra walked the only other female of age who had been among the bandits. The woman wore no shoes, and her feet were caked with dirt. Threadbare leggings that were ripped at the bottom dangled off her waist, barely held in place by a length of rope knotted below the woman's abdomen. Her dark hair was a tangled mess, almost certain to be riddled with fleas or lice. Sabra thought it best to keep a safe distance between herself and the bandit woman.

At the front of the column walked Gheric, who chatted affably with the bandit leader, their conversation too distant for her to make out. Sabra imagined it had to do with the agreement they had struck.

One of the bandits, a man of medium height and build, strode quietly behind them. He had not spoken at all. His downtrodden face looked vaguely familiar to Sabra, but for the life of her, she could not place him.

How do they stand the smell of one another? she thought, wrinkling her nose in distaste at the woman walking next to her. *The lot of them need to bathe.*

"Will we get to stay in a house?" the woman asked, interrupting her thoughts.

Sabra looked over at the bandit woman and saw lines of exhaustion on the woman's dirt-covered face.

"I have farmhands' quarters out by the fields," Sabra answered cautiously. "Those will be given over to you and the rest of the bandits—" She cleared her throat. "Farmworkers," she corrected, embarrassed at her slip.

"These . . . quarters," the woman said, fumbling over the word, "they have walls made of wood?"

"No," Sabra corrected. "The walls are made of stone."

"That . . . is a relief," the bandit woman said, giving Sabra a weary smile. "That will keep the animals out. Maybe the men too?"

"What do you mean?" Sabra asked, her voice sharp.

The woman cast a fearful look over her shoulder at the quiet man behind them.

"What's your name?" Sabra asked.

"Grada."

"Grada," Sabra repeated, giving her an encouraging smile. "Did the man behind us try to force himself on you?"

"Silence?" She scoffed, giving the man a warm smile. "No. None of the men in Yetter's group are like that, but . . . I have been in other bandit camps where such acts are common. The women are treated like little more than whores."

Sabra pursed her lips in thought. "I will make certain you and . . ." She paused and looked up at the young waif on Gheric's horse.

"Drei," Grada said.

"Drei," Sabra continued, "are given quarters separate from the men."

"That would be wonderful," Grada replied, seeming to relax. "Can I ask you something, Mistress . . . Sabra?" the bandit woman continued, looking at the farmer with a pair of weary brown eyes.

"Of course," Sabra answered.

"How long have you and"—she nodded toward Gheric—"your man been together?"

Sabra felt a flush of heat at the question.

"We are not together," Sabra answered, fanning her face with her hat.

"Why not?" Grada asked. "Is he cruel?"

Sabra shook her head.

"Does he beat you? Mistreat you in some way?" the bandit woman persisted.

Sabra wiped the sweat from her brow and placed the hat back on her head. "No, nothing like that."

"Is he lazy?" Grada continued.

"No," Sabra answered, wishing the woman would stop asking questions. "I've only just met him."

"Ahh, you find him unattractive," Grada surmised, nodding her head.

"Not at all," Sabra whispered, looking at Gheric's handsome features.

"I don't understand." Grada frowned in confusion. "Has he proven to be disappointing in some way?"

"Actually, it's the opposite," Sabra answered without thinking. "He was the only person in Caldor to speak up for me at the marketplace. He defied the baron's merchant, and he got me an incredible price on my . . ." Sabra trailed off, knowing she had revealed too much.

"Is he kind to you?" Grada asked.

"I don't want to discuss it," Sabra said, shaking her head. She absently touched the bandage still wrapped around her forearm.

"Did he do that to you?" Grada questioned, gesturing at Sabra's arm.

"No . . . Yes," Sabra stammered.

Grada looked at her in confusion. "Which is it?"

Sabra cursed herself under her breath. "It's both. No, he did not injure me, and yes, he bandaged my arm," she explained.

Grada gave Sabra a long look. "Are you attracted to him?"

Sabra's face flushed red. "No, I—" She paused, looking again at Gheric's handsome features. "Yes, I suppose so, but we aren't like that; he's just helping me with my farm."

"I see," Grada said, giving Sabra a sidelong look that clearly implied she did *not* see.

"I'd rather not talk about it," Sabra said again.

"I am sorry if I have offended you, Mistress," Grada

apologized, "but I find the whole thing between you two fascinating."

Sabra did not answer, and the two walked along silently for the span of a few heartbeats.

"I think you like him," Grada said, staring straight ahead with a tiny smile on her face.

"I barely know him," Sabra argued a little too defensively.

Grada's smile widened, and she leaned closer to the blue-eyed farmer walking beside her. "I do not claim to be a smart or wise woman, Mistress. My life has not turned out the way I hoped it would. But I have known love in my lifetime." She leaned in close and dropped her voice to a whisper, "But I'd wager everything you own that Gheric likes you too. Why else go through all this trouble to help save your farm?"

Sabra said nothing. She did not have time to think about any man with everything that was going on around her.

Despite that, she could not ignore the thrill of excitement that ran through her at Grada's words.

CHAPTER 6

*B*aron Niles Turner looked at the heavyset merchant kneeling on the cool stone tile in front of him, and his lip curled in contempt.

"Let me see if I understand you correctly . . ." the baron said, his voice sharp. "You somehow managed to let a newcomer to Caldor dupe you into thinking he had twenty silver eagles with which to pay Sabra Billerton?"

Nervous streaks of sweat ran down Varfore's face as he stared up in fear at his liege lord. "There was no way for me to know—"

Niles struck him across the face.

"That was not my question," the baron stated, as the merchant was knocked to the floor. "The question is, how did this stranger, one wearing the lowest quality of threadbare clothing, manage to trick you into thinking he had twenty silver eagles in the first place?"

Varfore looked up at Niles, his eyes pleading. "He said his backer—"

"What backer?" the baron spat, his eyes furious. "By the gods, you are a stupid man. This is what your greed has cost you. What possessed you to think you could underbid the value of Widow Billerton's crop so badly? Did you think so little of me that you believed I was unaware of what you've been doing?"

Varfore visibly paled as he tried to get up. His eyes were watering from the baron's strike across his face.

"My lord, I have no idea—"

Niles stepped forward and struck him again. "Do not play me for a fool!" he snapped. "You have been overpricing my rates for weeks. You pay out nine silver eagles to my coffers but report ten. Your avarice has cost me 137 eagles these past months, an acceptable loss to keep these peasants in line."

The baron stopped and nodded to his guards, who then lifted Varfore to his feet.

"Now I learn that you cost me twenty silver eagles on a single transaction. More importantly, you have embarrassed me *and* yourself in front of the entire market square."

"My lord, please, I—"

"Because of you, I looked weak to the people of Caldor," the baron continued coldly. "Fear and respect keep the peace here, not greedy little shits like you." The baron stopped, staring down at the merchant with revulsion. "Because of your actions, an example must be set, don't you agree?"

Varfore began to weep, a pathetic blubbering sound that echoed throughout the room.

Niles reached out and grabbed Varfore by the scruff of his neck. "I asked you a question," he snarled between his clenched teeth.

"I . . . I'm sorry, my lord!" the merchant cried out. "I will pay you back the money, I swear it."

Niles let go of Varfore's neck and gave the man a malicious smile. "No, it's too late for that."

Looking at his guards, he issued them an order.

"Take him outside, cut his head off, and stick it on a pole in the market square."

At the sound of the baron's command, Varfore exploded into action.

"No!" the heavyset merchant howled, rising to his feet and thrashing away from his captors.

The guard to his right was knocked over, landing heavily on the stone tile of the floor with a cry of pain. The other guard, a slighter man with long sideburns, hurled himself onto the merchant's back, trying unsuccessfully to bear the heavier man to the ground. After a momentary struggle, Varfore managed to throw his attacker clear. Free of the guards, the corn merchant ran for the exit, desperately trying to escape.

The whistling sound of steel cutting through air preceded a terrified gasp that burst out of Varfore's mouth. The merchant, mere inches from the doorway, fell to his knees and collapsed to the floor with a steel knife embedded in his back.

"Fetch my knife and clean that up," Niles said calmly to his guards, both of whom were climbing slowly to their feet. "Afterward, report to Captain Harmon. Let him know of your failure here today. Pray he doesn't recommend the same fate suffered by that obese idiot."

"Yes, my lord," both men answered, giving the baron a sharp salute. Quickly, the larger of the guards dragged Varfore's body out the door, while the other returned the baron's knife. Without another word, the guard left the room.

"What do you think, cousin?" Niles asked over his shoulder without turning around.

The sound of light footsteps sliding across tile came from behind him.

"I think you should have paid more attention to the

mayor's warning . . ." a sultry voice sounded from behind the wooden chair at the back of the room, " . . . instead of skulking about in a foul mood all day."

Niles wiped the merchant's blood from his knife and slid it back into its sheath. "About that stranger?" he asked, raising an eyebrow in question.

"The stranger who assisted the Billerton widow in the market square—not once, but twice," the feminine voice answered as its owner stepped out from behind the chair. "Tamalin said he had the look of a soldier about him. A real soldier, not these half-trained idiots my father sent you."

The baron turned around to stare at the curvaceous silhouette of his cousin, who was still standing in the dim light at the back of the room. "Tell me, Aurelia, what would you have me do?"

A wicked laugh emanated from the darkness in front of Niles. "Learn as much as you can about this stranger. Who is he? Where did he come from? Who did he visit while he was in town? What does he want? Money? Perhaps you can buy him off."

The woman stepped closer, her beautiful figure covered in a tight-fitting dress of black satin. Her face was hidden in the depths of a green cloak. "Most importantly, find out where he is now. There was a report he'd been thrown out of the Bad Apple Inn last night."

"Why was that?" Niles asked, reaching out to touch his cousin's face.

"My understanding is he refused to work for his meal," she answered, avoiding the baron's attempt to touch her. The sensuous woman made her way behind Niles, running her hands along the sides of his hips.

The baron chuckled softly. "I think we can rule out any

connections with the innkeeper. He's known to toss out anyone who offends him."

"Don't be so sure," Aurelia purred in her cousin's ear. "This man, this stranger, has all the makings of a formidable foe. Perhaps he was thrown out on purpose, to keep us off his scent. After all, my report says he was near Gyles in the marketplace."

Niles canted his head to the side in question. "That is not likely." He scoffed.

"Still, my instincts tell me he is dangerous," she insisted.

"Perhaps I should go kill him now," Niles rasped, his tone dark. "I could cut him to ribbons in the street."

The baron could almost *feel* his cousin smiling from underneath her hood. "Do I detect a hint of jealousy?" she asked, breathing heavily on the back of his neck.

"I don't get jealous of peasants," he answered.

"You can kill him anytime," Aurelia chided. "But your uncle, Malhallow, my dear father, will not like it." She laughed lightly as he sniffed at her in disdain. "You are in for an earful already, having slain Varfore. My sources tell me he was Father's favorite toy for a time."

Her hands ran along the top of Niles pants and slipped upward, her fingers exploring underneath his red tunic. The baron felt her soft fingers run along his lean, muscular torso.

Niles let out a groan. "When are you going to give in to me?" he whispered, his voice husky. "I yearn for more than your hands upon my skin."

"You can have all of me when I get what I came here for," Aurelia answered, striding away. "My advice to you is to gather what information you can about this stranger. My instincts tell me he is more trouble than that farmhouse bitch you covet so much."

"Now who's jealous?" Niles asked, giving her a dark smile.

"I would watch you take her a thousand times to keep the girl from stealing what is rightfully mine," Aurelia rasped as she disappeared behind the wooden chair of the baron once again. "As long as you leave her to my father when you're done."

Baron Turner's sour mood lifted at the thought. "Two more days, perhaps less," he muttered to himself, striding with purpose toward the room's exit.

"Guards!" he cried out. "Fetch me Captain Harmon!"

There was work to be done.

CHAPTER 7

Gheric sighed as he made his way into the village. It had been a long day, and he was more tired than he cared to admit. *One last matter of business, and I can get some sleep*, he thought, seeing the last light of the setting sun set behind the foothills to the west.

At least my gamble was successful, he mused. The six extra pairs of hands they had procured would go a long way in helping harvest Sabra's crops. He knew it would be slower going than he might want, as the former bandits were not farmers—nor were they used to working all day out in the sun.

"I'll worry about that in the morning," he muttered to himself with a grunt, musing back to the first moments the bandits had arrived at the farm.

The very first order of business was for each of them to bathe in the stream that ran along the back side of the property. Gheric had rarely seen any group enjoy cleaning themselves as much as the bandits had. Sabra had doled out plenty of soap and brushes, insisting that each of them wash every part of their bodies as thoroughly as possible.

"By some miracle, they are free of lice, though I think at least one of them was crawling with fleas," she'd confided to Gheric.

After the new farmhands had dried off, Sabra brought them all inside the main house and let them root through generations worth of clothing left by the former occupants of the farm.

"Armison once told me dozens of Billertons and their workers lived here," Sabra had told him. "These clothes have been laying around for decades waiting for someone to come along and bring them back to life."

The former bandits had pawed through the garments, sharing more than one laugh at one another's expense.

"Gods, there are enough clothes here to dress an army," Gheric had said. "Wigs, uniforms, I even saw an old cavalry saber lying about."

"I told you," she had explained in a huff. "Some of these clothes and artifacts have been here for more than a century."

After washing the farmhands clean and clothing them, Sabra had gone about the task of preparing a meal. It was a simple stew made of vegetables and bacon, but to the former bandits, it was like ambrosia.

Once everyone had eaten, the farmhands went to sleep, the novelty of lying in a bed rather than on the ground wearing off quickly.

"Keep your doors locked and sleep with that knife you tried to stick me with last night," Gheric warned Sabra. "I trust most of them, pretty girl, but that Othar is another matter."

"I thought him sufficiently cowed after your demonstration at the camp," she replied.

"But I won't be here," the warrior explained. "I need to speak with Gyles and see if he has any information about the baron. You get some sleep. Tomorrow, we will be busy bringing in your crops."

Sabra paused, her face unreadable. "Be careful," she said at last, her voice neutral.

"Are you worried about me?" he asked, giving her a smile. "I'm flattered."

"I'm not worried about *you*." She huffed, shoving him out the door. "I'm more concerned about the half dozen hardened criminals you've dumped on me! My guess is you will abandon me to my fate at the first sign of trouble!"

She promptly slammed the door in his face.

I can't say I blame her, he mused to himself, moving close to the outskirts of town. Slowing his pace, Gheric moved off the road, knowing it might be watched. Carefully, the big warrior picked his way to the back of the Bad Apple Inn, making sure he stayed out of sight.

Gyles was wary. He knew the baron would be inquiring about Gheric's whereabouts, and he was happy his old friend had refused to tell him.

"That way, you won't have to lie," Gheric had said, moments before the innkeeper tossed him out on the street.

It was now well past an hour after the sun had set the following day, and he had heard nothing from his old friend. Irritably, the innkeeper took out the trash, dumping the kitchen scraps and leftovers in the trough outside his establishment.

"I should have my head examined for thinking he could pull this off," Gyles muttered under his breath.

"I agree," came a soft voice from the shadows behind the inn.

"Gheric!" The innkeeper gasped, glancing at the surrounding area, searching for his friend.

"The stables," was all the innkeeper heard before the sound of footsteps moved away.

Just like old times, Gyles thought, carrying the bucket he used for scraps back inside.

A FEW MINUTES LATER, THE INNKEEPER WAS ABLE TO STEAL away from the common room. He carefully ducked inside his stables and closed the door behind him. From under his cloak, he brought out a lantern and removed its cover.

"Gheric?" he whispered into the darkness.

"Here," came a voice from the shadows to the right of him.

Stepping into the dim light of the lantern was his old friend.

"Good to see you," the dark-eyed warrior said, clapping Gyles on the back. "Is there any news?"

"Oh yes," the innkeeper said, his face serious. "The baron has his guards out asking questions about where you went. There is talk of trying you for your seditious behavior."

"Seditious behavior?" Gheric scoffed. "Since when is haggling considered seditious?"

"Since Niles was appointed as baron," Gyles answered with a shake of his head.

"That's to be expected, I guess," Gheric acknowledged. "Tyrants don't like anyone standing up to their authority—they cannot afford to look weak."

Gheric stopped speaking and looked at the long face of his friend. "What is it? What's happened?"

Gyles pressed his lips together somberly. "The merchant

you challenged, Varfore—they killed him. His head was placed in the marketplace for everyone to see."

The swarthy warrior gave a low whistle of surprise. "You were right about him. This Niles Turner is a sadistic pig. I think it's safe to say the baron won't abide any failures."

"It's worse than that," Gyles muttered. "He has squads of guards out asking questions, under the guise of looking for you, but . . ." The innkeeper leaned in closer, his voice dropping to a whisper, " . . . I think they mean to kill you."

"Well, it won't be the first time I've been the subject of a manhunt," Gheric replied evenly. "I'll keep out of sight until it's time to make an appearance."

"You need to be careful, move only at night," Gyles warned. "Even meeting like this is dangerous."

The warrior turned his eyes upward, searching the shadows of the stable.

"You are right, of course," Gheric concurred. "I expect things to get worse before they get better. But that is a worry for me, not you. You are a good man, Gyles. Get back to the inn. Take care of your wife and any others you hold dear. I'll keep my distance for a few days. I've no desire to put you in danger."

"That might be for the best," Gyles agreed. "Incidentally," he continued, trying to keep from grinning. "How are things going with Widow Billerton?"

Gheric shrugged his broad shoulders in response. "I am making progress," he offered.

"How so?" the innkeeper queried.

Gheric canted his head to the side. "She's calmed down quite a bit in the last day or so," he explained.

"What happened?"

"Well, she's eased up since she tried to knife me in the

heart last night," the dark-eyed warrior remarked sarcastically.

"Has she now?" Gyles smirked.

"Aye, but she's calmed down a great deal," Gheric explained, sarcasm dripping from his tongue. "Not an hour ago, she had regressed to merely slamming a door in my face. Improvement, don't you think?"

Gyles began to laugh quietly. "It's like you said, she has spirit."

"Can't say I blame her," Gheric acknowledged. "She wasn't too happy about the farmhands I brought in . . . but, like it or not, that group of ruffians is her best chance to harvest her crops."

"Farmhands?" Gyles asked in bewilderment. "Wherever did you find them? Surely not from here in Caldor?"

"No," Gheric said. "I found them outside the village. Poor folk with no allegiance to any but themselves."

"Outside of the village?" the innkeeper questioned. "There's no one out there but . . ." He trailed off, giving Gheric a hard look. "Tell me you didn't."

"I did," Gheric answered. "It's all I could think of."

"It's a risk," the innkeeper pointed out. "Though I doubt it will matter much to Baron Turner *where* they came from. As far as he's concerned, anyone found working that farm will be put to death."

"I guess we will see," the broad-shouldered warrior muttered grimly. "Now, best if you get out of here. I'll stay for a bit . . . make sure no one is watching."

"Good luck, Gheric, stay safe."

"You too."

The innkeeper exited the stable and reentered the Bad Apple Inn without incident. Gheric waited for more than a half turn of the hourglass before following after. Quieter than a the sound of a wasp walking on a windowpane, he stole his way back to the Billerton Farm.

Despite his precautions and intense scrutiny, Gheric failed to notice the cloaked figure that was hiding on the second story of the stable.

If he had looked back, the dark-eyed warrior would have seen a curvaceous female dressed all in black exit the stable and make her way back across the village commons, heading toward the baron's keep.

CHAPTER 8

The next day, the tenants of the Billerton Farm woke to the sound of a steady drizzle falling across the landscape. After a hasty breakfast of bread and cheese, Sabra and her new farmhands got to work, despite the rain. Gheric slept in and was left with the thankless task of feeding the livestock, while the others moved into the fields. Sabra was giving instructions on the proper way to pick corn as well as pulling the empty stalks from the ground, cutting them, and adding them to the compost pile she would use for fertilizer next year.

It was hard work, and she allowed her new hands a break at noon, just as the rain turned into a downpour.

"That's a fine horse," Yetter said, admiring Gheric's mare.

"Aye," Grada agreed, patting Kat's neck. "Her fur is so soft."

"He grooms her twice a day," Sabra said, dipping a metal ladle inside a water bucket. She tilted the ladle back and drank deeply from it.

"I'd guess she is battle trained," Yetter put in, biting into a piece of warm bread.

Drei stumbled in with an armful of corn. "It smells so good," she gushed, inhaling the aroma of a piece of newly picked corn.

"Eat as much as you like," Sabra encouraged, shooting a smile toward the smallest farmworker. "This is when it tastes best," Sabra said, taking the corn and peeling away the husk. "Fresh off the stalk. Tonight, we can cook some and flavor it with butter and salt."

"There is so much." Marn blinked, looking out the barn door and taking in the field around them with wonder.

"It is a big farm," Gheric agreed, walking up to join them. "The crops that grow here are wonderful. I was able to examine some of your harvest yesterday afternoon. I've never seen anything of the like."

"What do you mean?" Grada asked curiously.

"Take a look at these ears of corn," the warrior said, picking out a piece from the nearest basket and holding it in front of him. "The kernels are huge, twice as large in comparison with the corn grown by the other farmers I saw at the market the day before yesterday."

He paused a moment studying the cob Drei had in her hand. "Most corn harvested this late in the season is fit only for draft animals and the like. This," he continued, pointing at Drei's piece, "is fit for a kings table." Gheric looked at Sabra, his eyes studying where her arm had been bandaged. "It's almost as though . . ." He trailed off, staring at Sabra as though she were a puzzle he had not solved.

"Someone is missing," Sabra commented, looking past the men and women gathered in the barn. Her eyes turned toward the field.

"That's Silence," Yetter offered, scratching under his chin. "He's only been with us for a few days. He's a bit peculiar, not sure he's right in the head. Don't worry, he'll come in when he's ready."

"But it's dumping rain," Sabra protested.

"You live in the open as much as we have, you get used to it," Marn added.

Othar, covered in droplets of sweat and rain, looked sharply at the broad-shouldered warrior standing across from him. "Where have you been anyway? Sleeping in while we work the fields?"

"He's been feeding my livestock," Sabra said coolly. "Along with other tedious chores you haven't learned yet."

"Sounds easy," the pockmarked man complained. "He gets to sit around and feed the animals out of the rain while we work the field getting soaked to the bone? Probably been brushing his horse the whole time."

"I'd leave Kat out of this if I were you," Gheric warned. "However, you are right. I did sleep in this morning. Lucky for me, I have only one chore left to complete. Seeing as how you got up earlier than I, I'll offer to trade places if you like?"

"Deal," Othar said, smiling in victory. "What's your last task? Listening to the raindrops fall on the roof?"

"Shoveling manure," the dark-haired warrior stated with a smile. "There's a whole pen of it where the sheep have been staying. Make sure you cart it out next to the compost pile. The farm will need it for next year's crops."

Othar stared at him, openmouthed. "That's not what I . . . You tricked me!" he stammered.

"You're the one who wanted to do my job, now you have it." Gheric shrugged.

The tall bandit's face turned red and twisted in anger. "You son of a bitch!" he thundered, swinging a fist wildly at Gheric's face.

The dark-haired warrior dodged it easily and snapped off

a right hook that caught Othar in the stomach, knocking the bandit from his feet.

"Gentleman, enough!" Sabra shouted, stepping between them both. "There will be no fighting among ourselves on this farm. Should it happen again, our deal is off. Is that understood?"

"Of course," Gheric said, offering Othar a hand.

"Sod . . . off . . . you shit," the tall bandit cursed, trying to catch his breath.

"Do you understand?" Sabra repeated, grinding her words at Othar.

"I've . . . quit better jobs . . . than this," the former bandit gasped, his angry eyes fixed on Gheric.

"I will have your word," Sabra demanded, the sound of her voice unwavering.

"Fine," the former bandit muttered, glaring at Gheric. "Just keep that lying asshole away from me."

"That's another thing," Sabra continued, still focused on the lanky farmhand. "I don't want to hear that kind of talk in my presence again. Save it for your quarters."

Othar seemed ready to respond with a nasty retort, but the look on Sabra's face told him she'd meant what she'd said.

"All right," he growled, clearly embarrassed by his thrashing.

"Let's get back to work," Sabra ordered, stepping out from underneath the shelter of the barn. She made it three steps out the door before skidding to a halt. "By Chara," she cursed, looking back at Gheric. "We've got trouble."

"Does this mean I can bloody swear again?" Othar chirped sarcastically.

"What is it?" Gheric asked, ignoring Othar. He moved his head to the side and looked past Sabra, staring down the lane that led to her farm.

"A squad of the baron's guards are riding up the road," she answered. "It looks like they have a pack of dogs with them."

For a moment, no one moved.

"They must have heard I was here," Gheric muttered. Striding toward the back of the house, he called out behind him. "Sabra, go and greet them as you normally would. Invite them in and offer your hospitality. Show them there is no reason for you to be defensive. The rest of you, stay in the barn."

"Or what?" Othar sneered.

"Or they might kill you," Sabra answered, walking toward the back of her home, following Gheric.

She increased her pace until she was alongside the broad-shouldered warrior. "What of you?" she asked.

"I don't want you to have to lie," he said. "I'll get my things, grab Kat, and go. Tell them you have no idea where I am, but you've heard I've been skulking about in town. That is, after all, akin to the truth."

"What if they ask if you've been here?" she questioned.

"Tell them yes, you saw me walk past yesterday morning, and I was heading north toward Rathstone."

"What about the dogs?" she demanded. "Won't they pick up your scent?"

"They might, but a downpour like this could ruin the trail. Let's hope so."

"Are you certain?"

"No, not at all," he answered, giving her a smile as rainwater trickled along the contours of his face.

"I'll do my best to get rid of them," she said, bracing herself for what was to come.

"Kat and I will be gone as soon as I grab my things from the house."

"Will I see you again?" she asked, feeling a tightness she did not expect form in her chest.

"I certainly hope so," he answered as they slid through the back door of the house. "I've been meaning to ask you something, but it will have to wait."

She gave him a bewildered look. "What do you need to ask me?"

Gheric, despite the danger of their situation, gave her a mischievous smile. "I wouldn't want to spoil it, but . . ."

He leaned in close to her and gently ghosted his lips across her cheek. Despite the cold rain, they were soft and warm. Sabra felt the hair on the back of her neck rise. He slid his lips next to her ear and softly whispered, "You have a good heart, Sabra Billerton. I have wanted to ask you to kiss me since we first met. But that choice belongs to you."

A flutter of excitement ran through her body as he pulled away and gave her a last smile. "Be safe, pretty girl. I'll see you soon."

The swarthy warrior grabbed his belongings and was out the back door before Sabra could gather her wits.

He wants to kiss me? She shuddered in both trepidation and excitement, but that feeling vanished as she cast her gaze out the window and saw the group of guards drawing close to the entrance of her farm.

One thing at a time, she thought, bracing herself for her encounter with the baron's men.

LIEUTENANT JORRELL WAS IN A FOUL MOOD. HE HAD NEVER wanted to visit Caldor, but circumstances dictated that he must.

"*You are the best swordsman I have,*" his father had explained. "*It has to be you, you understand?*"

Jorrell *had* understood, as his own personal interests were at stake.

Still, at that moment, he was regretting his father's request for a variety of reasons. It was bad enough he was forced to ride out in the pouring rain on the orders of Baron Turner. Now, he had been tasked with bringing in the rabble-rouser who had caused so many issues at the marketplace.

Another regret was the company of the baron's guards. The raven-haired lieutenant glanced at his three companions with something close to revulsion. Each wore a tunic of leather armor with the silver emblem of a stag burned onto the front. All were draped in wool cloaks, now sopping wet in the downpour.

They, like the lieutenant, were not happy to be here.

"Ten to one he runs for the hills," the brutish sergeant to Jorrell's left said, wiping droplets of water from his face.

"You're crazy, Orms," voiced a second guard. He was a small, wiry man who went by the name of Ace. "I'll take that action. I think this newcomer will prove to be a scrapper. He'll rush out, hoping to take us by surprise. Then . . ." He stopped speaking and slowly drew a finger across his throat.

The brutish sergeant laughed and looked to the last member of their quartet. "How 'bout it, Frams?" he asked, looking at the tall guard next to him. "You want a part of this action?"

"I'll pass," the tall guard answered with a shake of his head, keeping a steady hand on the leash that restrained the dogs they'd brought with them.

"He's more interested in the widow, I'd wager," Ace snickered. "She's a nice piece of ass, wouldn't you say, Lieutenant?"

Jorrell frowned at the wiry guard. "There will be none of that," the lieutenant replied, somewhat stiffly. "Duke Turner wants her alive and unspoiled."

"Aww, come on now," Orms protested in his deep baritone. "She was married, wasn't she? Been spoiled already by the old farmer's sausage."

"That's enough," Jorrell said in disgust as they approached the farm's entrance.

Walking out to meet them was Widow Billerton, holding a blue cloak over her head to shelter her from the rain. She waved at them in a welcoming manner.

"Damn, but she is a fine-looking woman," Orms jeered at the others.

"I said enough," Jorrell commanded, his face hardening.

"Careful, Lieutenant, you just got here," Ace warned, his sour face turning with a sneer. "This ain't Rathstone. We do what we want down in these parts. You'd best learn that . . . else you'll go the same way as your predecessor."

Jorrell was not stupid. He knew the previous lieutenant, a man named Horval, had been removed for sympathizing with the people of Caldor. None of the guards he'd spoken to knew what had happened to him, but there was enough talk among the men that Jorrell suspected he was dead.

"We are here to bring the stranger named Gheric in for questioning, nothing more," Jorrell instructed. "Anyone disobeying their orders will answer to me."

The other guards muttered complaints under their breaths, but they did not challenge him further. He might have been new to Caldor, but Jorrell carried the reputation of being a master of the sword. The quartet remained quiet as they walked through the gate.

"Lieutenant," Gheric heard Sabra say from his place behind the barn. "Might I offer you and your men some refreshments inside, out of the rain?"

"That would be appreciated," the lieutenant answered, dismounting from his horse.

Gheric did not wait to hear the rest. Instead, he ran toward the back of the stable and led Kat away from the cluster of buildings that sheltered Sabra's new farmhands.

The constant sound of the rain thrumming all around muffled the sound of his escape. He made his way into the cornfield, water running down his face. Kat whinnied softly in protest as the rain-soaked leaves drenched both horse and master.

"Easy, girl," he whispered to the mare. "We've suffered through worse than this. It's just a bit of rain . . ."

At the edge of the farmland, they slid to a halt.

Standing in front of them was the wild-eyed Silence, the last of the new farmhands who had remained in the field. He stood nearly as tall as Gheric and had the lean, whipcord body of a swordsman.

"Damn it, man, you nearly got a knife in the eye," Gheric swore, surprised to see the former bandit.

Silence was rapidly fluttering his eyes and shaking his head as though he was in pain.

"Are you all right?" Gheric asked, letting go of Kat's reins and grabbing the farmhand by the shoulder.

Instead of answering, Silence pulled the warrior close so his mouth was next to Gheric's ear. Silence was breathing heavily, gasping as though he were choking on something.

Gheric tried to push himself away, but the former bandit was surprisingly strong. Silence took in a deep breath and managed to utter a single word.

"C-Cu-Cursed."

Gheric, who was employed by one of the most powerful spellcasters on the continent, knew immediately what Silence meant.

"You've had a spell cast on you?" the broad-shouldered warrior guessed, grabbing hold of the sides of the man's head.

The new farmhand nodded in relief.

"You're not really a bandit, are you?" Gheric reasoned.

Again, Silence shook his head.

Behind them, they could hear the sound of dogs barking.

"Shit," Gheric swore, with a quick look toward the farmhouse. "Who cursed you?"

Silence began gasping again, but he knew there was not enough time. Looking down at the ground, he saw a twig sticking in the mud. He reached down, picked up the twig, and scrawled a name in the mud.

Aurelia

"Aurelia?" Gheric asked. "Who is that? Is she with the baron?"

Silence nodded his head vigorously.

The barking behind them grew closer.

"Stay hidden if you can, and get to the barn," Gheric ordered, clapping Silence on the shoulder. "You're a good man."

Silence shot a brief smile at him and pointed into the forest.

"Yes, once I cross the stream, I'll hide in the woods. Don't worry about me," he said, grabbing Kat's reins. They took a few steps, and Gheric looked back at Silence, who was watching him closely.

"You were a swordsman, weren't you?" Gheric asked.

Silence held up a fist and gave the fleeing warrior a fierce smile.

CHAPTER 9

*B*aron Turner panted with excitement as he faced the soldier in front of him. Both men had their swords drawn, and neither had given an inch.

"You are good, Jorrell," the baron acknowledged as he lunged forward with a lightning attack. "Your reputation is well earned."

The lieutenant said nothing as he blocked the baron's thrust with a metallic clang of steel on steel.

"Excellent footwork, quick hands. It looks like my uncle sent one of his best," Niles continued.

"You are kind to say so, my—" Jorrell began to reply just as the baron attacked again. The lieutenant was a fraction late in his defense and felt his opponent's sword point tap him on the chest with a murderous riposte. Beaten, the officer gave the baron a strained smile.

"A fine move, my lord," Jorrell said, trying to hide his disappointment.

"You lack focus, Lieutenant," Niles chided, setting his sword on the ground.

"A fault my instructors have failed to drill into me," the lieutenant admitted, somewhat sheepishly.

"It will get you killed one day," came a cold voice of disapproval.

From the doorway came a figure of the largest man in the barony. Stepping into the light, the lieutenant saw a mountain of a man with a rigid face and square jawline. Upon his right cheek was an angry white scar that marred his otherwise plain face.

"As you say, Captain," Jorrell conceded, glancing at the hulking form of Harmon, the commanding officer of the baron's forces here in Caldor. The massive soldier filled the room, his arms and shoulders bulging with corded muscle.

"Something for you to work on." Niles sniffed, taking a drink from his cup of wine. "Now, to other matters."

Using a soft linen, the baron mopped his face of sweat . "I received information that this stranger, Gheric, was staying with Widow Billerton last night. Yet you tell me, Lieutenant, that there was no sign of him at the farm?"

"That is correct, my lord," Jorrell answered, wiping perspiration from his face with another linen. "Three of us searched the house, while Corporal Frams loosed the dogs into the fields. We found only the widow's workers taking a midday repast inside the barn. The man Gheric was nowhere to be—"

"Her workers?" interrupted Harmon. "What workers? When I last heard, Baron Turner had forbidden anyone in Caldor from assisting her with her crops. You must be mistaken, boy."

"There is no mistake," Jorrell stated, eyeing the captain evenly.

"Even if what you say is true . . . what townsfolk would

dare defy your orders?" Harmon asked, his baleful gaze resting on the baron.

"I don't know," Niles replied, his eyes hot. "You'd best find out, Captain. Whoever they are, they will burn for their disobedience."

"They are not townsfolk," came a sultry voice from behind them.

The three men turned to see the dark silhouette of Aurelia enter the room from behind the baron's chair.

"How do you know this?" Niles asked.

"These village folk have no backbone," the captain put in. "None would dare risk your wrath."

"That is true," Aurelia agreed. "However, this Gheric is smart. He's no run-of-the-mill soldier."

"Who is he?" Jorrell asked softly.

In answer, Aurelia stepped into the light of the room. A pair of brilliant blue eyes the color of the midmorning sky took them in. Her face was covered in a veil of black satin. From underneath her cloak, she produced a scroll tied neatly with a green ribbon.

"I sent word to my people in Rathstone last night," she explained. "I asked the same question you did, Lieutenant: 'Who is this Gheric?' This was their response."

She handed the scroll to Niles, who opened it immediately. Scanning the contents, his face turned down in a frown.

"My lord? What does it say?" the towering captain asked.

"His name is Gheric Carlow, known as Gheric the Fox," Niles answered. "He has been employed as an officer in a mercenary company that works throughout the Crystalline Sea."

"Which group of mercenaries is he employed with, my lady?" Jorrell asked.

"The information I received doesn't specify," Aurelia answered. "My sources will need more time to gather a complete report."

"What does it matter which group he's with?" the captain growled, his scarred cheek twitching angrily. "Enough with the pandering. Tell me where to find this Gheric, and I'll tear him apart!"

"Discovering his employer may give us the advantage we seek," Jorrell pointed out. "You know nothing of him—not the way he thinks nor the way he fights."

The captain looked down at the smaller man with contempt. "What do you know of it, boy? These warriors for hire are all the same. They answer to only one master: gold! The lot of them are worthless as soldiers; I have seen it many times."

"That is not always the case," Jorrell argued. "In my experience, these mercenary groups can change the course of a battle in an instant . . . and while they are paid fighters, they are loyal to their employers."

"In your experience?" the grizzled captain mocked. "Exactly how many battles have you fought in, Lieutenant?"

Jorrell's dark eyes held the captain in disdain. "More than a provincial captain of some backwater village," he answered coolly. "Besides, wasn't it a mercenary who gave you that scar?"

"*What* did you say to me?" Harmon raged, his face going red.

"You heard me just fine," Jorrell retorted, reaching for the hilt of his sword.

The massive captain responded in kind, his hand coming to rest on the pommel of his blade. "Let's see if all the dancing you do is enough to best me," Harmon said with a growl.

"Whenever you are ready," Jorrell hissed, his anger rising.

"As much as I'd like to see how such a fight might end, we have other matters to attend to," Baron Turner cut in, stepping between the two men.

Both officers glared at one another, neither wishing to back down.

"I said enough!" Niles barked.

"As you say, my lord," Jorrell responded, letting his hand fall to the side.

Casting his eyes toward Aurelia, Niles pursed his lips in thought.

"What is this mercenary doing this far south of his usual area of employment?"

"I don't know," Aurelia confessed.

"It's likely his downtime," Jorrell offered, with a last look at the captain. "Most mercenaries are employed in the warmer months. Winter is fast approaching. I'd say he's off for the season."

The captain gave Jorrell a hateful glare. "What do you know of it?" he sneered. "You couldn't even find the man, despite having information telling you *exactly* where he was hiding."

"The fault lies not with Jorrell," Aurelia interjected. "If Gheric is as well trained as I suspect, I doubt he would stay in one place for long. Even if he was at the Billerton Farm, chances are we missed out on finding him there. He's likely in the wind."

"Then we need to draw him out," Niles suggested. "If only we knew how."

No one in the room could see Aurelia's smile behind her veil.

"I have an idea," she offered.

"What is it?" the baron asked.

"We could capture his friend," she offered. "He is, after all, the reason Gheric came to Caldor in the first place."

The others looked at her with a mixture of surprise and confusion.

"Who is his friend?" Jorrell asked.

Aurelia walked behind the hulking captain of the guard, running her hands along the massive breadth of his shoulders. "Captain Harmon, I need you and your men to pay a visit to the Bad Apple Inn."

GYLES LOCKED THE FRONT DOOR TO HIS INN AT THREE HOURS shy of midnight. His wife had gone to bed already, and he was close to exhausted after a long day of work. Gyles finished up in the common room, preparing it for the next morning's business. There were a dozen mindless tasks he needed to attend to, which, while tedious, gave him time to muse about the excited talk among the villagers that had been discussed that day. There had been two items of interest that had been the topic of conversation in his common room that evening.

The first was that Baron Turner had apparently dispatched more than half of his guards in what turned out to be a futile search for someone. Several of the baron's soldiers had come into the common room, wet and miserable, asking for information about a new stranger in town. Most of the townsfolk suspected it had something to do with the confrontation in the market, but no one knew for certain.

The other rumor was even more surprising. An hour till sunset, the rain finally stopped, and the market square came alive for business. Sabra Billerton brought *five* wagons full of corn—350 bushels of the thickest, juiciest corn Caldor had ever seen. She had been paid sixty silver eagles by the baron's new merchant, a fair man by the name of Pyle. The surprise wasn't so much in the payment, but rather in trying to figure out how a single woman had managed to pick so much corn in the pouring rain.

The innkeeper swept his red hair from his eyes in wonder. *Ahh, Gheric,* he thought. *It didn't take you long to stir up the—*

Gyles's thoughts trailed off as he looked out the window. He noticed the stable door was unlatched and swinging on its hinges in the faint breeze outside. "That's odd," he murmured softly, opening the back door to investigate. The portly innkeeper grabbed hold of a lantern and eased his way across the muddy road that led to his stable. Stepping inside, he searched the darkness. There was a hooded figure sitting on the same rick of hay Gheric had rested upon only two days ago.

"Gheric?" the innkeeper asked, peering closely at the dark figure in front of him.

The hooded man slipped off the hay and stood, his vast height telling Gyles exactly who he was.

"Harmon," the innkeeper breathed, feeling a shiver run down his back.

The massive man in front of him took off his hood. "You should have stayed out of it," the captain of the guard hissed, the scar on his cheek glowing pale in the lanternlight. "But you couldn't let it lie, could you? Now, you and your mercenary friend are going to die."

The innkeeper took a step back right into the arms of four of the baron's guards.

"Take him," the captain ordered, his voice glacier cold.

Gyles felt a blow strike the back of his head, and he knew no more.

Sabra waited anxiously in the small space of her living room. When she heard a knock at the back door, she quickly stood and walked over to open it, relief flooding through her as she took in the sight of the broad-shouldered warrior standing in front of her.

"You're alive," she breathed.

"Hello, pretty girl. Did you miss me?"

For a moment, Sabra was too overcome with emotion to speak. When she did find her breath, she said the first thing that came to mind.

"Why do you call me that?" she snapped.

"Pretty girl?" Gheric questioned.

"Yes, there is more to me than the way I look, you know."

Gheric pressed his lips together firmly in an attempt to keep from smiling. "I apologize, Mrs. Billerton. I had no idea it would offend you. Tell me . . . how would the average-looking woman in front of me, with her mediocre hips and plain face, like to be addressed?"

"That's not what I . . ." she began, trying to regain her senses. "Why must you make everything so difficult?"

"I'm actually quite a simple man," he answered. "You, on the other hand, have a way of deliciously complicating everything around you."

"I do not!" she snapped, feeling her anger rise.

"Really?" he countered. "Because all I did was say hello when you opened the door. You took my compliment as some kind of negative insight into my character. In the meantime, you have refused to answer my very simple question."

"What question?" she demanded.

He smiled at her, drawing close enough to where she could see tiny flecks of gold in his eyes. "Did you miss me?"

"Yes . . . No!" she shouted, shoving him away from her.

"Well, that clears it up," he said with a laugh. Gheric wrestled his way out from under his backpack, setting it gently on the ground. "How did it go with the guards?" he asked, stripping off his tunic and hanging it on the post of his bed to dry. "I kept an eye on things as best I could. I saw them leave not long after their arrival."

"You stayed in the woods?" she asked, trying not to stare at his well-muscled torso.

"I thought it best, considering they might have come back to search for me again."

"What have you been . . . What happened to your beard?" she stammered, unable to look away from his face.

He smiled as he stumbled out of his pants. "Finally had time to shave," he said with a grunt, hanging the wet garment on the opposite post.

"By the grace of Chara . . . what are you doing?" Sabra gasped, turning away from him, her face burning red.

"Getting ready for bed," he answered. "I don't want to sleep in wet clothes."

"Don't you have the least bit of decency?"

His rich laughter rolled in from behind her. "I thought you were married once? Did you and your husband never see one another without clothing on?"

Sabra whirled around, her temper flaring. "You don't know anything about my marriage!" she yelled. "You are just like every man I've ever known. You let your cock do your thinking! Why, if you had an inkling of decorum—"

Sabra blinked, and he was there, well inside her personal space. Gheric was so close, she could feel the heat of his body emanating off his skin. He'd grasped the back of her neck with one hand, firmly, but without discomfort. With the other, he placed a single finger over her lips, quieting her with a look.

"I missed you too," he said simply.

The genuine sound of his tone and boldness of his statement caught Sabra off guard.

"I told you never to touch me . . ." she began, shaking away his finger.

"I stayed close by in the woods to keep you safe," he continued, placing the finger back over her mouth. "I watched to make certain no one, neither the guards nor your new farmhands, caused you any harm."

Sabra felt a heat rising inside her, one that she'd not experienced in a long time.

"And for the record," he continued, "yes, I think you are beautiful . . . but that is not why I am helping you."

The sincerity in his voice touched a chord with Sabra. Unconsciously, she reached up and touched his clean-shaven face with her hand. Slowly, he removed his finger from her lips. "Why did you . . .? Why are you helping me?" she managed to ask, her heart hammering in her chest.

Gheric gave her a smile. "Because you are brave in the face of danger, and that kind of courage is rare in this world," he answered. "I would not stand idly by when there was something I could do to help."

Sabra looked deeply into his eyes, seeing that his words came from the heart.

"Are you a hero, then?" she asked softly.

He shook his head in genuine humor. "No, pretty girl, *you* are the hero. I'm just here to help."

Sabra reached up with her other hand and gently caressed the side of his face.

"I missed you too," she admitted, feeling a weight lift

from her. "I was afraid the baron's guards would find you and take you away . . . from me."

Gently, Gheric stroked her cheek, his touch like fire on her skin.

"I'm sorry I presumed anything about you and your husband," he said. "I suppose I don't like the idea of another man being with you—even if it was before we met."

She reached out and brushed a strand of hair that had fallen over his eyes. "Do you still want to kiss me?" she breathed, her anger falling away.

She saw his beautiful lips turn up in a smile. "I thought I wasn't supposed to touch you at all?" he questioned.

"Little good that did me," she answered, longing to feel the press of his lips against hers.

"Of course I want to kiss you," he answered, leaning in close to her. "The real question is, what do you want?"

Sabra felt the last of her willpower drain away as she touched her lips to his.

Their passion started slowly, neither in a hurry, both wanting the moment to last. The warmth and softness of Gheric's lips surprised Sabra, almost as much as the gentleness of his touch. As the seconds passed, she could feel her desire begin to grow. His kisses, tender at the outset, had become urgent, more intense. Sabra, her body coursing with excitement for the first time in years, came vibrantly alive. She kissed him back fiercely, her passion equaling his own.

"What . . . are you doing?" she breathed as she felt his lips move away from her mouth.

"You are about to find out." He moaned, slowly working his way downward. She felt his lips kiss her chin, her throat, the side of her neck.

Sabra felt the heat of his touch, and a carnal desire stirred from somewhere deep within her chest. Her passion building, she wrapped both of her arms around the back of his head and pressed his face hard against the skin below her neck.

She felt the left side of her dress fall off at the shoulder. It was then that Sabra became aware of what Gheric was doing. His tongue moved from the flesh below her collarbone down to the front of her chest.

"Gheric," she whispered, feeling his hot mouth envelop her hardened nipple.

An ecstasy Sabra had never dreamed of swept through her like a driving rain that would not stop. She felt a wetness build between her legs, intensifying rapidly as Gheric kissed his way from one breast to the other.

"By the gods," Sabra breathed, as she felt the fingers of his hand move to her groin. As her desire heightened, she felt him slide his fingers carefully inside her.

"Gheric, I . . . By Dourn, what are you doing to me?" She gasped for air.

He did not answer. Instead, he took the nipple of her left breast fully in his mouth and began to suck on it. Simultaneously, he moved his fingers in and out of her, increasing their pace across the most sensitive part of her womanhood. Sabra could feel a tightly wound knot of passion building inside of her. Higher it grew, until Sabra opened her eyes in astonishment and looked down upon the beautiful man next to her as the ecstasy rising inside her neared its summit.

"Gheric—" She panted, rapidly losing control. "By the gods . . . *by the gods, what are you—*"

Like the steady rise of an ocean wave before it breaks, Sabra took a final long, deep breath. The sight of his mouth wrapped around her nipple coupled with the incredible feeling of his fingers inside her proved to be more than she could bear.

The wave crashed.

Sabra's head snapped backward as she felt the shuddering pleasure of her first orgasm. She cried out in ecstasy as a sensation she had never dreamed possible coursed through her body. It was the most incredible feeling she had ever known. From her head, all the way down to her toes, Sabra's blood burned like molten lava. On and on the sensation went, a never-ending volcanic eruption that seemed to last both forever and not long enough.

At last, bathed in sweat, the sensation faded, leaving Sabra breathless and wanting more. She became vaguely aware that she was still crushing Gheric's face into her chest.

Regretfully, she loosened her hold, and he kissed his way back up to her lips.

"What, in the name of the gods, was that?" she asked, nearly unable to speak.

"Just the beginning," he promised, kissing her deeply on the lips once again.

"There's more?" she asked, gasping in disbelief between kisses and feeling her passion rise a second time.

"Oh, Sabra, you have no idea . . ." he said breathily, moving her to the bed.

She felt Gheric's hands on her hips. Firmly, he turned Sabra around. Pushing her gently, the left side of Sabra's face hit the mattress, while her feet remained rooted to the floor. She could feel his hands moving up the skin of her naked back, and, somehow, she heard him whisper in her ear.

"Do you want me?" he asked, his voice filled with longing.

Sabra tilted her head backward and looked behind her. She saw Gheric had kicked his undergarments to the floor; he was completely naked now. Sabra could feel the hardness of his penis resting on her backside between her buttocks. The sight of him naked and aroused sent the unfamiliar sensation of desire coursing through her.

"Do you want me?" he asked again, this time with more urgency.

"Yes," she whispered hoarsely, her skin alive with his touch.

She became aware of his manhood easing its way inside of her.

"By the gods," she whimpered, desperate for him to power into her.

"You want more than that?" he teased, standing above her.

"Yes," she said with a moan, a carnal need flooding her senses once more.

"What was that?" he asked, pulling back out again.

"Yes!" she screamed, reaching back with her hands, trying to force his hips forward.

Sabra felt his fully erect penis enter her, and she let out a cry of pleasure.

He filled Sabra completely with his warmth as her desire reached new heights. She was acutely aware of his hands grasping her hips as he slid into her with a primal desire they both felt. She began to moan, softly at first, as Gheric moved slowly. As his excitement grew, so did his pace. Faster now, Sabra felt another orgasm building, and her moans became louder. She became intensely aware of his manhood hardening and knew he was close to his climax. Sabra reveled in it, knowing she was about to bring him to his fall.

With a primal cry of ecstasy, Gheric rammed his cock into her, his wetness exploding deep within Sabra as she shuddered in rapture with an orgasm of her own.

For the length of several heartbeats, Gheric continued, gasping uncontrollably for breath. Finally, he came to a halt, his ardor having run its course. Reluctantly, he pulling his manhood from inside of her.

Sabra nearly wept at its absence.

"Lay with me," he said between pants, taking her by the hand and crawling on top of the mattress.

Moments later, their bodies bathed in the sweat of lovemaking, they lay on the bed wrapped inside the warmth of a blanket.

"That was . . . incredible," Sabra said, looking up at Gheric's handsome face.

"It was," the warrior agreed, kissing her lightly upon her lips. "How long has it been since you felt the pleasure of a man's touch?"

"A long time," Sabra answered, her eyes misting over.

He pressed his lips together and shook his head. "I am sorry, Sabra. It is none of my business."

"No," she answered, wiping away a single tear. "It has been far too long since I've spoken of it."

"Was it . . . your husband?"

Sabra smiled and shook her head. "No, Armison was a good man, but he was well past seventy when we wed. We never consummated the marriage."

She took a deep breath and closed her eyes. "When I was seventeen, I fell in love with one of the blacksmith's sons. Trevor was his name. That summer, we spent our nights together, laughing and sharing in one another's company. We were to be wed that autumn."

"What happened?" Gheric asked.

"He died," she answered, burrowing her face into his chest. "A group of bandits had raided our farm, and he was killed by a stray arrow in the night."

Gheric shook his head. "A senseless death."

"Yes. Well . . . his mother was heartbroken. Told me it

was my fault, that I was cursed, that her son had paid for our sins. She said if it hadn't been for me, he never would have been at our farm in the first place."

Gheric wrapped his arms around Sabra and held her tightly.

"I'm sorry, Sabra. That was cruel of her to say."

"I know. I don't blame her, but . . . I've not let anyone close to me since."

"Until now?" he questioned.

"Until now," she affirmed, giving him a smile.

"I am flattered—" Gheric began to say before he was interrupted by a fist pounding on the front door.

"Widow Billerton!" yelled a voice on the other side. "I need to speak with you right away!"

"By Dourn, that's immaculate timing," Gheric huffed, clearly irritated.

"Hide," Sabra hissed, scrambling out of the bed and yanking her dress back on.

"Let me see who it is," he insisted, disentangling himself from the bedding and pulling on his wet pants.

Pulling a knife from his pack, Gheric crept over to the window and looked outside. "It's one of the baron's men," he whispered, gripping the hilt of the knife tightly.

Sabra pushed him aside, looking for herself. "That's Lieutenant Jorrell," she said softly, her face worried.

"Why is he here?" Gheric asked, looking to see if the man was alone.

"What do you want?!" Sabra asked, her voice loud enough to hear through the door.

"Thank the gods you are home," Jorrell replied, his voice sounding relieved. "I must speak with you, and time is of the essence."

"What is this regarding?" she asked, still uncertain of the man's intentions.

There was a pause on the other side.

"It's about Gheric," the lieutenant answered. "Somehow, the baron discovered that he's friends with the innkeeper at the Bad Apple Inn."

Gheric blanched at the news.

"Tell me truly, Sabra, because our lives depend on your answer," Gheric whispered. "When you spoke to him today, did you feel this Jorrell was a man you could trust?"

Sabra blinked once in hesitation and nodded. "Yes, he was professional, and he would not let his men hurt any of the farmhands, despite having orders to kill anyone they found working here. He seemed a decent sort to me. I believe he is a man to honor his word."

Without hesitation, Gheric opened the door, grabbed Jorrell by the tunic, and dragged the lieutenant inside. "What happened?!" Gheric demanded, smashing Jorrell up against the wall, holding his knife to the man's throat."Gheric, wait!" Sabra warned.

"Easy now," Jorrell said, looking calmly at the warrior in front of him. "I'm here to help you."

"Start talking," Gheric said with a growl, keeping his knife in a ready position.

"The baron's cousin, Aurelia, found out that you and Gyles are old friends," the lieutenant explained, licking his lips nervously. "They've brought him to the keep, hoping you will be drawn out into the open. I came to warn you to get away as soon as you could."

"What of Gyles?" Gheric demanded. "What will they do with him?"

Jorrell tilted his head to the side but said nothing.

"Shit," Gheric cursed, knowing Gyles did not have long.

"Why are you warning us?" Sabra asked.

The lieutenant let out a deep breath. "There are many reasons. Foremost among them is that I have seen the corruption in Rathstone under Baron Malhallow. It is even more prevalent here. Your friend, Gyles, is an innocent man who does not deserve to die as a pawn in the nobles' game. I am sick of seeing men of avarice get their way because they have power."

Jorrell's voice took on a venom that surprised both Gheric and Sabra.

"It is past time to stand up to these tyrants!" Jorrell barked. "That goes for both the murderous wretch in Rathstone and that monstrous beast that rules here in Caldor."

Jorrell paused and looked at Gheric. "I know who you are, Gheric the Fox. I know who you serve. Your master's reputation has reached even as far south as Rathstone. It is because of this I know that you are a man of honor, and I am at your service. Tell me what to do, and we can try and save your friend."

Gheric cast a glance at Sabra, surprised the baron's man was so willing to turn against his master. "How do I know we can trust you?"

"You don't," Jorrell answered. "But Gyles doesn't have much time. If it helps you believe in me, I called off my soldiers today when they suspected you were hiding in the woods."

Gheric processed the lieutenant's words and slowly lowered his knife. "All right," he decided, sheathing his weapon. "I will trust in you for the time being, but answer me one question: why do you hate Niles so?"

Jorrell's face turned red, and he struggled to maintain his calm. "I do not wish to speak of it, save to say it is a personal matter of great importance."

"Fair enough," Gheric replied, exhaling deeply. The swarthy warrior rubbed absently at the back of his neck. "When was Gyles taken?"

"Less than a half hour ago," Jorrell answered.

"How is it you are here?" Sabra questioned.

"I was relieved of duty by the captain of the guard," the lieutenant replied.

"Harmon?" Sabra whispered, a catch in her throat.

"Aye." Jorrell nodded. "That scarred devil was placed in charge of abducting Gyles."

Gheric rubbed absently at his chin, his mind chewing on the problem. "The baron is not expecting me to find out Gyles has been taken until tomorrow, is he?" he asked.

Jorrell shook his head.

Gheric began to gnaw on his bottom lip. "Sabra, could you go and summon Silence from the farmhands' quarters?"

"Silence?" she questioned.

"Yes, and we will have to see about getting him a sword."

"There's the old saber in storage," Sabra offered.

"Yes, that's right." Gheric nodded. "Well remembered. Now . . . two of us are going to have to go inside the baron's keep and release Gyles before the other guards know he's been taken."

"How?" Sabra asked.

"By distracting the baron with something he wants more than me," Gheric said, his voice grim.

"What do you think he possibly covets more than your capture?" Sabra asked.

Gheric gave her a tight smile and headed for the storage rooms.

"You."

CHAPTER 10

Captain Harmon was in the midst of delivering his report to Niles in the baron's private quarters when a firm knock came at the door.

"Go see who it is," Niles muttered, taking his boots off and letting them fall to the floor.

"Yes, my lord," the captain replied, moving across the room. When he opened the door, Harmon came face-to-face with Lieutenant Jorrell.

"Begging your pardon, Captain, but there's someone here to see the baron," Jorrell informed the huge man at the doorway.

"It's an hour till midnight," Harmon said with a growl, his anger apparent. "The baron is indisposed, and you, as I recall, are off duty."

"I understand sir, it's just—"

"It's just what, Jorrell?" Harmon snarled, cutting him off. "Did you misinterpret what I said? The baron is not seeing anyone!"

The dark-haired lieutenant glanced at the baron,

addressing his liege lord directly. "There is a visitor driving a wagon from the Billerton Farm," he explained. "If you'd like, I can tell her you are"—he paused, looking with contempt at Harmon—"*indisposed*."

The baron blinked in surprise. "Sabra is here?" he questioned aloud. "Is she alone?"

"As far as I can tell," Jorrell replied.

The baron looked from the lieutenant to the captain. "Harmon, fetch my cousin. Tell her to meet me in the courtroom."

Niles gave the lieutenant a hungry smile. "After all this time, she has come to me at last. Go, Jorrell, bring Sabra to the courtroom and leave her at the entrance with the understanding she has my permission to enter. After that, make certain we are not disturbed."

"Yes, my lord," Jorrell answered, snapping off a sharp salute.

With a withering look at Captain Harmon, the lieutenant turned around and left.

"I would like to cross swords with that smug little bastard tomorrow, my lord," the huge captain growled, his eyes following the retreating figure of the lieutenant.

"You may kill him for all I care," Niles answered, sliding his boots back on. "There is something familiar about him, something I've seen before, but I cannot put my finger on it." Niles shook his head. "Besides, he's too much like his predecessor for my liking . . . Horval, was it?"

"Another soft fool." Harmon grunted. "I'll let Aurelia know you've summoned her. Once the Billerton girl submits, this town will truly be yours."

"And you will get exactly what you want," the baron said with a wave.

"Your cousin's hand in marriage and a link to the barony here in Caldor," Harmon affirmed, his eyes fierce with the thought.

"And I will get Rathstone, if anything . . . untoward were to happen to my uncle," Niles said, shooting a malicious smile at the captain.

"What of the Billerton widow, and her . . . lackey?" Harmon asked, scratching at the scar on his cheek.

Baron Turner's eyes narrowed in hatred. "I will see the bitch in chains, her spirit broken. After she begs for mercy, I will execute her publicly in the market square. Her death will serve as a final warning to the last vestige of resistance during my reign. That should make the populace easy enough for you to govern in the years to come."

The baron paused, pursing his lips in thought. "As for the scrapper, Gheric . . ." He trailed off, flicking his gaze toward the captain. "You can kill him. Now go, let us put an end to this once and for all."

"Your will, my lord," Harmon answered, snapping off a crisp salute.

As Harmon was about to leave, the baron said, "Captain, you never did tell me how you got that scar on your face."

The captain snorted, looking for all the world like a picador bull. "When I collect the head of the bastard responsible, I'll tell you all about it."

Chuckling to himself, Niles slipped on his other boot as the door closed behind the captain. He glanced at his bed, imagining Sabra Billerton bent over it while he violated the girl long into the night.

"You will soon know the consequence of spurning my proposal of marriage," he muttered, brushing off his tunic and making his way to the courtroom.

At the front gates of the keep, Jorrell returned, issuing his orders to the guards. "I'll take it from here," he said to the trio of men standing watch nearby.

"She don't talk much," one of the night watchmen said, looking at the hooded figure sitting atop the wagon.

"The girl is not here for you," Jorrell said stiffly. "Now go, leave her with me."

"Look at that hair," commented another, staring at the wisps of blonde tufts spilling down the sides of Sabra's neck. "It's like spun gold, both on top and below, I'd wager."

"Have some respect!" the lieutenant barked, his voice commanding.

The other guards ignored him, laughing raucously at the second guard's quip. All three were leering at Sabra, openly admiring her form.

"Come with me, Widow Billerton," Jorrell said, pushing past the baron's men and offering a hand to the farm woman.

"I'd like to see more of what's under that dress," stated the third guard, staring hungrily at the figure stepping down from the wagon. He was a plain-faced man in his twenties with a crooked nose and a receding hairline.

Stepping foot on the ground, the figure in the blue dress walked over to the night watchman who had just spoken.

"I don't think you can handle what's under this dress," a soft, feminine voice teased.

The watchman laughed in surprise. "Oh ho . . . did you hear that, lads? The lass here thinks she can handle me!"

The guard moved closer, lowering his hand. "Give us a taste, then," he demanded, reaching under her dress.

"You got it," came a masculine voice from under the hood.

"What the—" the crooked-nosed guard rasped in confusion.

The figure in the blue dress yanked the hood off their head. The guard froze as he stared into the dark eyes of the stranger who had come to town. He was wearing a wig made of long blonde hair.

"What the hell is going on?" the man gibbered softly as Gheric slashed a knife across the guard's throat. The man's hands shot upward to clutch at the wound, failing to stem the flow of blood. The guard fell heavily to the ground, writhing in place and gasping for breath.

Jorrell did not hesitate. He lashed out with his sword, wounding the guard closest to him with a quick thrust to the chest. A second attack of his sword severed the watchman's windpipe as the lieutenant delivered a quick strike to the neck.

The third man was the only one to actually place a hand on his sword. He managed to draw the weapon halfway out of his sheath when a knife thrown from the back of the wagon struck him in the shoulder. Moving like a wraith, Gheric ran over and stabbed the last guard through the ribcage, his sword piercing the man's heart. The warrior held him tightly until the guard ceased his struggle. He eased the man's body to the ground, taking care not to get any blood on his dress.

"Jorrell, quickly, let's move them inside the guard room." Gheric grunted, dragging the corpse of the man he'd just killed.

"I must be out of my mind for letting you talk me into this," the lieutenant muttered, straining under the weight of the second watchman. His eyes darted to the surrounding area, looking frantically for more of the baron's guards.

"What about us?" Sabra asked, standing from where she had been hidden in the back of the wagon.

"As we discussed at your farm," Gheric answered, dumping the body inside the stone cubby, "I'll head to the courtroom and buy you as much time as I can," he instructed, wiping his hands clean on the dead guards tunic. "Jorrell and Silence will go to where Gyles is being held and bring him back here. Once they arrive, you four will ride for the farm. I'll meet you there when I can."

From his place next to her, the dark figure of Silence leaped softly from the back of the wagon and lifted the shoulders of the first man killed off the ground. Following Gheric's lead, he dragged the guard over to the cubby and stacked his lifeless body on the corpses of his fellow watchmen.

"That was a hell of a throw," Jorrell remarked at Silence, looking at him carefully.

Silence shrugged and pulled his knife free of the dead man's shoulder. Wiping it clean, he replaced it and strode over to Gheric.

"By the gods," the warrior swore, straightening the blonde hairpiece on his head. "It's hot as bloody hell under this thing."

Once satisfied with how it looked, Gheric pulled the hood back over his head. "Sabra, get that wagon out of sight. Park it next to the outer wall. Keep it in the darkness of the shadows."

He reached up and patted his mare fondly on the nose. "Kat will let you know if anyone approaches. All of you, move quickly about your business, but don't run. Running will draw unwanted attention. Be smart, and we will see one another again."

"What about you?" Sabra asked, concern in her voice.

"Don't waste time worrying about me," Gheric answered, his tone serious. "Now go, and good luck."

The broad-shouldered warrior watched as the others moved to follow his instructions. So much of this depended on him stalling long enough for the others to rescue Gyles. As for his own safety . . .

"I'll be lucky to see the dawn," he muttered, knowing it was a risk he had to take.

CHAPTER 11

Baron Turner waited inside the opulent courtroom, his patience wearing thin.

"Where the hell is she?" he spat, staring at the doors that led into the room from the outside.

"Perhaps she had second thoughts?" Aurelia suggested from her place next to him.

The Lady of House Turner had changed out of her figure-hugging black dress. She now wore a low-cut gown of emerald green trimmed in white lace. Her long blonde hair had been plaited behind her in an intricate love knot, and her veil had changed as well. The black satin had been supplanted with ivory-colored silk, leaving only Aurelia's brilliant blue eyes uncovered.

"Harmon!" the baron snapped. "Find out what's taking so long!"

"Yes, my lord," the huge captain answered, turning, walking toward the door.

Captain Harmon was only a few feet from the entrance when the door began to swing inward.

"Finally," the baron rasped, as the hinges shifted with a

high-pitched creak. As the doors swung wide, they boomed to a stop, and the trio inside the courtroom looked to see Sabra's hooded figure standing in the doorway. The baron could hear her feet shuffling nervously under her faded blue cotton dress.

Slowly, she ambled past Harmon without gracing the man with so much as a glance.

The hulking captain of the guard trailed behind, staring at the hooded individual trundling along in front of him. Ten feet from the baron, the slouching figure dropped to her knees, her head bowed low.

"Take off your hood," Harmon demanded, his powerful hand reaching for the dark cowl.

Sabra flinched away from him in apparent fear, swatting at the captain's hand with surprising strength.

"You little bitch," Harmon swore, looming over her.

"Stop," ordered the baron, his lips turning up in amusement.

"My lord . . ." the captain began to argue.

"It seems Widow Billerton has developed a distaste for you, Captain," Niles commented with a sharp laugh. "Be a good fellow and leave us. I would not have the pristine reputation of Sabra Billerton sullied by your hand."

"But, my lord," the captain protested. "It would not be wise to leave you unprotected."

"From a single farmgirl?" the baron barked out in laughter. "I am one of the foremost swordsmen in the world, Captain. I think I can handle this child."

"My lord—" Harmon argued again.started.

"Get out," Niles cut him off, waving the captain away. "Go! Check on our prisoner. See if the guards have broken him yet. I would like to hear what he knows about Gheric's whereabouts. The last thing I want is that bastard mercenary sneaking in the keep thinking he can cut my throat while I sleep. Wherever he is, I want to know."

"Yes, my lord," the captain answered, his voice cold. With a last look at the kneeling figure in front of him, Harmon spun around and left the courtroom, closing the door behind him.

"Now," the baron said, leaning back in his chair. "Tell me, whore . . . before I decide whether or not I beat you into submission—what brings you to cower at my feet?"

Lieutenant Jorrell led Silence through the front gates to a brick-and-mortar building located twenty paces away from the main structure of the keep. At the front, they found a closed heavy oak door, but it was unguarded. Lifting the latch, the pair eased their way inside, and they walked easily along the main corridor, Jorrell in front of Silence. The hallways were quiet, though they could hear a group of the night watchmen gambling with dice in a room nearby. Walking past, the pair took a right turn to the staircase that led to the building's underbelly.

"Lucky for us, they are an undisciplined bunch," Jorrell muttered, making his way down the stairs. At the bottom step, they came to a short hallway that branched to the left and right. The lieutenant hesitated, uncertain of which way he needed to go.

"Right, I think," he mumbled, trying to remember the building's layout. Uncertain, he took a step in that direction.

A slight tug on his sleeve stopped him. Glancing at Silence, Jorrell saw the lean farmhand tilting his head to the left.

"You sure?" the dark-eyed lieutenant asked.

Silence nodded, looking behind them. Both men could hear the sound of footsteps approaching from the stairs they'd just descended.

"I hope you have Arianal's luck," Jorrell whispered, inciting the name of the goddess of gamblers. Both men moved quickly down the corridor, leaving the sound of footsteps behind them. The approaching footfalls echoed dully inside the corridor, and Jorrell placed a hand on the hilt of his knife. If they were discovered, he knew they would have to make quick work of the guards before an alarm could be raised. Their luck held as the footsteps faded to the other side of the hallway.

Jorrell gave his companion a grateful nod of thanks, and they continued on their way.

Shortly after the close call, the two men came to a second set of stairs leading downward once more.

This has to be it, Jorrell thought, trying unsuccessfully to appear like the confident soldier he was supposed to be. Taking a deep breath, he calmed himself as much as he could and led Silence down the steps.

The bottom of the staircase opened into a small room made of dusky granite bricks. Inside was a wooden table covered in playing cards, and there were four guards seated around it. Across from the stairs was a heavy oak door, both bolted and locked.

The cells, Jorrell thought.

The four guards looked up from the table where they sat, and without thinking, Jorrell walked from the shadows into the lanternlight. The leader, a short man with sideburns down to his chin, stood, seeing the lieutenant walk into their midst.

"Sir?" the guard asked, looking nervously at Jorrell.

"What's your name, Corporal?" Jorrell asked, his voice crisp with command.

"Eynes, sir," the guard answered, his face flushing with embarrassment.

"Tell me, Corporal Eynes . . . were you going to go all in with only two towers showing?" Jorrell questioned, looking at the cards in front of him.

The tension in the room eased considerably. "I thought about it sir," the corporal admitted. "Ain't had no luck tonight. Perhaps it's best if I fold."

"You do what you like," Jorrell said, forcing himself to smile. "Me? I'm not much of a gambler. At least not when it comes to cards."

"Everything all right sir?" a second man with a thin mustache asked. "Captain Harmon told us to sit tight, let the innkeeper stew for a while."

"Everything is fine," the lieutenant lied, changing his tone to sound more formal. "I'm here to escort the prisoner to the main keep. If you would be so good as to unlock the door and fetch him, that would be appreciated."

"Of course sir," the first man responded, fumbling at his belt for the keys.

Silence peeked his head around the corner, his eyes taking in the room.

"Hey!" a potbellied guard sitting at the table said as he saw Silence. "I know you! You're—"

Silence drew his saber, rushed into the room, and rammed the iron blade through the potbellied man's chest. The guard looked at him in shock, blood bubbling out of his mouth.

Everyone in the room froze, stunned at the turn of events.

"Kill them!" Corporal Eynes shouted, leaping toward Jorrell.

"Shit!" hissed the lieutenant, drawing his sword, blocking a clumsy thrust from Eynes.

Silence had already moved on to the next guard, stabbing

wildly with his knife. The guard fell backward, upending the chair he was sitting in and toppling to the floor. Silence leaped forward with a snarl on his face, driving his knife downward and killing the man with a pair of savage thrusts to the heart.

Jorrell had wounded the guard in front of him twice already. Eynes was bleeding heavily from cuts on his hip and torso. The last man took one look at his companions and bolted toward the stairs. The lieutenant kicked a chair toward the fleeing man, where it slammed into him, causing the guard to trip to the floor.

"Silence!" Jorrell yelled at his companion. "Don't let him escape!"

The former bandit was already moving. Silence threw himself atop the dazed guard and slashed at the man's neck. Blood spurted from the wound, and he fell across the bottom two steps. Blood drained onto the floor, and Silence released his hold, letting the guard fall to the cool stone tile.

Corporal Eynes stared at them both in fear.

"Take whatever you want!" he gibbered, throwing the keys at Jorrell. "Just let me live. I won't say a thing about what happened, I swear it!"

Contrary to his words, Corporal Eynes panicked and hurled a knife at Jorrell.

Not expecting the attack, the lieutenant twisted his body backward in an attempt to avoid being struck. The butt end of the knife glanced off his jaw, and Jorrell fell to the floor, his face exploding with pain.

Silence did not hesitate. He returned the throw with one of his own. His aim was truer, slamming into the corporal's chest right above the heart. Eynes fell back with a gasp, his lifeblood oozing out of him.

Jorrell's jaw ached from the hit he'd taken, but there

seemed to be no lasting damage. He felt a strong arm reach under his armpit and lift him to his feet.

"You just took out four guards without breaking a sweat," Jorrell said the Silence, rubbing at his jaw. "Who are you?"

In answer, Silence pointed at the keys that lay on the floor.

"We will discuss this later," Jorrell decided with a nod. Picking up the key ring, the lieutenant found the right one and opened the door.

Light spilled in from the broken room behind him, revealing a short hallway with six metal doors running adjacent to it. Five of them were unlocked, but one, the last door on the left, was bolted shut. Jorrell and Silence hurriedly made their way down the corridor and looked inside. On the hard stone floor was the beaten and battered innkeeper of the Bad Apple Inn.

"No more," a weak voice croaked at their approach.

"Gyles," Jorrell whispered, opening the cell. "We are with Gheric. We've come to take you out of here."

The bloodied innkeeper tried to focus on the speaker through his puffy, swollen eyes. "Lieutenant?" he asked, looking at the pair of men looming above him. "Is that you?"

"Yes, it is," Jorrell answered, feeling relieved. "I'm going to help you, but I cannot do it alone. Can you walk?"

"I think so," Gyles said, shifting his gaze to Jorrell.

"Silence," Jorrell said, motioning to his companion. "Move those bodies to this cell while I help Gyles out of here."

The lean farmhand nodded and headed back to the room at the end of the hall.

Helping Gyles stand and leave the cell took longer than Jorrell had expected, but the innkeeper's legs were in a bad way.

"They beat them with a wooden cane," Gyles croaked, taking a drink of water from Jorrell's proffered flask.

"I'll have Silence carry you if I must," Jorrell said, knowing time was running short. He turned back to his companion.

"No, I can manage," Gyles said, climbing to his feet with a grunt of pain.

Jorrell began to sweat profusely. He wiped the sweat from his eyes, smearing a line of his victim's blood across his brow.

"Silence, scout ahead," Jorrell ordered. "Make sure the corridor is clear."

The farmhand nodded once and made his way quietly up the stairs.

"Why do you keep calling him Silence?" Gyles gritted through clenched teeth.

"He doesn't say much," Jorrell answered, placing his arm under the innkeeper's and helping him into the jailor's room.

"Haven't seen him in a while." Gyles panted. "I heard the lieutenant was dead."

"You heard I was dead?" Jorrell asked in confusion.

Despite his pain, Gyles barked out a laugh. "I'm not talking about you."

Jorrell was at a loss. "Then who are you . . .?" He trailed off as he saw a wide-eyed Silence racing down the stairs.

"By the high god, someone's coming, aren't they?" Jorrell cursed.

Silence nodded, pulling them back down the hallway leading to the cells.

"Who was it?" Jorrell asked.

The farmhand flexed his arms, exaggerating his muscles, then took both hands and raised them over his head. He made a bestial face and dragged a finger across his right cheek.

"Shit," Jorrell swore as a knot of fear formed in his stomach.

"Who is it?" Gyles gasped.

Seeing the body language Silence had used, Jorrell knew it could be only one person.

"Captain Harmon."

CHAPTER 12

As he knelt in front of the wooden throne, Gheric decided that he had heard just about enough from Baron Turner. It had taken all of his willpower to resist attacking the massive captain when he entered the room. There was something familiar about him. Gheric had an eerie suspicion he had seen the hulking man somewhere before, but his peripheral vision was partially blocked by the hood he wore over his head, and he'd failed to get a proper look.

Inwardly shaking his head, Gheric dismissed the captain from his mind. The only thing that was important at the moment was rescuing his friend and getting the rest of the people who had come with him out of the keep safely.

At the moment, he was down on one knee, listening to Baron Turner's taunts and promises of pain to the person he believed to be Sabra Billerton. Once again, Gheric held on to his patience, knowing every second he bought for his friends brought them all closer to success.

"I expect an answer, girl," Niles continued, his voice scathing.

Gheric did the only thing he could think of to buy more

time. He tilted his head forward till it lay flat on the ground and began to make high-pitched weeping noises, as though he was a foe who had been broken.

"How disheartening," he heard Niles utter in disgust.

Gheric heard the baron step closer to him.

"Aurelia, have you ever seen anyone in such a pathetic state?" he asked the woman who had come up next to him.

"After hearing she had a fiery reputation," a sultry voice replied, sounding disappointed, "I expected her to be more formidable. After all this time resisting you, she just bowed down in front of you and gave up."

The warrior in disguise heard the distinct sound of steel being drawn from its sheath.

"It must be our mother's blood," Aurelia nearly spat.

Our mother? Gheric thought, keeping up the act as the tread of light footsteps drew near.

"Stand up, girl," the sultry voice ordered.

Gheric stayed where he was.

"I said get up!" the woman snapped, placing a foot on Gheric's shoulder. She kicked outward, thrusting him backward.

Gheric went with the kick, tumbling away from the woman in his confining blue dress. Slowly, he climbed to his feet, staying hunched over to mask his height, making sure his face remained deep in the recesses of his hood.

"Who . . . who are you?" Gheric sniffed, hoping his voice sounded feminine enough to keep up the charade.

The woman stepped in front of him, her countenance covered in an ivory-white veil. "Time to meet your destiny," the woman hissed. With her right hand, Aurelia slowly unhooked the clasp holding her veil in place. The covering came off, showing Gheric the woman's face for the first time.

Inside the depths of his hood, the swarthy warrior blinked, completely stunned by what he saw.

In front of him was the face of a beautiful woman. She held a pair of sky-blue eyes and a finely sculpted jawline. Long blonde hair hung behind her in a plaited braid. However, it was not the woman's beauty that had taken away his breath. It was that he had seen this woman's face before. In fact, he'd kissed lips exactly like the ones on display in front of him less than two hours ago.

This woman was Sabra's twin.

"Your turn, sister," the woman hissed.

"Yes, do show us your face, Widow Billerton," the baron sneered from his place behind Aurelia. "I want to see your fear as you grovel before me."

"To hell with this," Gheric muttered under his breath, recovering from his shock. Standing upright, the tall warrior rose to his full height, towering over the woman in front of him. "Your day is going to be full of disappointments," he warned, speaking in his own deep baritone.

Aurelia's eyes widened in disbelief. Quickly, she thrust her hand in front of him.

"*Ventus!*" she shouted, using her magic.

Gheric felt a gust of air hit his face, blowing the hood off his head.

"You!" the baron snarled, his face twisted in surprise.

Gheric launched himself into a backward roll, tearing the dress from his body. Eyes glittering with anger, he drew his sword with a steely rasp. "I hear you've been looking for me?" he asked, his voice casual. "Here I am, Turner, face-to-face."

"Where is Sabra Billerton?" Niles snapped, his eyes filled with both rage and confusion.

"On her way to Kath with half of my forty-man

company," Gheric lied. "The rest are awaiting my arrival back at her farm."

"You're lying!" Aurelia shrieked, her eyes blinking nervously.

"You sure about that?" Gheric queried. "She carries a letter I penned for Duke Mays. I'm certain he will be interested to hear what you are doing in his barony." Gheric paused and gave them both a cavalier smile. "I wonder what Baron Malhallow will do when he finds out? You'll both have quite a bit to answer for."

A momentary silence filled the room.

"You blackhearted bastard!" the baron screamed, standing from his chair and drawing his sword. "Guards!"

"They won't be able to help you," Gheric taunted, stoking the baron's anger, hoping he'd fall into a fit of unbridled rage. "I've killed several of them already."

Aurelia's eyes narrowed, and she raised her hand once more. "*Conicio*!" she shouted.

A powerful magical force made of concentrated air raced toward Gheric.

"*Eludere*!" he countered, throwing up a magical shield of his own making.

The force of air deflected off his defenses with a jarring explosion of sound and slammed into a wall on the left side of the room. The collision was hard enough to where the attack cracked the mortar holding the walls together.

The two cousins glanced at one another, startled at Gheric's magical display.

"Who are you?" Aurelia breathed, her face stunned.

"Come and find out!" Gheric hissed as the battle began in earnest.

Captain Harmon looked on in dismay upon reaching the jailor's room at the bottom of the stairs. There was blood splashed all over the walls and floor. The tables and chairs had been overturned, and there wasn't a guard in sight.

"No," he hissed, ripping open the door that led to the cells. He sprinted to the end of the corridor and looked in the cell Gyles had been held in. Piled on the floor were the bodies of the four guards who had been on duty.

"Son of a bitch!" he thundered, searching the corridor for the missing innkeeper.

Narrowing his gaze, the huge captain gathered his thoughts. *I did not see him go past me*, he reasoned. *That means he must still be . . .* His eyes widened as he detected movement from the cell behind him.

"Yahhh!" cried a voice as two figures slammed into him unexpectedly, pushing the huge captain into the cell formerly occupied by the innkeeper. Harmon tumbled to the ground, tripping on the dead bodies of his underlings.

Behind him, the captain heard the slamming of the cell door, followed by a the sound of a key turning, bolting it shut. He looked up and locked eyes with Lieutenant Jorrell.

"You traitorous whoreson!" he bellowed, trying to grab his former lieutenant through the bars of the cell. "This is not the end of it, you treacherous bastard! I'll hunt you down to the ends of the earth!"

The huge captain slammed his formidable bulk into the cell door in a concentrated effort to smash it open.

"Let's get out of here," Gyles gasped, willing his legs forward.

"When I get out, I'm going to rip the head off your bloody neck!" Harmon roared, ramming his shoulder into the cell door again.

"Silence, help Gyles," Jorrell ordered, trying to ignore the captain. "I'll deal with anyone who stands in our path, one way or another."

Silence nodded, and the three men made their way up the stairs, leaving the raging Harmon howling behind them.

SABRA FELT AS THOUGH SHE HAD BEEN WAITING FOR HOURS. She'd moved the wagon into the shadows against the wall on the outside of the keep and positioned herself close to Kat. The horse was far calmer than Sabra, as Gheric's mount stood peacefully nipping at the tufts of grass nearby.

She had heard two groups of guards walk past the entrance, though neither had noticed anything amiss. Kat had ignored them both, steadily focused on her meal. Sabra continued to listen intently, straining her ears in the hope she would detect her companion's approach.

She did not have to wait long.

In less than a quarter turn of the hourglass since they'd left, Sabra saw Lieutenant Jorrell emerge from the darkness.

"Did you find him?" Sabra asked, relief flooding through her.

"Yes," he answered, keeping an eye out for any sign of trouble. His face was smeared with blood, and his voice was tight with nervousness.

Silence came around the corner next, supporting the badly injured Gyles.

"Thank Chara," the innkeeper said, nearly weeping in relief.

"Let's get him on the wagon and go," Jorrell said softly, grunting as he helped the innkeeper slide onto the back of the wagon.

"What about Gheric?" Sabra asked, looking back at the keep.

"You heard what he said," Jorrell replied, climbing into the front of the wagon. He picked up the reins, ready to be off.

"We can't just leave him," Sabra argued.

"Yes, we can," Jorrell replied. "That is what he told us to do."

"But you are a lieutenant of the guard," she insisted. "Surely you can—"

"The captain saw me," Jorrell snapped. "He knows I've betrayed the baron. I cannot return. Now, climb up here. We must be off."

Sabra hesitated only a moment before making up her mind. "Ya!" she said as loudly as she dared, striking the back of Kat's hindquarters as hard as she could with the flat of her hand.

"What are you—" Jorrell exclaimed before jolting forward, nearly falling out of the drivers seat.

She watched as the lieutenant, Silence, and Gyles rode off toward the relative safety of her farm.

Turning around, Sabra took a deep breath. She fingered the knife under her trousers before pulling the hood of her cloak over her head. *Damn you, Gheric*, she thought, knowing she should leave. Bracing herself, she walked toward the entrance of the keep, doing the best she could to move in the shadows.

CHAPTER 13

Gheric was breathing heavily now, his magical powers nearly depleted. He had fought against both adversaries for several minutes, buying his friends as much time as he could. He was bleeding from a wound trailing from his bicep to his shoulder, where the baron had scored hits with his sword. The broad-shouldered warrior was lathered in sweat, close to exhaustion.

Opposite him was Niles Turner, his face hard with rage and determination. He, too, bore wounds, one on his hand and another on the back of his calf. Neither were mortal, but both, Gheric knew, would prove to be painful.

Gheric was getting desperate, knowing he had to incapacitate at least one of his enemies if he had any chance of escaping.

"You are good," the baron admitted, his voice hoarse.

"I try," Gheric managed, struggling to catch his breath.

I must do something they won't expect, he thought, keeping an eye on the mage across from him. Aurelia was partially hunched over from a kick Gheric had landed to her ribs. He could not finish her off with Niles protecting her. He knew it was only a matter of time.

Knowing it might exhaust him, Gheric rolled the dice.

"*Infligo Tergum!*" Gheric shouted, sweeping his hand in front of him.

A wave of force billowed outward, slamming into Aurelia and the baron. It struck hard enough to send the pair sprawling to the ground.

A bout of dizziness ran through Gheric as he turned and stumbled for the door. He reached out and wrapped the cool iron handle in his fingers. Using what was left of his strength, Gheric yanked on the latch as hard as he could.

The door swung open with a loud creak, and he looked out into the serenity of the moonlit night. For the length of half a heartbeat, he felt the glimmer of hope.

It did not last, as two of the baron's guards rose from the surrounding darkness and blocked his escape.

"Kill the bastard!" Gheric heard the baron wheeze from behind him, as the ruler of Caldor was still struggling mightily to rise to his feet.

Without a word, the guards drew their swords and attacked. Gheric managed to parry the first blow, knocking the guard's sword away. The second man's blade struck the side of Gheric's torso, the cold iron slicing a deep gash under Gheric's arm near his ribcage.

The broad-shouldered warrior felt a jolt of pain shoot through his side. Ignoring it as best he could, he lashed out with his fist, knowing he had to act fast if he wanted to survive.

His fist hit the second attacker in the face, driving the man backward and stunning him.

The first guard had overextended his initial attack and was left slightly off-balance. Recovering quickly, he struck again, his sword going high this time. Gheric ducked under it at the same time as the second guard kicked out, tripping Gheric to the ground. The warrior-mage's sword fell from his hand to the ground. Out of energy, Gheric lay helpless on his back as the two guards loomed over him.

The first guard lifted his sword to deliver the *coup de grâce*. Focused as he was, he never saw the knife that slammed into the side of his neck from behind him. Knocked of balance, the guard's sword clanged on the stone steps, missing its mark. Bellowing in pain, the guard dropped to the ground and touched his hand to his neck, unsuccessfully trying to staunch the flow of blood.

"What the—" the second guard snarled, seeing a blur of movement next to him.

It was at that moment Gheric saw his savior.

Sabra, with a wild look on her beautiful face, lashed out, striking the second guard in the groin with her bloody knife.

"No!" the guard cried, dropping to the ground and clutching at his wound.

Gheric climbed unsteadily to his feet, aware that the baron was still in the room behind him.

"Come on!" Sabra pleaded, casting her gaze through the doorway.

Time slowed for Gheric at that moment as Sabra saw her twin for the first time.

Standing once more, Aurelia was looking out the doorway with her eyes blazing in fury.

The two looked at one another, both equally surprised to see the mirror image of themselves only a few paces away.

Aurelia recovered first. Gheric watched in exhaustion as she raised a hand up in front of her face.

"*Ardeat*," the mage hissed.

A white bolt of flame shot from Aurelia's hand, heading straight for her sister.

"No!" was all he could manage to say as death came for them both.

"*Contra*!" Sabra shouted, her voice steady, despite the danger.

A shield made from solid water sprang up, intercepting the flames in the air and turning them to vapor.

When the mist cleared, the two sisters locked eyes with one another.

"Run!" Gheric wheezed, scooping up his sword, knowing more guards would be coming. Willing his legs to move, he grabbed Sabra by the hand. Even through his fatigue, his mind was working furiously. "We must go before Niles recovers from my spell."

Turning her eyes from Aurelia, Sabra latched onto his arm, and the pair staggered off into the night.

In the bedlam of the courtroom, a pair of sky-blue eyes watched as the lovers faded into darkness.

"What have I become?" Aurelia gasped, collapsing to the floor, blacking out in exhaustion.

IT WAS NEARLY AN HOUR LATER THAT SABRA DRAGGED HER wounded companion through the front door of her farm. Lieutenant Jorrell was there keeping a lookout along with Grada, who was caring as best she could for Gyles.

Sabra led Gheric to his room where he laid down on the bed. Jorrell gave him a brief accounting of the rescue and then stood up and headed for the door.

"Thank you for your warning, Lieutenant," Sabra said before he left.

She saw him sigh and turn back around. "I don't know whether to laud your rescue efforts or scold you for acting on your own accord."

"I did what I needed to do," Sabra replied coolly. "I need no permission from you."

Jorrell raised his hands defensively. "You are right, of course. You do not need my approval, nor do I wish to condone your actions. They were courageous, certainly—though I'd advise a more . . . cautious approach from here on out."

Sabra gave him a slight nod. "My apologies, Lieutenant," she offered. "I am out of my element with all this. I did not wish to insult you."

"That is quite all right." He smiled. "If you need anything else tonight, you have but to ask."

"Thank you," she said, returning his smile. "You were wonderful tonight, in both your warning and during the innkeeper's rescue."

Jorrell nodded but did not reply.

"She's right," Gheric agreed, struggling to sit up. "We could not have done any of it without you."

"Silence did his part too," the lieutenant put in. "It was a close thing, but we can discuss the matter further tomorrow. Get some rest, the both of you. We aren't out of the woods yet."

"We will see how matters stand in the morning," Gheric agreed.

"Until then." Jorrell nodded and left the room.

"Good man there," the black-haired warrior stated, looking up at Sabra.

"You both are," she replied.

His face creased in disapproval. "It was insane of you to come back for me," he chided her.

"I could say the same of your actions tonight," she countered, clasping his hand tightly.

Gheric let out a deep breath. "But I thank you. There is no question in my mind that you saved my life tonight with your heroic actions," he acknowledged with a smile.

Sabra stared down at him, stroking his forehead. "You are welcome."

His smile faded. "The lieutenant is right . . . We are not out of the woods yet. Tomorrow will be a crucial day."

"What do you mean?"

Gheric's head sank back in the pillow with exhaustion. "I managed to wound Niles tonight, though I'd guess he will bring in a healer to see to it. If we are lucky, that will take most of the day tomorrow. The baron will surely gather what's left of his forces. It will take a day or two to order them all back to the keep. Once they are all together, he will come after us. From what Jorrell told me, he has more than sixty loyal guards left, and that's accounting for the nine we killed tonight.

"He has at least a dozen more scattered throughout the barony," Sabra reasoned.

"So, seventy soldiers, more or less."

"You don't think he'll come tonight?" she asked.

Gheric shook his head. "My spell knocked him down with enough force to render him unconscious. "With Harmon locked away there is no one with the authority to mount a search for us."

"He could come tomorrow," Sabra reasoned.

"He might," Gheric answered skeptically. "But to do so would mean he will field only a partial force, one that must attack us here. Also, he has no intelligence on our numbers. While he is angry, he is not stupid."

"There are only a handful of us," Sabra said.

"Yes," Gheric agreed, "but the baron doesn't know that. Tomorrow, he'll be gathering reports about how we infiltrated his keep, stole his prisoner out from under him, and fought him and his mage to a standstill. Niles might believe there was a score or more of us involved. After his losses tonight, my guess is he will be more cautious. Besides, I told him twenty of my men were waiting here for my return."

"You lied?" she asked with a frown.

He gave her a weak wave of his hand. "You can lecture me later on my horrific ways."

Gheric paused and gave Sabra a thoughtful look. "Any success we might have in the next two days depends solely upon you."

"On me?" Sabra asked, sounding surprised.

"Yes, you. Tell me, how long have you been practicing earth magic?"

Sabra stared at him, removing her hand from his.

"You saw what I did in the courtroom?" she accused.

"Yes, but I knew before that," Gheric replied.

"How?"

Gheric smiled and took her hand in his. "Look at your corn, your apples, your grapes! They are twice the size of any other crops grown in Caldor. That corn you showed me in the barn the other day is the best I've ever seen. It is only grown in the early spring and yet you managed to grow it in late fall. I've encountered a few Druids in my time. You have the markings of great power."

She looked at him, her eyes unblinking for a long moment.

"Tell me how I tie in with our success," she demanded.

Gheric pressed his lips together. "You are a grower, but also a healer. Earth magic can mend wounds and take away exhaustion."

He tapped her on the forearm he'd bandaged only three days past. "I know you healed yourself the other day. You didn't want to reveal it to me, but . . ."

He unwrapped the bandage. The skin underneath was whole and unblemished.

"So, you knew?" she questioned, her face tinged with red. "What is it you want me to do now?"

"You need to heal Gyles," he explained.

"I . . . I'm not sure I know how," she admitted. "Bumps and bruises are one thing, but he carries far greater wounds than I've ever dealt with."

"From what I understand, the power comes from inside you. How do you get your crops to grow so well?"

Sabra hesitated. "I . . . My mother taught me a few words she learned while . . ." She trailed off.

"While she was in training at Rathstone?" Gheric guessed.

Sabra gave him a look. "How did you know?"

The warrior-mage shook his head. "It is too much to explain right now, and I am already weary. Please, pretty girl. Use your magic and see if you can heal Gyles. All our lives depend on it."

Sabra stroked his forehead with her finger and nodded. Without a word, she left the room.

"He thinks you can heal the innkeeper?" Jorrell asked moments later, sounding skeptical. "How?"

Sabra did not answer. She looked down at the swollen face of Gyles, knowing he had endured this torture because of his friendship with Gheric. His breathing was weak, coming in choked gasps.

"He's got fractures up and down his legs," Jorrell diagnosed, running his fingers along the innkeeper's side. "I count at least four broken ribs, partially ruptured lungs, and more contusions than I've ever seen outside of battle. It's a wonder he's still alive!"

Sabra ignored him. Instead, she knelt next to the innkeeper and laid both of her hands upon his bruised chest. She closed her eyes and concentrated, gathering her magic.

"*Magna mater, sana haec vulnera,*" she breathed, remembering her mother's lessons.

A white glow emanated from her fingertips, slowly enveloping the innkeeper's entire body. Incredibly, the wounds on his chest began to heal. The swelling around his eyes receded, leaving the flesh unmarred and full of color. The welts on his chest and legs disappeared, as though they had never been.

Gyles, who moments ago was wheezing in pain, sat up and smiled. "Damn me, that feels better," he said aloud.

Sabra took her hands off his chest and opened her eyes.

"You did it!" Grada said, looking at Sabra in shock. "It's a miracle!"

"You have been touched by the gods," Jorrell agreed, tapping his fingers to his forehead, kissing them, and raising a salute at Sabra.

"Do you feel all right?" Sabra asked the innkeeper tentatively.

"A bit sore," Gyles admitted, loosening his shoulders. "But I feel a good sight better than I did."

"I'll let Gheric know," Jorrell reported, his eyes wide with wonder.

Sabra felt tired but rose to her feet. She felt a pair of arms encircle her neck. Grada was embracing her fiercely.

"You . . . you are a spirit sent from the Forest Mother!" the former bandit woman breathed.

"I'm just a farm woman," Sabra replied, relieved at Gyle's recovery.

"Widow Billerton!" Jorrell cried from the guest bedroom. "Come quickly! It's Gheric . . . I don't think he's breathing!"

"What?" Sabra gasped in panic, racing to the guest bedroom. "He was fine just minutes ago!"

"Here," Jorrell muttered, lifting the warrior's bloodied shirt and examining his side. There was a deep gash oozing blood under Gheric's arm. "He's lost a lot of blood," the lieutenant surmised. "Dammit, that is a deep wound, almost certain to have bits of cloth inside. If we don't act fast, he will bleed to death. As it is, it is likely to fester with infection. How the hell did he manage to make it back?"

Sabra did not hesitate. She knelt next to Gheric as she had done for Gyles, closed her eyes, and whispered arcane words of power, praying it was not too late.

CHAPTER 14

𝒜urelia winced in pain as the Druid, Temper, gingerly examined her ribs the next morning in her private chambers.

"One, possibly two are cracked." The wizened healer sniffed, his green eyes carefully scanning the side of her torso. "There is something else wrong internally," he said, looking at her sharply. "Something my magic cannot fix."

"Can you heal my wounds?" she asked, pulling her dress back down and wincing in pain.

The Druid shook his head. "Not directly, no. I've already spent my powers on the baron," he answered. "Your cousin suffered a nasty concussion, along with the other wounds he received in battle."

The Druid stood up and placed his hands on his hips. "Getting late in the autumn for this kind of nonsense. I'd have thought Niles would have learned by now, force is not the answer to every problem." Aurelia could hear the man's old joints popping as he stretched his body. "I've an elixir that should accelerate the healing of your wounds . . . among other things," he offered. "Though it is costly, twenty silvers."

"Twenty?" she asked sharply. "I thought the price would be much higher?"

"Not for you," Temper growled.

"How long will it take?" Aurelia asked, not wishing to gainsay the old man.

Temper smirked at her through his drooping gray mustache. "The rest of today, maybe less."

Aurelia nodded and sent her maid to fetch the money.

"I've a question for you," the highborn woman said, shifting in discomfort. "Why do they call you 'Temper'?"

The Druid laughed lightly as he began to rummage through his bag of supplies. "In my youth, I was easy to anger. Always impatient, never satisfied."

"And now?"

"I'm older." He snorted, laughing again.

Finding what he was looking for, Temper took out a small glass vial filled with a dark liquid.

"May I?" Aurelia asked, reaching out her hand.

"After I get paid." Temper tsked, keeping the vial cradled in his hand.

She gave him a wry look. "Don't you trust me?"

"I don't trust anyone," the Druid answered, looking at her through disapproving hazel eyes. "Especially members of the nobility. All that money and they're cheaper than snow in the winter."

Aurelia furrowed her brow but did not argue, knowing he was right. Moments later, her maid returned with the coins, and Temper handed over the elixir, doffed his wide-brimmed hat, and exited the room. She drank the bitter contents of the vial and dismissed her maid once more.

Aurelia eased herself back into her bed, thinking about

the events of the previous night. Everything had happened so quickly. It was not the battle with Gheric that bothered her, though he had been far more dangerous than she'd expected. Disguising himself as Sabra had been an inspired—if desperate—ploy. His skill with the sword had been exceptional, as he had more than held his own against Niles. His magic though, that had been unexpected. A warrior that skilled who also displayed a strong understanding of magic? Well, that could only mean one thing.

Gheric was almost certainly employed by the Battle Mage, the most powerful mercenary company on the continent. He was not some random soldier of fortune. Killing him would almost certainly mean repercussions, as the Battle Mage was well-connected with every duchy in Rhone, including the one in Kath.

Aurelia felt a sharp pain in her abdomen. She placed a hand over the area until the discomfort receded.

"Damn Druidic healing," she swore.

Then, there was the problem of her sister.

Aurelia had been waiting most of her life to confront her twin. Abandoned by a mother she did not know, Aurelia had grown up in the politically volatile world of her father's court. Sabra, their mother's favored child, had spent idyllic days here in the south, with no knowledge of her ancestry. Sabra was a daughter of House Turner, one of the ancient houses that could trace its lineage back to the kings and queens of ancient Shaara.

Aurelia had always thought she would entrap her sister with some clever ploy and break the girl's spirit over time. She would make certain her twin knew she was nothing special—that their mother had made a mistake in keeping her instead of Aurelia.

But the elder twin was wrong. Sabra was more than special, she was gifted.

Like Aurelia, Sabra had inherited their mother's magic. That alone would have made her rare, but there was more. The older sibling had not accounted for Sabra's courage.

When Aurelia had first seen her twin struggling to rescue Gheric, all she'd wanted to do was incinerate the woman in a fiery magical blast. Unleashing her spell in fury, Aurelia watched, desperate to see her sister burn. Instead, Sabra had countered the magic easily, dousing her flames with a spell of water.

Now, sitting alone in her room, Aurelia felt differently. When she had directed her spell at Sabra, it was though all of the jealousy, hate, and envy that had built inside her over time had been cast out in one terrible magical burst. Afterward, nursing her wounds, Aurelia had been forced to take a long look at what her life had become.

I am a monster, she thought, realizing with disgust she had tried to kill the only living relative who remained of her mother. Replaying the memory of the previous evening in her mind, she again saw Sabra's valiant effort to save Gheric. She did not look like the spoiled child Aurelia had always imagined. Instead, Sabra had encompassed the very nature Aurelia had longed for her entire life: strong, independent, and above all, caring.

After the battle, reports had come in that Gyles had been rescued from his cell. A guard passing near the entrance had seen a wagon moving away from the keep. There was no doubt in Aurelia's mind that Sabra was supposed to be on that wagon riding to safety. Instead, she'd come to save the warrior from the north.

Aurelia exhaled deeply, knowing such noble character

could not have been learned without the guidance of a strong role model.

Their mother.

A knock came at the door, interrupting her reverie. "Enter," the noblewoman ordered.

Aurelia's maid timidly entered the room.

"As you requested," the girl said with a bow, handing her mistress a tightly bound parchment.

"Thank you." Aurelia sniffed, gesturing for the girl to leave.

The maid curtsied and exited the room, closing the door behind her.

Aurelia blissfully began to feel the healing effects of the elixir as the pain in her ribs started to fade. Finding a modicum of comfort, she scanned the contents of the parchment quickly.

"By Dourn, he's on his way here," she murmured in surprise, her voice barely above a whisper. "That can only mean one thing . . ." She trailed off, pursing her lips in thought.

Reaching over to the stand next to her bed, the highborn woman lifted a tiny brass bell and rang it. The door opened, and the maid walked back in. "My lady?" she asked.

"Prepare a horse for me," Aurelia commanded with a grimace. "I want to leave within the hour. Don't tell anyone I have requested it."

"Yes, my lady," the maid answered. "Is there anything else?"

Aurelia looked down at the parchment, studying the words once more. "Yes, send Temper back to me. I have a favor to request of him. If anyone asks, tell them I'm indisposed for the rest of the day because of my wounds. I am not taking any visitors, not even my cousin."

Aurelia paused and wrote a quick note on a spare piece of parchment. "Bring this to the mayor after you ready my horse. Let no one see it but him."

"As you say, my lady," the maid replied, taking the letter and tucking it into her dress. She gave Aurelia a formal curtsey and left the room.

The mage sat on her bed, thinking through her potential course of action.

"If I do this, there will be no going back," she murmured, rolling up the parchment the maid had given her and tucking it into her deepest pocket.

She took a deep breath, steeling herself against any doubt.

"It is time to find out if I am right about my sister . . . and my father."

She gingerly climbed off her bed and began dressing for the road.

CHAPTER 15

There was a faint light eking into the bedroom through the window when Gheric opened his eyes. His shirt had been removed, and his chest had been washed clean. Next to him, with her arm draped over his torso, lay Sabra, sleeping soundly.

Moving as carefully as he could, Gheric slipped out of bed. He gently kissed Sabra's brow and moved as quietly as he could out of the room, closing the door softly behind him.

In the main dining area sat Jorrell along with Gyles and Yetter. The smell of warm corn muffins baking inside the cast iron oven was wafting through the kitchen. Yetter inclined his head politely.

"Gheric," the former bandit said in greeting. "The other farmhands and I, we were wondering . . . what should we be doing today? Are we working the fields, or are we doing something else?"

The broad-shouldered warrior hesitated a moment before answering. "Have Grada and Drei take care of the animals in the barn. Marn can focus on the back fields until the ladies are ready to join him. It's less than a week before the last full moon of autumn. We need to get as much of the crop in as we can."

Yetter nodded and looked out the window. "What of Silence?"

Gheric walked over and put his hand on Yetter's shoulder. "I need Silence to stay here and keep an eye out for any trouble."

"How about Othar and me?"

"Help Marn get set up in the field, then both of you come back here. I have a special job that only the two of you can hope to accomplish."

If the former bandit had any feeling about what he'd been told, he kept it to himself. "Othar won't like it," Yetter reasoned, "but he bitches about everything anyway."

"Tell him if he wishes to stand out where the baron's guards can pick him off with a single arrow, by all means, join Silence near the front gate," Gheric said wryly.

Yetter stopped for a moment and gave Gheric a hard look. "I'll let him know," he replied as he walked outside.

Gheric sat down at the table and turned his gaze toward Gyles. "How are you feeling?"

"Quite well, considering I was at death's doorstep last night," the innkeeper answered with a shudder. He took a drink from the cup in front of him. "Mulled cider," he mused with a smile at the mug. "Sabra might have a small orchard, but those trees produce incredible fruit."

"You should get your wife out of the Bad Apple," Gheric warned. "She will be a target now."

"I went and got her last night," Jorrell answered. She's asleep in Widow Billerton's room.

"Well done," Gheric nodded, surprised at how resourceful the lieutenant had proven to be. "What happened in the cells last night? How did you escape?"

Jorrell glanced at Gyles and shook his head. "It was touch and go, believe me. I'll fill you in on the details later." He glanced at the innkeeper and then back to the bedroom, where Sabra still slept. "Not to change the subject, but how are *you* feeling?" the lieutenant asked Gheric. "That was a close call last night."

"What do you mean?" Gheric asked in confusion.

"Widow Billerton," Gyles put in. "She saved you. Brought you back from death's door."

Gheric looked at them, stunned. "No, I—"

"You had a deep wound under your arm," Jorrell said, pointing at the spot near Gheric's ribcage. "It punctured your lungs. You nearly bled to death."

Gheric thought back to his battle in the courtroom and how the guards had him down and helpless. "I'll be damned," he said, rubbing at his side. "She rescued me *and* saved my life."

Gheric looked at the bedroom Sabra still slept in. "How did she heal me?"

"She used her magic," Jorrell answered. "It was something to see, I can tell you."

Gheric sat still for a long moment. He began to rise from his chair, knowing he needed to thank his savior.

"Let her rest," Jorrell suggested, reading Gheric's intent. "The ordeal wore her out. She insisted on staying in the room with you in case you woke in need of more healing." The lieutenant stood up and walked over to the oven. "I don't know which of you snores louder, but my money is on her." He chuckled, opening the iron door and taking out a metal cooking pan.

A wave of heat ran through the cool air of the room and hit Gheric. With it came the delectably sweet smell of corn muffins.

"I recognized that recipe," Gheric said with a smile at Gyles. "You are a damn fine cook, and a brave man."

The innkeeper gave Gheric a weak grin but did not reply.

"I'm going to bring Silence some food and drink," Jorrell said. "When I come back, we can discuss our next move. I doubt Baron Turner is wiling away his time, and after last night, I expect I'll have to deal with that big Shar myself."

"What did you say?" Gheric asked, his memory stirring.

"The big Shar," Jorrell repeated, pouring Silence a mug of cider. "The baron's captain, Harmon. He comes from the city of Dagor, in the country of Shaara."

"Son of a bitch!" Gheric exclaimed, striking his hand to his knee. "*That's* where I've seen him."

"Who? What do you mean?" Jorrell asked.

"The baron's captain," Gheric explained. "I have run across him in the past. I've seen him fight too. Not an honorable bone in his body, from what I remember. I swore to him if he ever came against me again, I'd finish what he started."

"You fought him?" Gyles scoffed.

Gheric's lips turned down, his expression sour. "He wears the results of my efforts upon his face."

Both Jorrell and Gyles glanced at one another.

"*You* gave him that scar?" Jorrell asked in surprise. "When was this?"

Gheric shook his head. "A couple of years ago. We will speak of it upon your return. Go, see to Silence. I need to have a private word with Gyles anyway."

Jorrell gave the warrior-mage a perplexing look but left the room carrying a plate of steaming food and a mug of fresh cider.

Gheric looked at his old friend and gave him an

encouraging smile. "You are a good man, Gyles," he said simply.

The red-haired innkeeper shook his head. "I am a fool, and a coward to boot." His voice was low, filled with self-loathing.

"That's not true," Gheric argued.

"Do you know how close I came to breaking last night?" Gyles spat, his disgust clear. "I was ready to turn you in. I couldn't take any more." The innkeeper dropped his voice below a whisper, stating, "I'm not brave like you and the rest of the Battle Mage. Being around Khaine and the others, it made me feel nigh invincible, but I am a fool. Last night, I was so afraid. I knew then I was not like you."

The innkeeper sighed bitterly and looked down into his mug. "The hard truth is I am a lowly cook, nothing more."

Gheric was frowning at him. "What the hell are you talking about?" he snapped. "You withstood hours of brutal torture and said nothing! No one, myself included, could have endured what you did any better. Hell, man, I'm impressed enough that I'll be recommending you be given a commission should you ever return to the Battle Mage. You are far more than just a 'lowly cook.' You are one of the bravest men I have ever known."

"That is kind of you to say, but—"

"But nothing!" the fierce-eyed warrior cut him off. "You think because you were scared last night that you are a coward? Let me tell you something, Gyles: *Everyone* gets scared, especially under duress. Despite that, you stayed the course. Mark my words, Gyles, that is what bravery is, and you have it as much as any man I have ever known!"

"You are wrong—" Gyles began to argue.

"Shut up!" Gheric snapped, clearly annoyed. "I'm not done. Where was I? Oh yes—stop saying you are a fool. You are quite the opposite! You knew the risk you were taking when you summoned me. You knew I'd come here and stir up the hornet's nest. But did that stop you? Hell no! You did it anyway, and do you know why?"

"Because I'm an idiot!" Gyles hissed, his anger flaring.

"The gods be damned, enough with your self-pity!" Gheric roared. "You did it because you'd not stand idly by and watch this village fall under the control of that sadistic sociopath. I've said it once, and I'll say it again: You are a good man, Gyles, one of the best I have ever known. Yes, your cooking is superb, but that is not *who* you are. You are a man people listen to, a man who people trust. Why do you think I came all this way to see you? By the gods, you almost died last night to keep me safe! If that isn't an example of trust and bravery, then I don't know what is!"

The innkeeper was looking intently at his old friend, searching his face for any trace of dishonesty. All he saw was genuine admiration and concern for the innkeeper's well-being.

"Thank you," Gyles said sincerely. "I still don't feel proud of my actions, but . . . you do make a fair point."

"Yes, well, I am sorry to say this, but I am going to need to call upon your courage one more time."

Gyles held his breath. "What do you need from me?"

"I need you to do what you do best," Gheric answered.

"You want me to cook something?" the innkeeper asked sheepishly.

Gheric chuckled and shook his head. "No, I want you to stir up a rebellion."

CHAPTER 16

The sun had risen above the horizon for half a turn of the hourglass when the matriarch of the Billerton Farm awakened from a fitful night's sleep.

Opening her eyes, she took in the unfamiliar setting of the guest bedroom. After a moment's confusion, she remembered why she was not sleeping in her own bed.

Gheric, she thought, sitting upright in a panic.

"It's all right," she heard a voice say from the chair next to the bed.

Sabra turned and saw her broad-shouldered house guest fully healed and looking none the worse for wear.

"Gheric," she rasped, staring at him in surprise. "How . . . how are you feeling?" Her voice was higher pitched than normal and strained with concern.

"I'm feeling fine, thanks to you," he replied, his lips turning up slightly in a half smile.

Thank the gods he is alive, she thought, leaping out of bed and throwing her arms around him. His chest was bare once more, but at the moment, she did not care to ask why.

"How are you?" he asked, moving away from her.

"I'm all right, though I'm a bit nauseous from the power I expended last night."

"An old Druid by the name of Temper came to examine you while you slept," Gheric said, looking at her strangely.

"He's the village healer," Sabra explained with a shrug. "And an old friend of my mother's."

"He had just come from the keep," Gheric continued. "It seems he was sent at the behest of Aurelia, someone who bears a striking resemblance to you. He had some other news to tell me that I found rather disconcerting."

"He came at the behest of Aurelia?" she questioned.

"Aye, it seems she has had a change of heart."

Sabra put her hand up to keep him from saying any more on the subject, unwilling to discuss the matter with anyone. She moved away from him, her cheeks flushed red in anger. "Where is your tunic?" Sabra asked, wishing to change the subject. "Why is it you always have your shirt off whenever I am around?"

"It's being mended," he answered. "There was a hole in it, just here," he pointed underneath his armpit. "Gyles's wife is sewing it closed as we speak.

Remembering the events of the previous evening, Sabra stepped back and punched him in the stomach. "Why did you not tell me of your wounds last night?" she chastised him, shaking her hand in pain. She felt as though her fist had hit a rock wall.

"I did not realize their severity," he answered, raising his hands defensively.

Sabra's face darkened. "How could you not know?" she snapped. "I thought you were some kind of almighty warrior?"

"I was a bit busy, if you recall," he pointed out. "I didn't really have time to take stock of my situation."

She stared at him, her anger apparent. "Why did you stay in the courtroom for so long?" she huffed. "Surely you could have escaped before I showed up?"

The warrior frowned at her. "I wanted the baron's focus on *me*. The rest of you needed time to make your way to safety."

"You could have been killed!" she shouted. "You should have stuck to the plan!"

"I did," he argued, his voice even. "You, however, decided to take things into your own hands. You never should have been near the baron's courtroom. You should have been with Jorrell and Silence."

"Was I supposed to leave you to die?!" she screamed in frustration.

"Yes," he answered. "Your life is far more valuable than mine."

"Why?" she questioned, her voice strangled. "Because you think I'm a simpering female who needs some big strong idiot to rescue her?"

"Of course not," he countered, his own anger rising.

"Is it because the great and powerful Gheric needed to be saved?" she continued. "There is no shame in it!"

"I know that," he sputtered, trying to regain his temper. "You saving me has nothing to do with it."

"Then what?" she stormed. "What is so important that you think I would leave you behind to die? Why would you not want my help?"

"Because I've fallen in love with you!" Gheric bellowed, his voice ringing throughout the room. "I would not see you risk yourself for me."

Both of them stood stark still, staring into one another's eyes.

"You love me?" Sabra gasped, her anger draining away.

"Yes," he admitted, "though only the gods know why."

"You . . . you don't even know me," she reasoned, her voice hesitant. "You're infatuated with me because you like the way I look."

"That has—" he began.

"I have known your type all my life," she hissed, cutting him off. "You lust after what you cannot have. Once you get what you want, you will be on your way, just like every man I've ever known." Her blue eyes looked at him with disgust. "A womanizer like you cannot know what love is."

Gheric rolled his eyes toward the heavens. "Dourn, give me strength," he cursed, trying not to lose his patience.

"You should go," she said bitterly, her gaze dropping to the floor.

"The hell I will," Gheric said with a growl, grabbing her by the shoulders. "Look at me," he ordered, his voice commanding. "Now, you listen, and listen well: I have been lucky in my lifetime. I had a wife once, a damn fine woman better than I ever thought to find. I loved her more than a fool like me should have been allowed."

He paused, his voice becoming strained.

"Four years ago, a sickness took her from me. It was a malady that no Druid, no healer on Quasa could counter. I buried her in a secret glade outside of the city of Adian, known only to me. It is the same place I asked her to be my wife."

Gheric sighed and cast his gaze out the window, his eyes focused on the past. "Since her passing, I have known the touch of many women, it's true—but I have not known the feeling of love again."

He stopped, letting go of Sabra, and wiped away a tear that had formed at the corner of his eye.

"I never thought to find that kind of woman a second time. It was a miracle to have it happen once."

He let out a deep breath and plowed on.

"Then I met you. A girl of enduring character, with the beating heart of a lioness. A woman brave enough to fight against a foe well beyond her capabilities to defeat, and yet you fight anyway. Rarely have I seen such courage."

"You just like me because you think I'm pretty," she argued again. "A piece of ass to satisfy your needs until you leave Caldor."

His face wrinkled in annoyance. "That's nonsense. Yes, I am attracted to you, but physical beauty only opens the doorway to my heart. It takes more than a pretty face, Sabra. I agreed to help you because I believe in what you stand for."

"I still don't—" Sabra began.

"Look at what you have done in just the last few days," he said, turning around and cutting her off. "You've faced down that merchant Varfore in the marketplace. Then, you brought in wanted men and women to work your farm . . ."

He trailed off as he turned back to her, lifting his fingers to brush away a lock of golden hair from her eyes. "You, with no formal training, took on a sorceress and a master swordsman to save a man you barely know. By the gods, woman, how could anyone not admire such valor?"

He let out a deep breath and let his arms hang at his sides. "Believe me, Sabra, I did not want to feel this way ever again; it has proven to be a gateway to pain that knows no end. Unfortunately, you have given me little choice in the matter. You have left your mark indelibly upon my very soul. I will love you, now and forever, no matter what your feelings for me might be."

He made to step away, but Sabra instinctively grabbed him by the hand. "Wait I . . ." She halted, suddenly terrified at the thought of him leaving. "Don't go," she blurted out, saying it in a rush. "I feel the same . . . I mean, why do you think I came for you last night? I . . . By Chara, I *have* become a simpering fool."

"What are you trying to say?" Gheric asked.

Sabra's cheeks flushed a deep red. "Must I spell it out for you?" she asked, casting her eyes downward. "You've already stretched propriety to the limit."

Gheric gently put his fingers under her chin and bade her to look him in the eye.

"Say it," he murmured.

"I . . . I am afraid," she admitted softly. "After the loss of Trevor, the smith's son—"

"Say it," he repeated, his voice insistent.

"I . . . love you too," she whispered.

"What was that?" he teased, giving her a smile.

"I love you! All right?" she shouted, her tone angry. "Are you happy now?"

"Yes," he answered, his voice rich and filled with warmth.

Gheric leaned in and pressed his lips to Sabra's, kissing her with all the built-up passion she'd awoken inside of him two nights ago. Her lips were soft and warm, stoking his desire. He wanted nothing more than to tear the clothing from Sabra's body and throw her on the bed.

Instead, he reached under her dress and lifted it gently over her head. He released his hold on the worn cotton, letting it fall in a crumpled mass to the floor. Gheric felt her hands slide down the front of his torso. Gently, she undid the belt holding up his pants. The worn leggings soon joined her dress at the foot of the bed.

Gheric's lips moved from Sabra's face to her neck as she moaned with pleasure in his ear. The broad-shouldered warrior kissed his way slowly downward until he came within reach of her hardened nipple. He gently caressed it with his tongue before taking it in his mouth, listening as Sabra's breathing intensified. He moved his lips further down to her flat stomach, kissing it tenderly and lifting her leg over his shoulder, pushing her gently onto the bed.

"What are you doing?" she breathed, now lying flat on her back.

"Just lay there," Gheric instructed, shushing her as he moved his tongue between her legs.

Sabra began moaning again, quietly at first, and then louder as her excitement began to build. She moved her hands to the back of his head and pushed him down gently, urging him to increase the pressure as her pleasure grew.

Gheric took the cue, increasing the force of his tongue upon her most sensitive area. As he continued, the pressure she exerted on him increased as her pleasure intensified. Finally, Widow Billerton cried out in an explosion of decadence as her orgasm hit with a violent intensity. Lost as she was in her hedonistic pleasure, she was unaware of how firmly she was pressing down on the back of his head. Sabra was willing him on, forcing him to bury his mouth inside of her.

Thrice more in the following minutes did Sabra climax, each time screaming more loudly than before. On it went, Gheric never slowing, never coming to a halt. The incredible sensation of her orgasms ran throughout her entire body. It was an exquisite feeling, one that came in waves. After Sabra's fifth orgasm, Gheric withdrew his tongue and kissed her stomach again.

"No more," she begged, gasping for breath.

"Never say that to me," Gheric taunted with a smile, climbing on top of her.

He pushed his manhood inside of Sabra, and the warmth

of his hardened cock filled her as she gasped in pleasure once more.

"What the hell . . . are you doing to me?" She moaned, her eyes rolling backward. Gheric sat up, taking in Sabra's perfect body. She looked magnificent, like a nubile goddess come to life.

The swarthy warrior lay back down and pressed his chest against hers, feeling Sabra's arms circle his waist. Gheric could feel her hands against his hips as his arousal heightened. Despite Gheric's experience, he felt himself building toward climax quickly. He tried to slow his pace, but that only heightened his ardor.

"Come for me," Sabra begged, sensing he was close.

Her words unleashed the rains.

In a rush, it hit. Snapping his head back, Gheric came, harder, more completely than ever before. Sabra cried out from underneath him, experiencing another blistering-hot orgasm of her own. On and on it went as he continued to power into her.

Finally, his ardor spent, Gheric collapsed on top of her. For some time, they lay together, unmoving, save for the gasping of labored breath, bathed in the sweat of lovemaking.

After catching her breath, Sabra turned onto her side and propped up her head with her arm.

"What did Temper say to you that was so disconcerting?"

Gheric hesitated, giving Sabra a frown. "That's the first thing you have to say to me after what we just experienced?" he lamented. "Not 'good job' or 'that was incredible'?"

Sabra began to laugh. "It *was* incredible," she admitted, giving him a dazzling smile. "But what did the Druid say?"

Gheric shook his head with a laugh, leaned in, and kissed her. "He just wanted to make certain you got your rest."

"Anything else?"

Gheric gave her a smile. "Yes, but it's from me, not the Druid. I love you, Sabra Billerton," he said, looking deeply into her blue eyes. "Now and forever."

"It's Hastings," she breathed, kissing him again. "Sabra Hastings—my mother's maiden name—and I love you too."

CHAPTER 17

It was an hour past noon when Aurelia and her companion reached the fork in the road that turned toward the Billerton Farm. She was dressed in the simple brown doeskin tunic and leggings of a common traveler. The highborn woman carried only a small pouch at her side, filled with what looked to be various parchments. Underneath her was a silver gelding, moving easily with Aurelia's expert guidance.

Next to her, nestled atop a light-brown pony, rode the village mayor, Tamalin. The mayor was wearing a heavy wool coat on top of his red tunic and black pants, and he was sweating profusely under the growing warmth of the midmorning sun. His sour face was shaded underneath a wide-brimmed hat of red felt. He looked none too pleased to be there.

"We are going to be murdered in broad daylight, riding out like this," Tamalin griped, peering at the farm ahead. "It's rumored this Gheric has more than twenty men with him."

"That is a possibility," Aurelia sniffed, her voice calm.

The mayor snorted. "What, in the name of Kelthane, are

we doing out here?" he asked. "Your cousin will have our heads if he finds out."

"Then you best not tell him," the mage replied.

They rode for a few more steps until an arrow buried itself in the ground only a few paces in front of them.

"Kelthane's beard!" Tamalin swore, turning his pony around. "My apologies, Aurelia, but I didn't sign up to be shot off my pony!" Without another word, the mayor leaned forward and shouted, "Ya!" The pony took off at a gallop, leaving Tamalin's companion alone on the road behind him.

Aurelia looked up and saw a familiar figure holding a bow in the distance. Slowly, she lifted both her arms, keeping them safely in the air over her head. The figure drew a second arrow and fitted it to the string. Slowly, the man made his way forward, keeping the blue-eyed beauty in his sight the entire time. He stopped some twenty paces away, looking balefully at the highborn mage in front of him.

"So, this is where you've gotten off to," Aurelia said in greeting. "I'd wondered what had happened to you."

The man holding the bow pulled back on the string, drawing a bead on Aurelia.

The mage tilted her head slightly forward. "I understand why you wouldn't trust me. However, I've come to speak with Gheric . . . and my sister."

The man in front of Aurelia did not move. He just stood there ready to kill her.

"We will see about lifting the curse from you and clearing your name," she added. "Would that satisfy you?"

Silence narrowed his eyes and eased his pull on the string. With his nostrils flaring, the former bandit jerked his head toward the farm, allowing her safe passage.

Tension was high outside Sabra Billerton's farmhouse. It stemmed from the woman who had been hellbent on killing two of the three people standing across from her the night before.

"Why are we listening to *anything* she says?" Sabra asked, acid dripping from her tongue.

"Diplomacy often works like this," Jorrell mildly put in.

"In case you have forgotten, she tried to kill us!" Sabra shouted, pointing an accusing finger at her twin.

"It will not hurt to listen," Gheric sighed, having expected the outburst.

Sabra glared icy-blue daggers at him. "You too?" she asked, angry. "Need I remind you, if it hadn't been for me, you'd be a charred corpse right now! All due to this . . . this . . . *bitch* standing next to us!"

"No one is debating that . . . " Gheric began, taking a step toward Sabra.

"Am I the only one with any sense left?!" Widow Billerton screeched, pushing Gheric away from her. "If you wish to speak with this treacherous *slag*, that is your business. I, for one, will not stand near her for one more second!"

"Sabra, be reasonable," Gheric pleaded, moving close to her once again.

She raised her hand and slapped him across the face.

"Just when I thought you'd found an inkling of decency, you'd let this harridan into my home? Get out! All of you!"

Gheric looked at Sabra, his face creased in a frown. "I'm not looking for a fight, but, technically, we *are* outside. You should go in."

Sabra's eyes narrowed in anger, and she struck him again. Gheric took the hit stoically and stood his ground.

"By Chara, you are the most egotistical, insufferable man I've ever met!" she thundered. Spinning around, Sabra stomped to the door. "Get that bitch off my property!" she screamed, slamming the door behind her.

The trio that remained stared at one another in silence.

"I saw that second slap coming," Jorrell said, chuckling softly. "You all right?"

"I thought it might make her feel better," the broad-shouldered warrior replied with a shrug. "She needed to hit something . . . Better me than either of you."

"I like her," Aurelia announced, speaking for the first time. "She's nothing like I had imagined. I thought to find some docile farmwife, soft-spoken and pampered. She's a spirited girl, much like me."

"The two of you might have the same face," Gheric growled, turning his attention to Sabra's twin. "But she is *nothing* like you. Everything she said is accurate. You did try to kill us both last night. Because of this, I have no reason to trust you at all. However, I have dealt with enough politicians to realize you are here for a reason. Speak your piece, mage, but know this—you severed any goodwill I might have shown you when you tried to kill Sabra last night."

Aurelia nodded, expecting his response. "I don't have much to say, but I do have something to show you, something I'm sure will garner your interest."

Aurelia reached inside the front of her dress and pulled out the parchment she'd been given earlier that day. She handed it over to Gheric, who unrolled it and began to read the contents.

"Baron Malhallow is coming here?" he asked, surprised.

"What?" Jorrell gasped.

"By the gods," Gheric continued, scanning the bottom of the parchment. "Someone tried to kill him."

"An assassination attempt?" Jorrell guessed. "There were rumors of such a plot before I left."

"By whom?" Gheric mused, his eyes flicking to Aurelia.

"There are only two people who would stand to benefit from Malhallow's death," Jorrell reasoned, resting his gaze upon the baron's eldest. "His daughter and his nephew."

Both men stared at the woman in front of them. Aurelia gave them a smile. "It wasn't me," she said in a honey-sweet tone.

Gheric snorted. "Forgive me if I don't take you at your word."

"You are missing the point of my visit," the noblewoman said. "According to my sources, my father is a day's ride away, perhaps less. He will arrive in Caldor early tomorrow at the latest with three hundred of his best men."

"You think we should run?" Gheric asked, inherently sensing that was not why she'd come.

Aurelia raised one of her eyebrows. "I thought you were smarter than that."

Gheric shook his head. "I'm not a politician," he said dryly. "I don't think the way you do."

Jorrell, however, opened his eyes in surprise.

"Dourn's beard," the lieutenant swore. "You want to rid yourself of them both, don't you?"

"Nice to see one of you has a brain," she quipped.

"With Malhallow and Niles out of the way, you will rule in Rathstone," Jorrell reasoned, seeing her line of thinking.

"Yes, and I will leave my sister here to govern in Caldor," Aurelia stated. "Those are my terms, gentlemen. Otherwise, my father and the soldiers he's brought with him will kill you all by this time tomorrow. Afterward, he will take Sabra's farm, spirit her away, and rule with an iron hand for the foreseeable future."

"He's your father," Gheric said, looking at her coldly. "Don't you care about him at all?"

More quickly than he thought possible, the swarthy warrior witnessed Aurelia undergo a complete metamorphosis in front of him. Her beautiful countenance twisted into a visage of hate.

"He's not my father," Aurelia spat, with venom in her voice. "He is the pig who forced himself on my mother, infecting her with his seed . . . but a father? No. Malhallow Turner is many things, but a father is not one of them."

"Have you no love for him at all?" Jorrell asked.

Aurelia gave the lieutenant a look of disgust. "Does a father use his little girl as a tool to curry favor with his underlings? Does a father whore his daughter out to others so he can gain some political advantage? Does a father use his child to garner information? Does a father train his own flesh and blood as an assassin to eliminate his rivals?"

Her sky-blue eyes were glacier cold.

"You have the audacity to ask me if I care about him?" she hissed. "Let me tell you something, the both of you—Malhallow is not worthy of being called a father. He is a narcissistic monster who cares only about himself."

She took a deep breath in an effort to steady her nerves. "To answer your question, no, I do not care for him at all. He is unworthy of love—not from his people and certainly not from me."

The two men were stunned to see such vehemence from the slender woman in front of them.

"I had no idea. I'm sorry," Gheric apologized.

"Nor did I," Jorrell put in.

An uncomfortable moment of silence hung in the air.

Jorrell cleared his throat. "Not to change the subject," he began tentatively, "but how are we supposed to defeat that many of Malhallow's soldiers? We are already grossly outnumbered by his nephew's men."

"We don't need to defeat their soldiers," Gheric reasoned. "We only need to kill Niles and his uncle."

Jorrell looked at Gheric, his face skeptical. "I doubt they are going to offer up their necks in sacrifice."

"No," the warrior-mage agreed. "We will have to isolate them, kill them when they are alone."

"Why would they choose to fight personally when they command scores of able-bodied soldiers?" Jorrell scoffed. "There is no reason for them to take such risks. They can sit back and let their guards hunt us down."

"I think at least one of them will take the bait," Aurelia countered. "Niles's arrogance is colossal." She motioned toward Gheric with her hand. "Word has gotten out about how you, a lowly peasant, nearly defeated him in hand-to-hand combat."

"It was one against two," Gheric muttered, eyeing her coolly.

"All the more reason he will challenge you publicly," she agreed. "He cannot afford to have his precious reputation tarnished."

"A trial by combat?" Gheric queried, absently rubbing his jaw. "They still have that here?"

"In these backwater baronies, they are common," Aurelia answered.

"It is all but extinct in the duchies," the broad-shouldered warrior mused.

"While that's all well and good, what about your father?" Jorrell asked. "He's nearly sixty years old. Malhallow is not about to step from behind his guards and duel with anyone."

Aurelia pressed her lips together, trying to hide a smile. "That's true, but he wants Caldor in one piece. Firing the town and destroying the fields to flush you into the open will catch the eye of Duke Mays in Kath—so will initiating a barony-wide manhunt to search for you. Malhallow wants to keep this quiet and out of the duke's court. He will choose a champion to fight for him. He has done so many times in the past."

"I hope that is true," the lieutenant nodded.

"You want to fight his champion?" Gheric asked.

"I was the best man under his command in Rathstone," Jorrell scoffed. "I don't think he's got anyone who could beat me."

"He won't pick anyone he's bringing with him," the noblewoman warned.

Jorrell frowned. "Then who will he . . . " The lieutenant's voice trailed off, and his face paled.

"They found him underground last night, battering the door of the cell you locked him in," Aurelia said tightly. "It took eight men to keep him from hunting you down. Only a direct order from Niles has kept him inside the keep."

"Who?" Gheric asked in confusion.

"Captain Harmon," Jorrell answered, his voice strained.

"Yes." Aurelia nodded. "He used to fight in the gladiator pits of Tal-Mur. He is both fast and strong. Harmon has already fought for my father in three trials by combat, one of which won Malhallow the barony here in Caldor. He will certainly choose the captain as his champion if it comes to a duel."

Gheric eyed her suspiciously. "Even if your father and cousin agree to this, you've asked Jorrell and me to take all the risk. What do you bring to the table? And what if Malhallow fails to live up to his end of the bargain?"

"That's why I invited the mayor," she explained. "He will oversee the combat and write up the papers making it legal and binding."

"That's not going to be enough to keep Malhallow from

breaking his word," Jorrell argued. "Even if we manage to win, he'll have more than three hundred soldiers at his disposal to kill us and take Caldor."

"It won't do him any good if he's dead!" she replied, her words shocking them into silence.

"Who is going to kill him?" Gheric dared to ask, his eyes wild with surprise.

"The very man who can condemn his actions to Duke Mays."

Aurelia snapped her fingers, and Silence appeared from the barn behind them.

"Gentleman, I'd like you to meet Lieutenant Horval. He's the finest shot with a bow in the duchy."

"Nice to formally meet you both," Silence said in a low baritone, giving them a rapturous smile.

CHAPTER 18

Sabra heard the door to her farmhouse open and knew Gheric had come inside. She was still fuming and did not want to speak to him.

"Go away!" she shouted, slamming the drawer of her nightstand in frustration. "I don't know how you could possibly listen to a word that traitorous bitch has to say!"

She heard footsteps approach her door, and her ire doubled.

"Don't you dare come in here!" she screamed. "Why don't you go cozy up to that psychotic rag you seem to be so enamored with!"

Sabra heard a soft creaking sound as the door to her bedroom swung inward.

"Are your ears full of cow dung?!" she screeched, whirling around.

Her twin sister stood in the entryway.

"You must really care for him to hate me this much," Aurelia said, her voice calm.

"What are *you* doing here?" Sabra spat.

Aurelia raised her hands defensively in front of her. "I'm not here to fight with you, sister, only to ask you a question."

Sabra stared venomously at the woman in front of her, wanting nothing more than to grab the woman by the scruff of her neck and throw her from the room.

"One question," Sabra snarled, her voice quivering with rage.

Aurelia nodded and clasped her hands in front of her. She looked at Sabra, took a deep breath, and spoke, "The woman who . . . No, *our mother*," she began, her voice uneasy. "What was she like?"

This was not the question Sabra was anticipating. "Our mother?" she asked in confusion.

"I never knew her," Aurelia said. "I just wanted to know . . . What was she like? Slender and beautiful like us? Was she a good cook? What were her favorite flowers?"

Aurelia paused, absently smoothing the folds of the dress in front of her. "This is one of the reasons I came to your farm today . . . to ask you about our mother."

Sabra's eyes narrowed in suspicion. "You rode from the keep under pain of death to talk to me about our mother? Wouldn't a letter have been more efficient?"

Aurelia pressed her lips together, as though she had anticipated this kind of resistance from her twin. "I expect that it would have," the noblewoman admitted. "At the time I was sent to Caldor, I was angry and, I'm ashamed to say, jealous. All my life, I was taught to believe that I was alone in this world, that any member of my family would be a threat to my way of life."

She shook her head. "I thought if you found out your true lineage you'd go after our father's position as baron of Rathstone."

"What has changed since last night?" Sabra hissed, her

anger flaring again. "It was only yesterday that you tried to kill Gheric and me."

Aurelia hesitated and cast her eyes to the floor. "I was a fool," she admitted. "I let rage and ambition blind me. While we were raised in different places by different people, you are my blood. I should not have assumed anything about you. When I saw you come to rescue Gheric . . . I came to know the error of my ways."

Aurelia lifted her eyes and looked at her twin. "I don't know you, Sabra, and I know I have created chaos for you, but someday, if you could forgive me, I would like to know you as a sister."

She halted her speech. Sabra was surprised to see tears welling in Aurelia's eyes.

"I . . ." Sabra began before Aurelia cut her off.

"It's okay," the noblewoman said, waving her hand. "I don't expect forgiveness anytime soon. It's just . . . "

She paused, casting her eyes downward once more. "The moment I cast that spell last night, I knew it was a mistake," she confessed. "I lay awake most of the night, replaying the event in my mind. I thank the gods you were able to counter the spell. By some miracle, I have been given another chance . . . a chance to make amends for what I have done."

"You expect me to believe you?" Sabra challenged.

Aurelia shook her head. "No, but I hope that you will give me the opportunity to prove that I am more than what you have seen me to be."

Sabra looked long and hard at her sister, trying to discern the truth. Uncertain, she raised a finger and spoke a single word under her breath.

"Veritas."

Utilizing her magic, Sabra cast a simple cantrip. To her astonishment, she did not detect an inkling of deceit coming from the woman in front of her. For better or for worse, Aurelia was speaking the truth.

Sabra looked outside the window and caught a glimpse of Gheric talking to Jorrell.

"What did you say to them?" she asked.

Aurelia quickly outlined the planned duels she had discussed with the others.

Sabra stared at her, knowing such an idea was fraught with peril . . . for Gheric more than anyone.

"Gheric agreed to this?" she finally asked.

"Yes," Aurelia answered. "He, along with Jorrell and I, believe it will cause the least amount of bloodshed. But none of us will agree to it without your consent."

A knot of fear came to rest in Sabra's stomach at the thought of Gheric fighting a duel for his life. She also thought of the villagers her choice would affect. Sabra knew, whatever course of action she chose, it would affect every person in Caldor. It all came down to a simple truth.

Do I trust Aurelia or not? Sabra thought. This plan already had the backing of Gheric and Jorrell.

Knowing time was short, Sabra came to a decision.

"Our mother's name was Fiora," she began. "Fiora Hastings. She loved a flower that used to grow on the walls of our old house. It blossomed a pale violet and smelled of sweet honeysuckle. The leaves would turn a bright yellow in the autumn."

"Wisteria," Aurelia breathed, giving Sabra her first smile. "That's my favorite too."

Aurelia nodded and turned. "Thank you," the noblewoman said, preparing to exit the room.

Sabra, wrestling with the battle of wills raging inside her watched her leave.

"Aurelia!" she shouted, lurching toward the door.

"Yes?" her twin asked, looking over her shoulder.

Sabra stopped, her eyes searching the woman in front of her. "When this is over, if we both survive, perhaps we could discuss our mother a bit more."

Aurelia nodded. "I think I'd like that, Sabra . . ." she said shyly. Hesitating a moment, Aurelia flashed her twin a wicked smile. "I . . . have an idea I'd like to run by you, but it may prove to be extremely dangerous, particularly for us. However, if it is successful, it may spare Gheric some risk."

"Why should I trust you?" Sabra questioned cautiously.

Aurelia stepped close to Sabra and took her sister's hand. "Because I can see that you care for him a great deal."

Sabra felt her heart begin to pound, and she made to pull her hand away.

"I know what you risked for Gheric last night," Aurelia continued. "The others told me how you would not leave his side after healing him."

"I don't know," Sabra whispered, reluctant to give in to her sister so easily. "It would be simple for you to betray us all."

Aurelia straightened and looked deeply into Sabra's sparkling eyes. "He's coming, you know," she said. "Our father. He and his three hundred men will be here by sunrise tomorrow."

"He's coming here?" Sabra gasped, her eyes widening in surprise.

"Yes, and he's ordered me to capture you and bring you to him," Aurelia stated. "You think things are bad now? Wait until Niles has full control of the village. The people of Caldor will live in misery for the rest of their lives."

Sabra detected nothing but the truth rolling off her sister.

"Father will order anyone who resisted Niles to be put to death," Aurelia continued. "That would mean Gheric, at the least. Malhallow is a ruthless warlord who brings nothing but pain and suffering to anyone who defies his rule."

Sabra blinked in shock, unsure of how to respond.

"All your friends, Gyles and Jorrell . . . even the bandits you've brought in to help harvest your fields . . . he will hang them from the battlements if they do not comply with his demands."

Sabra felt a jolt of fear at Aurelia's statement. "Even Little Drei?" she asked softly.

"Everyone," Aurelia answered, her truth evident. She squeezed her sister's hand in her own. "But together, we can stop him."

"How?" Sabra asked.

Aurelia gave her twin another smile and unveiled her plan.

GHERIC WAS SPARRING WITH LIEUTENANT JORRELL IN THE open space behind the barn as the sun passed its zenith. The two men, both excellent swordsmen, had attacked and defended against one another for nearly an hour. Grada, Drei, and Marn were watching nearby, each basking in the midst of their afternoon repast. The trio of farmworkers looked on in wonder at the speed and skill of the two warriors in front of them.

"Dammit, Gheric," Silence chided, looking at the swarthy warrior in annoyance. "How many times do I have to tell you —Niles is murderously fast on the riposte. You keep leaving yourself open! Jorrell has killed you three times in the last five minutes!"

Gheric was wincing from the blow to his ribs. "I heard you before," the barrel-chested warrior muttered. "I can't resist it. Jorrell keeps luring me in, leaving a gap in his defense."

"I do it on purpose," the lean swordsman replied. "The baron bested me twice on that very move only yesterday."

"And you," Silence said, shifting his gaze toward the lieutenant. "Harmon is stronger than any of us and just as fast. His tactics were learned in the arena. I've seen him fight before, don't underestimate the man. All it takes is one solid strike and you are done."

"Aye," panted Jorrell. "He has that reputation."

"Let's take a break," Gheric suggested, his face red from exertion.

Both men lowered their practice swords and walked inside the shade of the barn, escaping the warmth of the midday sun overhead. Jorrell dipped an earthenware mug into a pitcher of cool water Marn had carried from the stream.

"Where are Yetter and Othar?" Drei asked, her high-pitched voice cutting through the afternoon heat.

"On a task I've assigned to them," Gheric said, panting and taking the mug from Jorrell with a thankful nod. He filled it with water and dumped it on his head. He stood up straight and let the cool liquid run down his neck. Shaking his head, water flew everywhere, causing Drei to squeal in delight.

"You three best get back to work," Gheric ordered. "The north field is nearly done. All Sabra will have left to harvest are the crops planted to the west."

"You think we will get all the corn in on time?" Marn asked, his voice filled with the enthusiasm of youth.

Gheric shrugged. "We will see. The full moon is in three days. If needed, we can work all that night."

He nodded at Grada and motioned toward the field. "I'll have Silence—Horval, bring the wagons around in an hour.

We can all pitch in and load them up before we take them to the market."

Jorrell looked concerned but held his tongue until the three farmhands left.

"You think it wise to bring the corn into the village today?" he asked. "Word will get to Niles. He'll be waiting there with his guards."

The swarthy warrior dipped the mug into the water a second time and drank from it deeply. "Maybe not, but today is the day Niles is supposed to implement his new tax."

"So?" Jorrell said, his eyebrow arched in question.

Gheric gave Jorrell and Horval a wicked grin. "So, I want to bait him, get the man to agree to the duel. Then, the people of Caldor will see him for who he truly is."

"Aurelia just came from the market," Horval argued. "She said it's nearly empty."

Gheric scanned the road leading up to the Billerton Farm. There was a portly figure in the distance making its way toward the barn.

"We will see," Gheric replied with a wolfish grin.

CHAPTER 19

Baron Turner looked sourly upon the parchment that he held in front of him, his eyes scanning the contents.

"You are certain?" he questioned, without looking up.

"My scouts saw his colors flying on the Old North Road," Harmon replied. "Unless there is some delay, your uncle will be here early tomorrow."

Niles did not respond. Instead, he let out a slow breath and placed the parchment upon the table in front of him.

"This says there was an assassination attempt," Niles stated evenly. "Who was it, do you think?"

The hulking captain shrugged. "Could have been any number of people. Your uncle has left a fair share of enemies in his wake."

Niles stood from the chair and walked over to his sword and quickly scanned the rest of the chamber. "Come now, Harmon, there is no one about. Do you think he suspects us?"

The captain shrugged his huge shoulders. "It's not likely. The man I used hailed from Gallanse. I received word that my courier was killed by the assassin, and now the assassin is dead. The funds are untraceable. Your uncle can suspect all he wants, but there is no proof."

"Hmmpt." Niles grunted, satisfied with Harmon's reasoning. "What of our men?"

"About half have returned," the captain answered. "The rest should be here after sunset. Several groups were quite far afield searching for Gheric."

The baron grunted, drew his sword, and began shadow fighting, moving flawlessly through his dueling forms.

"The Billerton Farm?" Niles asked, biting off the end of the question. "Were there any signs that mercenary bastard was telling the truth? Are there a score of men waiting for us?"

Harmon snorted, his nostrils flaring. "No one has gotten close enough to tell. My reports say that coward Tamalin was the only one to go near the property, though no one seems to know why." The captain laughed darkly. "One arrow loosed, and he ran with his tail between his legs. I doubt his threat has merit. He told me last night Sabra was half-way to Kath by now, yet my cousin tells me she was in the courtroom fighting with Gheric last night."

He paused, a scowl crossing his countenance. "Had I been able to, I'd have sent men to hunt them down last night. With Aurelia and I unconscious, they managed to escape."

Niles frowned, knowing things were unraveling quickly in Caldor. "What do you think of this duel Widow Billerton has proposed?"

The captain's eyes began to burn with rage. "Nothing would make me happier than to butcher Jorrell in front of the entire village. That whoreson murdered at least four of my men—perhaps more. Their souls cry out for vengeance. I would give it to them if you will allow it. Name me your champion, and I will gut the bastard."

"Yes," Niles agreed. "My uncle has never hesitated in using you before. I think you will be his champion against Jorrell. Of that, I have no doubt."

Niles remained quiet, moving smoothly through the forms and contemplating on his own battle from the previous evening. "The son of a bitch was well trained," Niles admitted, coming to a halt. "Better than I would have imagined."

"Who?" Harmon grunted.

"Gheric," Niles answered, picking up once again. "I should not have underestimated him."

Harmon frowned at his liege. "You are not suggesting he could best you?"

Niles froze in place, his sword extended in front of him. "Of course not," he answered scornfully. "There were a number of holes in his defense I might have exploited, but for his spell casting ability. That's what threw me off. Damn magickers, you never can tell what they will do."

"Are you agreeing to the duel, then?" Harmon asked.

"If I do, I will have to take him more seriously this time," Niles began. "I will insist on a restriction against his use of magic, but, yes, I believe I will accept. We will keep things nice and quiet in this little hamlet. No need for Duke Mays to . . ."

A knock at the door interrupted their discussion.

"Come in!" the baron said with a growl, putting away his sword.

The door opened, and in walked the mayor of Caldor.

"Ahh, Tamalin," Niles said. "We were just speaking of you."

"I'm sorry to interrupt, my lord," the mayor said with a bow, "but you asked to hear of anything unusual."

"Indeed, I did," Niles replied with a nod. "What news from Caldor?"

The mayor removed his felt hat and clutched at it unconsciously. "It's probably nothing, my lord, but . . . there are very few people at the market today."

"This is why you interrupted me?" Niles asked, his voice dangerous. "Because the market is slow?"

Tamalin's face paled. "I know it seems foolish, my lord, it's just—"

"It's just what?" Harmon barked, his voice harsh.

Tamalin gaped at the huge captain and swallowed nervously. "It's just, the market has been quiet all day," he explained in a rush. "It is rarely like this."

"Is there anything else?" Niles asked, clearly annoyed.

"Actually, yes," the mayor answered reluctantly.

"What is it?" Harmon spat the question. "Are all the cats barking like dogs?" he mocked. "Or perhaps it's beginning to rain shit?"

Tamalin shook his head, shrinking under the captain's words. "The Billerton Farm is stirring," he said. "There are six fully laden wagons heading this way. They are being driven by Sabra, Jorrell, Gheric, and three other farmhands I don't recognize. They are heading to the market."

Niles was surprised at the news. "The three of them are entering the village?" he questioned.

Tamalin nodded his head.

"No sign of other warriors? Mercenaries or the like?" Niles pressed.

"The roads are empty, save for the wagons," the mayor answered.

The baron's handsome face creased in a cruel smile. "Perhaps we won't need to fight a duel after all," he said, turning to Harmon. "Captain, gather whatever men have returned. Have them form up in the courtyard. Today, we put an end to Gheric and his troublesome ways. You can rip apart Jorrell too, while we are at it."

Looking toward the mayor, Niles issued another order. "Fetch my cousin. She should be healed enough by now to bear witness to my victory."

"Yes, my lord," Tamalin replied, fervently praying Aurelia had returned from her clandestine visit unscathed.

CHAPTER 20

The skies overhead were beginning to fill with clouds as the small convoy of wagons entered the marketplace. The first came to a halt as its driver pulled back on the reins. Dismounting, the warrior moved toward the back of the column, dressed and ready for battle.

"Just remember, let me do the talking," Gheric reminded Sabra as he walked past the blue-eyed farm woman, who was climbing off her wagon.

"This is the most uncomfortable thing I've ever worn," he heard her complain as she tugged in annoyance at the collar of her dress.

"Let us hope that is the least of our worries," Jorrell put in, coming up behind them and giving her a chastising look. Both men were dressed in armor, Gheric in his leather cuirass while the baron's former lieutenant wore his shirt of chain mail. Jorrell's wrists were fixed with finely etched leather bracers as well. Each had swords hanging at their sides, and neither looked particularly pleased to be in the market square. As they approached, Gheric cast the dark hood of his cloak over his head and partially obscured his face.

Jorrell cast him a questioning look. "Why the hood? It will limit your peripheral vision."

"I have my reasons," the warrior-mage answered, saying no more on the matter.

Upon their arrival, the fearful eyes of the townsfolk began to appear, nervously peeking out from behind locked doors and windows.

"Let's get this over with," Gheric muttered, casting his eyes at the buildings that made up the market square.

The trio walked over to the merchant in charge of produce.

"Hello, Pyle," Gheric said with a grunt. "Good to see you again."

"You as well," the plain-faced merchant replied, returning the courtesy with the bow of his head. "How may I help you?"

Gheric glanced to his beautiful companion, who nodded for him to continue. "We have 294 bushels of corn today," he reported. "If my calculations are correct, that's thirty-six silvers."

The merchant licked his lips nervously and glanced back toward the keep. "Normally, I'd give you that exact amount, however . . . with the new tax that has been implemented, your total comes to twenty-one silvers."

"Fifteen silvers in tax?" Jorrell scoffed, his eyes going flat. "That's preposterous."

"And yet you will pay it," came the oily voice of the baron. From behind the merchant's stall stepped Niles Turner, fully dressed in his chain mail armor. Next to him stood the towering captain of the guard—similarly attired—who glowered ferociously at Jorrell. Behind them, skulking in the background, were Tamalin and the baron's cousin, her face covered in a black veil of satin.

"No, we won't," Sabra challenged from her place next to Gheric. Her blue eyes were glittering in outrage. "You cannot make up these ridiculous rules whenever you see fit. There is a protocol to follow when it comes to raising taxes."

Niles looked at Sabra with scorn in his eyes. "I am the Baron of Caldor, Mrs. Billerton," he hissed in return. "I will do as I please!"

"This tax is illegal," Jorrell pointed out, stepping forward. "It has not been vetted by Duke Mays, nor has it been approved by your uncle. That is the proper protocol, is it not, Mayor Tamalin?"

The red-faced village official looked remarkably uncomfortable as all eyes turned to him. With a cautious glance at the baron, Tamalin cleared his throat and said, "I am . . . uncertain of what the proper procedure is," he squeaked. "I would have to look into the matter more thoroughly, given more time."

Niles flicked his eyes toward the mayor, his disapproval evident. "Be that as it may," the baron groused, "the tax stands. Either pay it or suffer the consequences."

"And what consequences are those?" challenged Sabra, sounding for all the world like an aristocrat at court.

Niles leered at her, failing to hide his lascivious desire. "I will take over your farm, and you will be arrested."

"You will not touch her," Gheric threatened, placing a hand on the hilt of his sword. The broad-shouldered warrior stepped closer until he was less than a foot away from the baron. Harmon closed ranks, looming over them all.

"Maybe you are used to terrifying the local populace, you blackhearted bastard," Gheric hissed, "but no one here is afraid of you."

He paused, turning his dark eyes upon Harmon. "Nor this oversized ape you call your captain."

Harmon's eyes went flat. "First you presume to challenge the baron's authority," the guard captain snarled, "and then you insult me?"

"I will challenge any man who would threaten the rights of the people he is supposed to serve!" Gheric shot back. "If your precious baron doesn't like it, the challenge has been issued. He and I can settle this right now in a fight to the death, him against me."

"I've heard enough of this seditious slander," Niles said with a growl. "Captain, summon your men."

"Company!" shouted Harmon. "Come forth!"

From the buildings inside the marketplace, the baron's guards came running. Nearly forty men, all armed to the teeth, filed into the square.

"You think I would risk everything I've worked for in single combat?" Niles barked at the implacable face of his adversary. "You are more foolish than I believed."

The baron looked back at his cousin, who had shrunk behind her veil. "My compliments, Aurelia, for bringing the idea of a trial by combat to these rebels. You were right. I should have known if anyone could draw them out from that cesspit they've been hiding in, it would be you."

"It was an honor to serve you," Aurelia managed to say, her blue eyes fixed on Gheric.

"I trusted you," the broad-shouldered warrior said, his eyes hot with a barely contained rage. "I vouched for you! What possible reason could you have for betraying Sabra? For betraying me?"

Eyes going flat, Aurelia gave her answer. "I did what I needed to do in order to keep those important to me safe," she answered. "No matter what the cost to your pride, I would not alter my actions."

Glancing at Harmon, Niles issued his final order. "Arrest them all. If anyone resists, kill them."

The baron's men began to move forward.

"You might want to hold off on that order," Jorrell said, staring balefully at the baron.

"Oh? Why is that?" Niles scoffed.

From inside the Bad Apple Inn, there came the sound of a shrill whistle, loud enough that it could be heard throughout the market square.

The door to the inn swung opened, and dozens of men spilled out into the market. Most were farmers or tradesmen, and they were wielding an assortment of tools ranging from quarterstaffs to pitchforks. A like number stood up from the half dozen wagons behind Gheric where they had lain hidden until needed. As a group, all of them moved forward, coming to a stop only a few paces from the baron's guards, and pushing his way to the front carrying a steel-headed glaive was Gyles.

"I won't be taken so easily this go round, you bastard!" he spat, glaring at Harmon. "It's high time to see what you're made of."

From behind the market square came the shuffling sound of footsteps pounding on the dirt road. Dressed in rags, a good three score bandits came running around the corner, blocking the way back to the keep. Most were armed with swords and knives, though a few grasped at the handles of axes and longbows. Standing in front of the group were Yetter and Othar, and they were looking at the baron hungrily.

Between them, with his feet planted firmly on the ground, was the stoney-eyed Horval, arrow nocked and held at the ready.

"You so much as twitch, and I'll bury a shaft in your heart," the former lieutenant hissed, staring at Niles.

In all, more than one hundred men of Caldor and half again as many bandits had surrounded Baron Turner and his guards.

Niles and his men froze in place, their eyes wide in disbelief.

"My offer stands," Gheric stated mildly. "One to one combat to see who lives and who dies."

The baron glanced furtively back to his guards. "My men are trained soldiers," Niles argued, contempt dripping from his tongue. "You have farmers with sticks, save for the turncoat Horval."

"Those farmers outnumber you almost five to one," Jorrell put in. "That estimate doesn't include our friends from the woods nearby," he continued, nodding at the bandits.

"Archers!" Horval bellowed, raising his bow. A half-score number of bandits followed his lead, fitting arrows to string, ready to loose their clothyard shafts at the baron's men.

"Then, of course, we have . . ." Gheric interjected, waving his hand in front of him. A ball of fire burst from his fingers and hovered over his head. ". . . a few other advantages as well," he finished.

The baron wet his lips, weighing his options.

"Personally, I'd wager that you will refuse my offer," Gheric taunted. "You're nothing but a bully and a coward; one who would rather send his men forward to die needless deaths—*if* they chose to obey their orders."

"They are soldiers of Rathstone," Niles contended. "They will obey any order I give."

"I'm sure they are fine men," Gheric admitted. "But how can you expect them to defend a man who is afraid to fight for them?"

Niles narrowed his eyes, his face seething with anger. Gheric suspected the baron knew he was being goaded into a fight. It was the warrior's hope the baron would grow angry enough to accept it.

"I agree to the duel," Niles finally spat, "on one condition."

"Name it," Gheric said with a growl, his hand grazing the hilt of his sword.

The baron's eyes shifted from Gheric to Jorrell. "My fight will be with you, Lieutenant."

"No," Gheric snarled, stepping forward. "It will be between you and me, you son of a bitch!"

"I accept," Jorrell stated, nodding his head.

"What?" Gheric hissed in protest. "That was not what we agreed to!"

"You have no choice in the matter," Jorrell explained. "This is why I was sent here."

Gheric looked at Jorrell in confusion. "What do you mean? Who sent you?"

In answer, Jorrell tore off his cloak to reveal a blue-and-white sigil on a thin chain worn around his neck. The sigil was embossed with the emblem of a kingfisher. "I am Jorrell Mays, youngest son of the Duke of Kath," he announced. "I have been sent by my father to deliver his justice."

Jorrell looked at Niles, who stood open-mouthed, his face incredulous.

"Six months past, you beat and raped my sister Adema," Jorrell said, choking back his rage. "Though she was sorely injured, her physical wounds have healed with time." Jorrell's face darkened, and his voice became a winter's frost. "The emotional scars, however, she will carry until the end of her days."

The former lieutenant drew his sword, his eyes cold with hate. "Today, you will know the taste of vengeance." The lean warrior flicked his eyes toward the mayor. "Tamalin, by order of the Duke of Kath, I command you to issue the challenge."

The mayor, looking terrified, pulled out a piece of parchment, his hands trembling in fear.

"As I bear witness, these men have agreed to a trial by combat," the mayor began. "Should the baron emerge victorious, he will receive all the rights and properties in Widow Billerton's possession. Should the baron fall, the debt owed to the barony will be terminated."

Tamalin paused and motioned for the combatants to step forward. "As this is a matter of both honor and finance, I am here to assure that you settle it fairly. There will be no interference from anyone on the outside. If mercy is asked for—"

"Mercy will not be asked for," Jorrell snarled, his face like stone.

"Nor will it be given," Niles agreed, his voice supremely confident.

The mayor glanced at both men and finished reading his prepared statement. "Then you may attend to your weapons and commence upon my signal. May the victor be favored by the gods and live free of any retribution. To the loser—"

"That will do," Jorrell said, raising his sword.

"I vaguely remember your sister . . . Adema, did you say?" Niles asked. "She had the look of a whore about her, as I recall—especially around the eyes. Nice to hear she remembers me."

The baron drew his sword and gave his adversary a mock salute.

Gheric stepped forward and spoke softly to Jorrell. "We will discuss this change of plan after you kill him," he growled. "Don't let him goad you—keep your cool and be patient."

Jorrell did not respond. Instead, he dropped into a fighting crouch while Gheric backed into the crowd of onlookers.

"You may begin," Tamalin ordered, scrambling away from the combatants.

Niles moved forward, his blade leading the way.

Jorrell was there to meet him.

CHAPTER 21

Sabra looked on in morbid fascination as the two men fought in the market square. Loathe to look away, she cast her eyes around the clearing. Nearly everyone was watching as the blades of Niles and Jorrell clashed over and over again, neither able to gain an advantage.

Nearly everyone.

She managed to catch her sister's eye. Aurelia was looking at her intently, moving her head imperceptibly to the side.

She wants me to leave, Sabra thought, knowing it was what they had planned from the beginning, no matter what the outcome of the fight might be.

For a moment, she hesitated, torn between abandoning the man she'd fallen in love with or trying to save his life. Her eyes came to rest upon Gheric, who was watching the battle in front of him intently. After nearly sacrificing his life last night, she did not doubt for a moment he would risk everything to save her.

That, she could not allow, even if it cost Sabra his love.

Widow Billerton let out a bitter sigh and made her decision, backing quietly away from the battle.

GHERIC NOTED MOVEMENT BEHIND HIM AND SHIFTED HIS GAZE backward. He saw his lover trying to ease away from the duel playing out in front of them.

"Get behind me," he ordered, grabbing her by the hand. Her palms—soft to the touch—were damp with sweat.

"I don't know what will happen, regardless of the outcome," the warrior absently said to her, his focus still on the fight. In the background, he saw Aurelia had eased her way next to the captain of the guards and was speaking to him softly. "Harmon might order his men forward even if the baron loses. Best if you stay close to me."

He felt Sabra pull her hand away but remained behind him as he suggested.

Gheric studied the baron with the eye of a professional soldier. He could see how Niles had done well at the Great Games the previous summer. His footwork was excellent, and his blade moved with viperous speed. Thus far, Jorrell was up to the task, holding his own against his deadly opponent.

The pace of the fight began to increase as the two warriors exchanged a flurry of attacks and counters. Ducking a swipe that would have decapitated him, the baron lunged forward, and the onlookers gasped.

The baron's blade came away dark, dripping with blood.

"The first cut of many," Baron Turner promised, seeing red ooze from the wound on Jorrell's upper arm. Though Niles smiled, his tone was biting. "Nothing to say, Lieutenant?"

Jorrell remained motionless, failing to rise to the bait.

Instead, the son of House Mays stayed back, keeping his defense in place.

"You *can* learn," the baron taunted, trying another tactic. "Too bad you didn't bring your sister with you. She was a bit young for my taste, but a comely whore, nevertheless."

Jorrell's face twisted in hate as the anger built inside him.

"Stay calm!" Gheric shouted out. "Don't let him play upon your emotions!"

Niles flicked his eyes toward Gheric, his face twisting in a snarl. "Stay out of it, mercenary! Your time is coming!"

Baron Turner ceased his speech and attacked with a sudden fury. Jorrell, expecting such a move, put up a blurring wall of defense.

It was not enough.

Nile's offensive had forced his opponent's sword blade high and to the right. The baron moved with enough speed where Jorrell's footing was off, and he was left out of position. In the blink of an eye, the baron's riposte struck flesh, and he drove the tip of his sword deep into Jorrell's shoulder. The former lieutenant gasped in disbelief, dropping his weapon in surprise. Niles kicked out and struck Jorrell in the chest, sending him sprawling in the dust.

"Is this the vengeance you promised me?" Niles mocked, his face triumphant. "You are no match for me, Jorrell. You never were."

"Stay focused!" Gheric shouted, willing Jorrell to his feet. "Pick up your sword, it isn't over yet."

"I'll deal with you momentarily," Niles said with a sneer, flicking blood off his blade and spattering it across Jorrell's face.

Jorrell gave Gheric a look of steady determination. He bent down and lifted his sword with his wounded arm. Blood was running freely down his right side, covering his torso.

"No good with your left?" Niles jeered. "Come, son of Kath, let us see if you scream like your sister did!" the baron crowed, raising his sword once more.

Niles attacked with a renewed ferocity. Jorrell defended as best he could, but even the most untrained eye saw he could not last. The baron wounded him twice more, lashing out once at Jorrell's thigh and again at his shin. The duke's son was bleeding profusely now, trying heroically to stay on his feet.

The baron was no longer defending himself. He was toying with Jorrell, much like a cat playing with a mouse.

"This has lasted long enough." Niles grunted. "It is time to end the lesson."

The baron's right arm moved back, and Gheric knew he was going for the killing thrust. Jorrell saw it too and brought his hands together, looking for all the world like he was preparing to block the attack.

Instead, unseen by all but Gheric, he transferred his sword to his left hand.

The baron thrust forward with his blade, and Jorrell desperately parried the attack with the bracer on his weakened right arm. Nile's eyes widened in shock as he registered the move that would kill him. With a cry of pent-up rage, Jorrell's left arm shot forward, and he slammed the point of his sword upward driving into the baron's neck. It tore through the skin and severed both the windpipe and jugular. Niles dropped his sword and fell to his knees, clasping at his neck with both hands.

"How's that for vengeance, you son of a bitch?!" Jorrell thundered, looking Niles dead in the eye. Placing the hilt of his sword in both hands, the youngest son of Duke Mays made one last attack.

With a sickening crunch, Jorrell took off Baron Turner's head.

The severed skull rolled across the ground of the merchant's square and came to rest twenty feet away, its lifeless eyes staring up at the guards.

The duel was over.

A great cheer went up from both the farmers and bandits alike.

The mayor was awestruck at the result, his mouth wide open.

One of the sergeants, a brutish fellow who had come looking for Gheric at Sabra's farm, drew his sword. "Have at the bastar—"

His voice was cut off as an arrow slammed into his chest and ripped through his lungs. The sergeant fell to his knees and toppled face first to the ground.

All eyes turned to Horval, the baron's former lieutenant.

"Sergeant Orms was a pig!" he stated loudly, nodding to the man he'd shot. Horval calmly nocked a second arrow to his bow. "He lived to inflict pain upon others."

The archer looked up, seeing the rapt faces of the remaining guards. "You all know me," he continued. "I served Baron Turner loyally for many months."

The archer's eyes flashed in momentary anger. "But he turned on me, left me for dead—all because I acted against his orders. Orders that proved to be illegal, just as this new tax is."

Horval sniffed, casting his gaze upon them all. "Now, it's up to you, but I'd consider laying down your arms and staying alive, otherwise . . ." He trailed off and pulled back on his bowstring.

The remaining guards looked at him then at the hundreds of men surrounding them.

"The hell with this," a short man with a red beard swore, dropping his sword to the ground. "I didn't sign on to kill my own people."

One by one, every guard in the market repeated the action, surrendering to their former officer.

Jorrell, blood oozing from him, staggered to one knee.

"Get the Druid," Gheric snapped, helping the wounded swordsman ease himself to the ground. He turned toward Sabra, concern etched on his face. "Stay close, we might need you."

"I will," he heard her promise, still stunned at Jorrell's victory. Looking across the way, Gheric's dark eyes searched everywhere for Sabra's twin.

Of Aurelia and Captain Harmon, there was no sign.

CHAPTER 22

A quarter turn of the hourglass later, Jorrell was being tended to by Temper inside the Bad Apple Inn.

"I haven't been this busy since the war up north twenty years ago," the old Druid grumbled, mashing herbs together in an age-stained mortar and pestle.

"Which war was that?" Jorrell managed, gritting his teeth in pain.

"I've lost track," the Druid admitted, shaking his head. "Idiotic things—there are always piles of dead on both sides. Thought I could escape such stupidity when I came south."

"With any luck, Caldor will return to being a quiet, peaceful barony," Jorrell replied. He shifted his weight uncomfortably, wincing in pain. "While I appreciate your administrations," the duke's son continued, "I don't understand why you or Sabra cannot heal me with your magic."

"Earth magic takes energy, boy," Temper flared. "I used all mine up this morning on the baron . . . Little good it did him."

"Sabra too, is weary, I'd wager," Gheric added,

looking across the room where she stood quietly speaking to Yetter and Horval. "Else she'd have offered her services by now. Temper's skill with herbs will have to do for the time being. We still have Malhallow to contend with."

"Gheric, wait," Jorrell said, taking hold of his arm. "About the duel . . ."

The warrior waved off Jorrell's words. "Had I known of your vendetta, I'd have passed the duty to you freely."

"Yes, well, I thank you for it," Jorrell said tightly. "Though I'm afraid I won't be in condition to fight the big Shar tomorrow."

Gheric offered him a smile. "You've done your part. Leave Harmon to me."

Jorrell offered Gheric his hand, and the swarthy warrior shook it.

"Infants, the both of you," Temper chided, his face sour.

Chuckling to himself, Gheric strode over to where Sabra was still speaking to Yetter and Horval.

"What news from the road?" Gheric asked, looking at the former lieutenant.

"It's not good," Horval answered, his face grim.

"Tell me."

With a sigh, Horval responded. "He's brought three hundred men with him, his elite soldiers."

"I take it they won't surrender to our peasant army?" Gheric voiced wryly.

"Not likely," the archer quipped.

"I'll deal with it as soon as I can," Gheric said, shifting his eyes to Sabra.

The beautiful farm woman nodded toward the back of the inn. "We need to talk," she said quietly.

Knowing Sabra wanted a private word, Gheric looked to

Yetter. "Find Othar and meet me back here in a few minutes," he said.

Yetter raised a knuckle to his forehead and gave a halfhearted salute. Sabra took Gheric by the hand and led him into the back of the room where they could speak without fear of being overheard.

"What's this about, pretty girl?" he asked.

Sabra looked around the room and saw they were alone. "This," she said, handing him a letter written in bold handwriting.

"What is it?" Gheric asked.

"It's from Aurelia," Sabra answered.

Gheric frowned. "She betrayed us both," he muttered, unfolding the parchment. "I'm not sure we can trust anything she—"

"Just read it!" she snapped, her face going red.

With a shake of his head, the broad-shouldered warrior took the letter and started reading it. His dark eyes widened as he scanned the contents.

"Do you know what this says?" he asked finally, looking back at Sabra.

"Yes," she answered grimly. "Malhallow is sterile. He has not been able to produce another heir since . . . my birth."

Gheric narrowed his eyes. "Well, he has Aurelia, I suppose. I'm sure she will bear him grandchildren."

Sabra's eyes flashed in a fleeting show of pain. "No, Aurelia informed me that she was barren."

"Impossible," he scoffed. "Evil she may be, but she is still young and—"

"By Chara, I thought you had a brain in that head," she cut him off. "Malhallow has invited a string of noblemen into Rathstone with the singular task of impregnating his daughter. None have been successful."

Gheric's face turned in confusion. "She told you all this?"

"Yes, while you were out sparring with Jorrell," Sabra answered.

He shrugged his broad shoulders. "I'm not sure any of this is relevant to our current—"

"By the sons of Kelthane, are you even listening?!" she snapped.

His mouth turned down in a frown. "What is the problem? So what if Malhallow doesn't have any grandchildren? I can hardly—"

"To think I believed you were more than a pretty face," she interrupted. "Malhallow's not marching three hundred of his best men south for Aurelia, he's coming so he can continue his line."

A cold feeling began to churn inside of Gheric's stomach.

"What are you saying?" he asked.

Sabra sighed. "According to Aurelia, Malhallow wants a male heir. He cannot produce one himself, and his elder child is barren. He is ready to exercise his only remaining option."

"Which is?" Gheric asked.

Sabra sighed, suddenly looking tired. "He will take me from Caldor and treat me as a broodmare until he gets what he wants—a male heir."

"Over my dead body!" Gheric stormed. "If he thinks he can come to Caldor and take you away from me, he is insane! I'll butcher him and every one of his soldiers if he so much as lays a finger on you."

Sabra looked shocked at Gheric's reaction. "You would . . . protect me? Even from the might of Malhallow's army?"

Gheric took her hand in his. "I told you, I am in love with you, girl. No power on the continent will keep me from protecting you."

The beautiful woman in front of him looked into his eyes with an expression of longing he'd not seen before on her face. "I . . . I fear I am not worthy."

"Nonsense," he whispered, reaching out his arms and holding her close. He gently brushed a strand of hair from her eyes. "You are the worthiest person I've ever known. I would defy the gods for you."

She looked up at him and stared deeply into his dark eyes.

"Kiss me," he heard her whisper.

Gheric dipped his head and touched his lips to hers. This kiss was different from the ones they shared in the past. While she was normally reserved, Sabra's lips now locked onto his with a fiery passion. Gheric felt her hand on the back of his head, crushing his face toward hers. He was acutely aware of the softness of her tongue lashing as she explored the inside of his mouth. Surprised, Gheric's passion began to rise as he kissed her back with a desire that matched her own. The faint noise of the inn faded away until he was aware only of the woman in his arms.

"Is this a bad time?" came a voice from nearby, moments later.

Gheric stopped and tilted his head toward the speaker. He saw Yetter and Othar staring at him and Sabra.

"Gentleman," he said, somewhat out of breath.

"I hate to bother you when you are . . . entertaining your . . . Widow Billerton," Yetter said with a grin. "It's just you mentioned that you wanted to meet with us."

"I do." Gheric nodded, regretfully stepping away from Sabra.

"I should go," Widow Billerton said, giving the former bandits a tight smile. With a last look at Gheric, Sabra strolled back into the common room.

"She's changed." Othar grunted, watching her leave. "She

seems a completely different person than the one that plucked us from the forest."

"Let's get down to business," Gheric said, brushing off the farmhand's comment.

"We did our part," Othar put in. "Yetter, Silence, and me, we went out and did what you wanted. Gathered up every bandit in the area, we did. It's time to get paid."

"You will get your silver," Gheric agreed. "However—"

"Ahh, for shit's sake," Othar grumbled. "You aren't going to pay us, are you?"

The warrior frowned at the tall farmhand. "Of course I am, I never fail to pay my debts. It's just . . . I have another job for you and the other bandits you brought in, if you are game."

"You take me for a fool?" Othar spat. "I heard what the others are saying! I don't mind banging away at a few of the local guards, especially when we outnumber them, but I'm not going toe to toe with three hundred soldiers of Rathstone. It's suicide!"

Gheric's face took on a bland expression. "I would not ask you to do that. However, I can see your mind is made up. If you'd like, I'll pay your wage to you right now."

"Damn right you will," Othar growled, nodding his head in determination.

Gheric reached into a small satchel at his waist and pulled out a single coin. "Yetter, would you have Gyles exchange twenty silvers for this? I'll need the silvers to pay your compatriot."

"You have a gold falcon?" Othar gasped, eyeing the coin greedily.

"No," Gheric replied, feigning a yawn. "More like a hundred or so. I buried them on my way into Caldor after my encounter with you lot on the road."

"A hundred?" Othar gaped.

"Aye, hidden in a satchel, not too far away." The dark-eyed warrior grunted. "Of course, if something were to happen to me, well, it would be like that gold just disappeared. A real shame too, I brought it in case I had to hire good men like you."

Othar narrowed his eyes. "You think I'm stupid? I know what you are doing. I'm not falling for that."

"That's fine," Gheric said agreeably. "I'm happy to pay you as soon as Yetter here exchanges the falcon for eagles."

The warrior turned back to Yetter. "Off with you, I need to pay this man his wages and speak with the rest of your men."

"Can I . . . Might I hold it?" Othar asked, transfixed by the gold.

"Of course," Gheric said, nodding at Yetter.

The elder farmhand suppressed a smile and passed the yellow metal coin over to the taller man, who stared at it in disbelief.

"I've never seen gold up close before," Othar breathed. "Never thought I'd get to hold a coin like this."

"Glad you got the chance," Gheric said, turning back to Yetter. "Once Othar is paid, I'll tell you how you and the other men you brought in can make double what I promised."

"Double?" Othar blinked and looked up, sounding stunned. "You didn't say anything about that."

"I'm sorry, Othar, I thought you were leaving?" Gheric asked.

"I . . . I am," the former bandit stated firmly, lifting his axe off the ground and tossing the gold back to Gheric.

"Oh, incidentally," Gheric said, turning back to Yetter, "I've spoken to the mayor. He's agreed that any of your men who assist us tomorrow will be given temporary citizenship here in Caldor. How does that sound?"

"Damn good to me," Yetter answered with a smile.

Othar looked at the warrior in front of him, his eyes narrowed in suspicion.

"Could be a permanent citizenship if they prove to be valued members of the community," Gheric continued.

Othar gave Gheric a look of pure frustration. "Goddamn it," he growled, releasing his hold on his axe. "I never should have bothered with you at all. You are just as likely to lead me to my death as pay me twenty silvers."

"You're staying?" Gheric asked, his voice mild.

"Just shut up and tell me," Othar growled. "What's the play?"

CHAPTER 23

Baron Malhallow sat inside his command tent, impatiently waiting for his report. He swirled a cup of wine in his hand before tipping it to his lips, barely tasting it. He frowned at the sudden commotion coming from outside his tent, followed quickly by the heavy rustling of the entrance flap being dragged open.

"My lord," said his attendant, a burly sergeant by the name of Bramon.

"What is it?" Malhallow asked, his voice commanding.

"Riders, my lord, coming from Caldor."

Malhallow shifted his considerable bulk uncomfortably in his cushioned chair. "Who is it?"

Bramon hesitated a moment. "It looks to be Captain Harmon and your daughter, Aurelia," he answered.

The baron pursed his lips as he tapped his fingers lightly upon the rim of the cup. "What word do they carry?"

The sergeant shook his head. "The captain wouldn't say. Claims he'll only speak to you."

Malhallow tipped his wine cup backward and drained it.

"My daughter?" he asked, refilling his drink from a pitcher of white porcelain on the table in front of him.

"She hasn't said anything at all," the sergeant answered.

The baron placed his hand on his white goatee and stroked it absently. "That's not like her. Send them in—and station your squad outside the entrance."

"Yes, my lord," the sergeant said with a bow. He exited the tent, leaving the baron of Rathstone alone.

Something's gone wrong, the old man thought, pursing his lips sourly. *Where is my idiot nephew? More importantly, where is my youngest daughter?* The baron of Rathstone sat at his table and mulled over these questions in his mind.

Malhallow did not have to wait long. It was only moments later when the massive captain of the guard entered the room with Aurelia trailing close behind.

"Keep your distance, the both of you," Malhallow growled. "I don't know who to trust these days."

Harmon stopped and gave the baron a cold stare. "You doubt my loyalty after all these years?"

"I doubt everyone after this last attempt on my life," the old man answered crisply. He moved his gaze on to Aurelia. "What of you, daughter? Have you no greeting for me?"

"I am glad to see you alive," Aurelia murmured, giving him an awkward curtsy.

The baron frowned at her. "Has it been so long you have forgotten how to pay your respects in the proper manner?"

"Apologies, my lord," she said. "I was injured last night. My wounds, I fear, have left me somewhat stiff."

Malhallow stood upright, his face grim. "Yes, I've heard of your battle with this . . . mercenary," the baron said. "It seems he has been quite the upstart."

Malhallow craned his neck, searching the empty space

behind them. "Where is Niles? Surely, he would not have sent you to my camp alone?"

Aurelia cast her eyes downward while Harmon shook his head. "He's been killed, my lord," the captain explained. "Slain by the youngest son of Duke Mays."

Malhallow's icy-blue eyes widened in surprise. "Slain?" he questioned in disbelief. "When did this happen?"

"Not three hours ago on the streets of Caldor," Aurelia answered.

The baron moved backward and slumped into his chair. He looked past them both, his thoughts churning.

"The arrogant fool," Malhallow whispered at last. "What possessed him to participate in a duel at all? He could have had his guards cut the man down."

"The villagers rose up against him," Harmon stated. "We were outnumbered five to one."

"I see you managed to save yourselves," the baron remarked sourly, refocusing on the captain.

Harmon furrowed his brow, his anger stirring. "I saw no need to stay behind and be slaughtered. I took your daughter and left. What would you have done?"

"I would have taken my youngest child on the first day like *Niles* was supposed to!" Malhallow spat. "Impregnate the bitch and continue my line! Instead, Niles let his anger get the best of him because the girl spurned his ridiculous proposal of marriage. Worse, I am now left having to pen a message to my sister explaining how her only child is dead because of his own stupidity."

The baron shook his head in irritation. "I should have sent you south earlier, Aurelia. Perhaps you could have dissuaded him from this folly."

"Speaking of folly," Aurelia said, looking at the baron coolly. "A second challenge has been issued."

"A second trial? Malhallow asked sharply. "By whom?"

"Jorrell, the son of Duke Mays."

For a moment, Malhallow was speechless. "Jorrell is the duke's son?" he asked in surprise. "The boy was part of my personal guard for the last three months."

"It seems he had an agenda of his own," Harmon growled. "Apparently, your late nephew raped and beat his sister. Duke Mays sent his finest swordsman to extract justice."

The grizzled face of the baron was implacable, lost in thought. "On what grounds is this second duel based?" he questioned.

Aurelia cast her blue eyes upon her father. "Jorrell wants control of your barony in Rathstone, as he has already assumed command in Caldor."

Malhallow's eyes narrowed in anger. "Of course he wants Rathstone, child! That's not what I asked. I want to know what legal grounds he has for this duel?"

Aurelia's eyes searched her father's face, as though seeing him for the first time. "It is said that Lieutenant Horval has proof of your treachery. He has a missive sent from you to Niles that shows you're planning a rebellion against the Duke of Kath."

"I thought the matter had been dealt with weeks ago," Malhallow snapped.

"No, Father," Aurelia answered. "Lieutenant Horval lives. If this proof comes to light, the duke will come after you himself. As it stands, Jorrell's challenge will wrest control of both baronies from you."

"Rathstone and Caldor are mine!" the old baron shouted, his anger rising.

"With respect," she offered, "Jorrell has already seized

control in the south. Caldor no longer stands under your jurisdiction."

Malhallow glowered at her coldly, knowing her logic was sound.

"Leave us, Daughter," Baron Turner commanded, waving Aurelia from the room. "Wait for my summons outside. I wish to speak with Harmon alone."

"Yes, my lord," Aurelia acquiesced, giving another awkward curtsy before exiting the tent.

Malhallow rose from his seat and moved toward the huge captain. "How many men does Jorrell command?"

Harmon snorted derisively. "No more than fifty guards, and twice that many farmers."

"The guards left behind . . . are they likely to follow Jorrell's orders?"

The big captain shrugged. "Hard to say, though I'd guess they will not offer much resistance should a larger force happen upon them."

The baron pressed his lips together and rubbed the back of his neck, trying to knead away the tension building there. "I intend to march into Caldor on the morrow . . . I have no desire to burn it down, but I will take it by force if I have to."

"It would be easier and less of a risk if I killed Jorrell's champion in a duel," Harmon offered.

Malhallow frowned in confusion. "I would have thought Jorrell would fight you himself."

The captain shook his head. "He was badly wounded today. Niles had him beaten, but his arrogance proved to be his undoing. I do not believe Jorrell will be fit to fight. He will choose the mercenary Gheric as his champion."

The baron clasped his hands behind his back. "How formidable is this Gheric?"

"I have not seen him fight," Harmon admitted. "But he

held his own against your nephew. No easy task. But I doubt he can stand up to my experience in the arena. I will fight him for you . . . for the right price."

The old nobleman narrowed his eyes. "What price is that?"

Harmon stood to his full height. "To wed Aurelia and become Baron of Caldor."

Malhallow grunted in surprise. "I won't allow it," he snapped. "You are a commoner. My daughter, despite her uselessness, is of noble blood."

"I understand your reticence," Harmon replied. "However, should things go awry tomorrow, my offer remains."

Malhallow shook his head. "Thank you, Captain, but I'd rather not incur the risk. I do wish Lieutenant Locke would report. I'd rather not advance blindly into Caldor without knowing what obstacles might lie ahead."

Harmon raised his eyebrows in surprise. "Your lead scout has not reported in?" he questioned. "It's not like Locke to shirk in his duty."

The baron shook his head. "I had him ferried across the Lesser Rhone earlier today to make certain there were no forces on the other side of Caldor. He may have been delayed in his return."

Harmon snorted. "So, you suspected Mays might have ferreted out your plans to rebel against him?"

Malhallow looked sharply at the captain and sniffed in surprise. "You are smarter than you look, Captain. Perhaps you *would* make a good ruler in Caldor."

"I'll remember you said that." Harmon grunted.

"We will use my forces tomorrow and end this nonsense once and for all," the baron reiterated. "Now go, get some rest. Send Aurelia in on your way out."

"Yes, my lord." Harmon nodded, giving the baron a salute.

Malhallow lifted his cup to his lips and drained it once more. As he placed the wooden container back upon the table, he heard the flap of his tent be drawn aside.

Aurelia entered once more but did not approach him.

"You have changed, Daughter," Malhallow voiced, slipping into his chair.

Aurelia shot him a glare that spoke volumes. "I'm happy to disappoint you," she answered coldly.

Malhallow let out a burst of harsh laughter. "You have been away too long. You used to hide your contempt for me better than this."

The blue-eyed woman moved forward a step until a raised hand from her father stopped her.

"Come no closer," the baron hissed. "You think I would let you approach? Your assassin nearly had me in Rathstone. A few seconds more, and I would be dead."

There was a momentary pause between them as Aurelia took in the information.

"So, the rumors are true," she said quietly. "Did the killer use a blade?"

"Poison," he snarled. "A woman's weapon."

Aurelia looked at him with genuine confusion. "It was not I who brought in the hired killer," she said. "Had I wanted you dead, I'd have used my magic and taken Rathstone long before this."

Malhallow leaned forward in his chair. "If not you, then who?" he asked, his grizzled face twisted in confusion.

"Niles?" she suggested as her father shook his head.

"Assassins are not his way," the baron disagreed. "Stupid he may have been, but the boy was a bonny fighter. No, this was something else. The killer came from the north, possibly

Gauth or Shaara. The money, however, we traced south of Rathstone."

"Caldor," Aurelia whispered, her curiosity piqued.

"Yes," the baron agreed. "Of all the people in Caldor, only you have contacts that far north."

Aurelia's face hardened. "I will say it one last time . . . it was not me. Besides, there is another in Caldor with ties to the north."

Malhallow stared at her and dismissed the issue with a wave of his hand. "If it is Harmon, as you are alluding to, it is a moot point. I need him now—more than he needs me."

"As you say," Aurelia murmured.

"No matter, child, it is by the by," Malhallow said. "Tell me, Aurelia, did your trip south bear fruit? Is your bitch of a sister in Caldor?"

Aurelia's face went red as she struggled to hold her anger. "I saw another woman bearing my likeness," she answered. "Sabra is her name."

"Was she with child?" he pressed.

Aurelia shook her head. "She is unwed, nor does she have any offspring of her own."

"Good," he nodded. "Tomorrow, we will go to Caldor, exchange you for your sister, and you can take over the barony until she supplies me with an heir."

The baron's daughter said nothing, fighting against the fury building inside her and straining to hold her tongue.

"If that is what you wish," she managed to rasp out, barely able to control her temper.

"It is," he replied. "I never thought your whore of a mother would provide me with another chance. I had always regretted not sending my men to hunt her down and kill her sooner than they did. Now, it seems your younger sister will finally be of some use."

Aurelia stared at her father, her breath coming in shallow gasps.

"*You* had her killed?" she managed to ask.

"Of course I did," the baron answered with a frown. "She deserved it. Running off on me, keeping the birth of our second child a secret. Had I not been involved in my battles to the north, I'd have had her killed years earlier."

Malhallow reached for his pitcher of wine. "You're dismissed, Aurelia. Tomorrow, you begin your reign as Baroness of Caldor—until a suitable replacement can be found."

The blue-eyed woman in front of Malhallow wanted to lash out at him, to strike him down where he stood. She could feel her magic building inside her. She focused her will as the words that would release the spell formed in her mind. *He killed my mother*, she thought, seconds away from unleashing her magic.

The face of one she loved in Caldor appeared in her mind and stayed her hand. She knew if she killed the baron now, Harmon would take the army and raze Caldor to the ground. That would result in the death and destruction of the entire village.

Letting go of her magic and whirling around, the youngest daughter of the baron listened to her father's mocking laughter trail behind her as she stormed from his tent.

CHAPTER 24

It had been a long day before Gheric turned in. The dark-eyed warrior knew that tomorrow would be even more harrowing. So far, they had not heard from Malhallow's camp, but the warrior approached the coming dawn as though he would be fighting for his life. As he often did before any battle, Gheric gathered as much information about his opponent as he could from those who knew the captain best. The results were not promising.

Harmon was abnormally big and remarkably fast. He could fight with almost any weapon but favored the sword or mace. With skills sharpened in the gladiator pits of Tal-Mur, the baron's champion had few weaknesses. He was almost always on the offensive, and once he had you down, you rarely got back up.

I will have to utilize my magic, Gheric thought, knowing the big Shar would have considered that possibility. Unfortunately for him, Gheric knew there were ways for other warriors to withstand a magical assault, and Gheric was not overtly powerful with his spell casting.

The more he deliberated the issue, the more he realized that he would need to be on top of his game.

"Enough thinking about it." He grunted to himself. *Malhallow may not choose the duel*, he thought. *He may just have his men sweep in and butcher us all.*

Gheric reached up and massaged his temples. *I need to get some sleep,* he told himself, his mind numb. The dark-eyed warrior kicked off his boots and heard them thud onto the floor. *Rest, what I need is rest,* he decided, dropping the rest of this clothing onto the wooden floorboards at the base of the bed.

He climbed onto the mattress and covered himself with blankets, but sleep eluded him. Tossing and turning with uncertainty, anxious thoughts kept him awake well into the night.

Outside his chambers, there was a soft shuffling of feet. With a quiet creak, his door opened. Sitting up, Gheric made out the silhouette of Sabra, who was carrying a soft-white candle.

"I can't sleep," she said, seeing he was awake.

"Nor can I," Gheric confessed, patting the empty place on the bed next to him.

Sabra hesitated only a moment before slipping onto the bed. She wore a soft cotton nightshift that glowed a pale yellow in the candlelight.

"What is troubling you?" she asked as she lay on her side, her head resting on the crook of her shoulder.

"More than I care to burden you with," he answered, reaching out and taking hold of her hand.

"Is it the baron's forces?" she asked.

Gheric shook his head. "No. The plan we have in place is a good one, though it is risky."

"Is it the thought of dueling the captain?"

Gheric smiled. "No. He will prove to be a formidable foe, I am sure, but I have been in many fights. I learned to control my fear long ago."

"Then what is it?" she persisted.

The handsome warrior looked at her and took in Sabra's exquisite form. "I am concerned about you," he said softly.

"Me? Whatever for?" she asked curiously.

"You really don't know, do you?" he questioned softly.

"Know what?"

Gheric sighed, finally coming to grips with what had been plaguing him all day. "I am afraid of losing you," he admitted.

"Losing me?" she questioned.

"I know, it's foolish," he continued. "I have only known you for a few days, but the thought of living the rest of my life without you unsettles me more than I thought possible."

He looked at her, withdrawing his hand from hers and placing it on her hip. He could feel the warmth of Sabra's skin underneath the cotton nightshift. Slowly, he moved his hand up toward her shoulder.

"You are a beautiful woman, born with the face of a goddess, the soul of a saint, and enough courage to shame us all. I do not wish to leave you, now or ever, though I am still uncertain how you feel about me."

The woman lying next to him looked deeply into his dark eyes as tears began to run down her face.

"No one has ever spoken to me that way before," she said with a slight catch in her voice.

"Well, barring my imminent death tomorrow, I plan on speaking to you that way for the rest of your life," Gheric promised. "Unless, of course, you don't feel the same—"

His voice was cut off as Sabra rolled on top of him and kissed him quiet.

Unlike their first intimate encounter where Gheric had dictated events, Sabra took the lead. Gheric could feel the heat of her lips upon his, the softness of her tongue as it teased his mouth. He wrapped his powerful arms around her body, slipping his hands underneath the nightshift and runninghis fingers along the warmth of her skin.

"Say you love me," she whispered in his ear, as she tore the gown from her body.

"I love you," he said hungrily, lifting his head upward and taking her nipple in his mouth.

Gheric saw Sabra's neck crane upward as arousal filled her. With surprising ease, she moved her hips downward and guided Gheric home.

"How does that feel?" she asked, leaning back, moving her pelvis slowly up and down on top of him.

"Incredible," he answered, his manhood swelling to its fullness.

Gheric reached forward and began to massage the inside of Sabra's most sensitive area with his thumb, knowing it would drive her mad with pleasure.

"Oh, yes," she whispered, leaning backward, her neck straining.

For the next several heartbeats, Gheric worked his thumb, slowly building her desire.

He felt her wetness grow and soak him completely. Slowly, ever so slowly, he reached out and cupped her naked breast with his hand. A jolt of energy raced through Sabra at this new, unexpected touch.

"By the gods," he heard her gasp, instinctively knowing she was near the height of arousal.

He focused on her most sensitive area, rubbing against it with more pressure than before.

"Look at me," he ordered, knowing she was ready to release her climax.

"No," she breathed, desperately trying to force her arousal higher.

"Look at me!" he commanded, pushing harder with his thumb.

With a cry of elemental lust, Sabra exploded and drenched his cock. Her cries of passion reverberated throughout the house, echoing even into the darkness of the surrounding night. On it went, her orgasm like an unquenchable fire sweeping across a field steeped in oil. Her shudders of pleasure shook the bed, knocking both down-stuffed pillows to the floor.

Finally, Sabra's ardor ran its course, and her body ceased its convulsions.

Gheric felt her collapse on top of him, her naked skin slick with sweat.

"How did you . . . " she started, looking at him strangely. "How is that possible?"

"It's possible," he answered, kissing her sweetly, "because I'm in love with you."

Sabra stared down at him, biting the bottom of her lip. "What about you?" she asked. "What of your pleasure?"

"I'm just—" he started to say before she began to gyrate her hips slowly up and down once more.

"You're just what?" Sabra teased, her eyes never leaving his.

"I'm just—" he tried again, as she forced his rock hard cock to slide in and out of her. "That's not fair," he complained, knowing she was tightening every time she pushed him back inside of her.

"Shut up," she whispered, kissing him quiet once more.

Gheric began to feel a tightness building inside him. He

moved his head to the side away from her kisses. "Where did you learn—" he gasped.

"I said shut up," she whispered, placing the hardened nipple of her breast in Gheric's mouth.

Gheric made to protest once more, but she pressed downward, filling his mouth with her soft flesh. She began to move her hips faster, all the while tightening every time she forced him inside of her.

Gheric was building more quickly than he was used to. He moved his hands to her shoulders and tried to lift her off him.

"Oh no you don't," she crowed, pinning his hands above his head.

The brief sensation of being helpless excited Gheric, almost to the point where he knew there was no coming back. Sensing this, Sabra slowed, teasing his manhood and building him further, heightening his arousal more than he had ever known. Gheric began to moan in protest, his mouth still stifled by the fullness of her breast.

She drew back, exposing her naked torso to him. "Stop your moaning and explode inside of me," Sabra ordered, thrusting forward once more. "You are mine, Gheric! I will hear you scream!"

Gheric's control detonated in a snarl of primal ecstasy. He unleashed his seed inside her with a soul-baring roar. His hips pushed upward, forcing his manhood deep inside the exquisite woman on top of him. Over and over, he thrust, driving himself into her. His carnal desire became so intense, he nearly blacked out from pleasure. It was a purely hedonistic indulgence of a like he had never known.

The feeling lasted longer than he expected, but slowly, ever so slowly, it ceased, leaving him gasping for breath.

Gheric came to lay still on the bed, completely spent and panting with exhaustion.

For several heartbeats, neither moved, entangled within the confines of both the sheets and their bodies.

"By the gods," Gheric muttered, his voice exultant. "How the *hell* did you do that to me?"

"Because," she hesitated, sliding off him and placing her head on his chest. "For the first time in my life, I felt what love is. I wanted to share that with you, in the best way I know how."

Sabra's voice was both melancholy and wistful at the same time.

"Don't be sad," Gheric said sleepily. "After tomorrow, we will have the rest of our lives to spend together."

The warrior's breathing slowed, and he drifted off to sleep, his mind finally at rest.

Her head still on his chest, Baron Malhallow's firstborn daughter, Aurelia, lay awake for some time. She wept silent tears, having experienced the feeling of true affection for the first time.

CHAPTER 25

Sabra opened her eyes in the darkness before dawn. Already, she could hear the camp stirring as the baron's men prepared to march upon Caldor. She closed her eyes again, knowing today would change everything in her life.

The memory of her conversation with Aurelia the day before was still fresh in her mind.

"Why would our father come to Caldor himself?" Sabra asked. "Doesn't he have a thousand soldiers at his command?"

Aurelia shook her head. "Not so many in Rathstone, though he could muster twice that if the need arose." The elder twin sighed. "Whoever tried to have him killed is almost certainly here in Caldor. It was not me, though he is paranoid enough to consider it a possibility."

"Niles then?" Sabra guessed.

"No, my source tells me the attempt was poison. That is

not my cousin's way. Niles is more likely to use a blade, preferably one he wielded himself. No, it was not Niles nor me, but Malhallow will not believe that."

"Who do you think it is?" Sabra asked.

"It had to be Harmon," Aurelia answered. "Probably working in cahoots with Niles. If our father had been assassinated, Niles would have ruled in Rathstone, and Harmon would have taken the barony here in Caldor." The elder twin brushed the front of her satin dress absently. "It does not matter now. Whoever sent that assassin got what they wanted, even if it was a byproduct of the assassin's failure. Malhallow may be alive, but he has left the safety of Rathstone. He's been flushed into the open."

"Surely he will not be traveling alone?" Sabra asked.

Aurelia shook her head. "You are right, of course. He will be surrounded by no less than three hundred men, possibly more."

"What will you do?" Sabra queried, curious.

The elder twin gave Sabra a questioning look.

"He's coming for you, isn't he?" Sabra had asked.

Aurelia smiled. "He's not coming for me," she said with a hint of bitterness in her voice. "I am of little use to him, as I am barren," Aurelia replied."

"Barren?" Sabra repeated, shocked.

"The gods know it is not for a lack of trying," Aurelia explained. "Dozens—even hundreds—of noblemen have tried to conceive a child with me, all to no avail."

"Hundreds . . .?" Sabra gasped, her voice trailing off.

Aurelia smiled bitterly. "That is what it is to be Malhallow's daughter," she explained. "I have been used because of my bloodline and then cast aside when I could not provide him with an heir."

"That . . . that's monstrous!" Sabra exclaimed in revulsion.

"It wasn't always bad," Aurelia said. "Some of the kinder ones were quite adept lovers. A few fell in love with me, or my body, I should say."

"Why doesn't Father just marry someone and have a child himself?" Sabra had asked.

Aurelia went quiet and exhaled deeply. "I cannot tell you the number of women he's brought into his bedchamber in the last twenty years. If I had to hazard a guess, it would number more than a thousand. He has consulted with Druids and mages of every shape and description. No matter what he has tried, no matter how many women he beds, Malhallow has yet to father another child."

Aurelia stopped and looked with great sympathy upon Sabra. "You are his only hope. He is sterile. He will not admit it to anyone, but Malhallow will not father any more children."

Sabra took in the information, and her breath caught in her chest. She finally understood the horrible purpose of her father's visit to Caldor.

"He's not coming for you, is he?" she breathed. "He's coming for me."

"Yes, sister," Aurelia agreed quietly. "He will lock you away in a tower and send one nobleman after another to your bed until a child grows inside you. Upon its birth, he will take it away and raise it as his own while you return to the tower and suffer the same fate as before."

Sabra felt the bile rise to the back of her throat. "Did you . . . Is this what you have endured these past years?"

"Some of it, yes," Aurelia admitted. "Though I was raised in the court, so I have other . . . uses . . . besides my body."

A great well of sympathy had grown inside Sabra, along

with an overwhelming need to comfort her twin. "I did not know," she said, taking Aurelia's hand in her own. "How could a father do such things to his child?"

"I would not see you suffer my fate, sister," the elder girl said, trying to keep control of her emotions. "I fear it would break your will."

"You are right!" Sabra hissed, suddenly angry. "I would rather die than suffer as you did!"

Aurelia, her face unreadable, looked at her twin. "There is another way," she said hesitantly. "But I must warn you, it is fraught with peril for us both, you more than I."

Sabra hesitated and looked out the window, watching as Gheric sparred with Jorrell. She walked over to the pane and touched the glass with her fingertips, listening to the sound of steel on steel. "Will it endanger him?" she asked, nodding at her lover.

There was a faint step behind her, and Sabra felt her twin's hand rest on her shoulder. "Far less than the danger he is already in," Aurelia answered.

"You must guarantee his safety," Sabra demanded. "Else, I will spend whatever time I have left by his side."

Aurelia lightly kissed the back of her sister's head. "I cannot make that assurance. At best, there will be no duel, and the two of you can live here happily with no one the wiser."

"The worst?" Sabra asked.

The elder twin let out a sigh. "At worst, our father's soldiers will butcher him in the street, and you will be locked away until you run out of use," Aurelia answered.

Sabra felt the cold hand of fear clutch her heart. She turned around and searched Aurelia's face. "You have known our father for years. In your opinion, how will the events of the next day most likely play out?"

"My idea is a longshot," Aurelia breathed. "But it would give us a chance at a favorable outcome. Most likely, Gheric will have to duel either Niles or Harmon at the least, but I will do what I can to keep that from happening."

Sabra watched Gheric face off against Jorrell, their swords moving at a speed she could scarcely follow.

"If I do nothing, he will have to fight anyway," she reasoned. "If I agree to your plan, it gives him a chance to avoid any combat."

"That is true," Aurelia agreed.

"I will give him a chance to avoid the duel," the younger sibling said softly. "No matter what the cost to me."

Aurelia looked at Sabra, her blue eyes touched with envy. "You must love him greatly, to risk so much," she'd said, her voice wistful.

"He has become everything to me," Sabra answered.

"Would he do the same for you?" the elder sibling asked.

Sabra turned back to the window, her eyes following Gheric's every move. "He already has."

Aurelia stepped closer, standing next to her twin and watching the broad-shouldered warrior outside.

"I have never known the feeling of love," Aurelia admitted. "I cannot advise you one way or another. The choice, my sister, is yours alone."

With a sigh, Sabra made her decision. She turned toward Aurelia and stared into her twin's beautiful blue eyes.

"What must I do?"

Now, Sabra lay in the middle of her father's forces, pretending to be Aurelia. The two had spent more than an hour going over what she would need to know in order to successfully impersonate her twin.

Pretending to be Aurelia was more difficult than Sabra had thought.

While they looked identical, Aurelia's mannerisms were completely different from hers. It had been years since the younger twin had practiced a curtsey. She certainly did not have the graceful style or courtly experience her sister had lived and breathed over the last twenty-three years.

Both women had decided the best course of action was for Sabra to say as little as possible and keep as far from Malhallow as she could.

Thus far, their plan had worked. Harmon had said little on their journey north the previous day, and Malhallow had been too distracted to see through Sabra's charade. Sabra had spent only a brief amount of time with her father before retiring for the night.

As she prepared for bed, a note had been delivered by the burly sergeant she'd seen when she was first brought to her father's tent. It was from Malhallow, telling her to be ready to ride before dawn.

Sabra slept little that night, hoping Gheric had come to his senses and fled ahead of her father's army. When sleep finally came, it was fitful, filled with flashes of Gheric being killed in battle. She awakened with a start, soaked in sweat, to the sounds of soldiers moving outside, preparing to depart.

As Sabra lay on the cot inside her tent, she knew within the hour the baron and his army would be riding south to subdue Caldor and its people. Sabra had not wanted to dupe her lover, but the thought of Gheric dying in a pitched battle was more than she could bear.

She rubbed absently at her stomach and took a deep breath, trying to calm her nerves.

With any luck, she and her sister could make the switch peacefully with no one the wiser. Sabra would remain in Caldor, while Aurelia traveled north with their father. If their luck held, by the time Malhallow discovered the ruse, Jorrell's father would march his forces upon Rathstone and place Aurelia on the throne.

This was the plan the elder twin had concocted with Sabra inside the confines of the Billerton farmhouse. Her thoughts turned fleetingly to Gheric, hoping he had not discovered the true identity of the woman posing as her.

Sabra thought back to their last dalliance together and blushed at the thought of Aurelia having to play the part.

"I do not care if he beds my twin," she whispered, trying to keep jealousy from overwhelming her. "Just let the Highgod keep him safe."

AURELIA WOKE AS THE SUN BEGAN PEEKING ITS WAY OVER the horizon. As she got her bearings, she realized she was in Gheric's bedroom. Alone. She quickly moved into her sister's bedchamber and threw on a worn dress, one dyed a navy blue. She brushed her hair before knotting it in a simple braid and strode out into the living area. Gheric was there speaking quietly to Horval and Gyles. He was wearing his leather cuirass once again, armed for battle.

"Are you sure about this?" Horval was saying, his face skeptical.

"It's the tallest building in Caldor, with the best vantage point," Gheric replied. "Go now, Gyles and the others will accompany you before the early risers wake."

Both Gyles and Horval made to leave, with the latter hesitating at the door. "When this is over, I owe you a drink."

Gheric gave him a wry grin. "I look forward to it."

Gyles gave out a barking laugh and clapped the archer on the back before exiting the room.

Aurelia cleared her throat, subtly announcing her presence.

Her lover turned around, giving her a smile. "Hello, pretty girl. I trust you slept well?"

"Very," Aurelia answered, wrapping her arms around him in a warm embrace. She inhaled deeply and took in his smell.

He let go of Aurelia and brushed his lips across hers. "I hope you don't mind, but I let you sleep in," he explained, somewhat apologetically. "You looked so peaceful; I didn't want to wake you."

"How did you sleep?" she asked, knowing the time had come for her to tell him who she really was.

"Wonderfully," he answered. "The house was so quiet . . . I didn't even hear you snore," he teased.

Aurelia expelled a deep breath, wanting to blurt the truth out. Instead, her voice caught in her throat, and her tongue remained still.

Gheric noticed, and his face twisted with concern. "Sabra? What's wrong?"

Aurelia's heart somersaulted inside her chest. By the gods, even the way he looked at her was filled with love. She was not ready, not yet. It had only been one night, not nearly enough time to sort out how this man made her feel.

I promised Sabra I'd keep him safe, she thought, knowing she could not hide the truth from him any longer.

"I . . . There's something you should know," she stammered, her voice trembling.

"What is it, my love?" he asked.

"I . . . That is, my sister and me, we both thought . . . "

"Gheric!" came a shout from outside the farmhouse.

"The gods be damned," the broad-shouldered warrior swore, flicking his eyes through the window. "Go on, dear heart, whatever is happening outside can wait."

"Gheric!" came the voice again, calling more urgently than before.

"It sounds important." Aurelia blinked, losing her nerve.

"Not as important as whatever it is you have to say to me," he assured, taking her hand in his.

He does not love you; he loves your sister, Aurelia thought, feeling an ache in her chest. With regret, she shook her head and let go of his hand. "It can wait," Aurelia replied. "Come on, let us see what is amiss."

The swarthy warrior frowned at her, but he moved to the door and threw it open. Outside, they saw Jorrell gingerly easing himself down from his horse.

"Dammit man, you shouldn't be riding in your condition," Gheric chastised, striding over to stand next to Jorrell.

"This could not wait," the former lieutenant answered, wincing as he dismounted.

"What is it?" Aurelia asked, her eyes moving up the northern road.

The new Baron of Caldor held onto his saddle as he made his report. "I sent a scout to keep an eye on Malhallow's forces last night. He rode in not ten minutes ago. He said Malhallow's camp was up before sunrise. He will be here with his forces within the hour."

"Any news from the mayor on whether or not he received word about the duel?" Gheric asked.

"No," Jorrell answered. "There was no response from the baron's camp last night. I fear a duel is not likely unless we can . . . persuade him otherwise."

"Our forces are in play," Gheric said with a determined

smile. "With a touch of Arianal's luck, we can be rid of Malhallow by the end of the morning."

"You could have sent us one of your men instead of coming yourself," Aurelia scolded, seeing Jorrell was barely strong enough to stand. She moved over to the side of the farmhouse and picked up a worn chair leaning against the wall.

"The guards who have stayed are busy preparing the keep for a siege, if it comes to that," Jorrell managed to answer, gasping for breath. "Damn this wound. Temper made me a healing elixir, but it has not yet taken effect."

"You did your fighting yesterday," Gheric said with a grunt, grabbing him under the arm and easing him into the chair Aurelia placed on the ground next to him. "You leave today's fight to me."

"Perhaps it will not come to that," Aurelia suggested. "He is only here for me, after all."

"Absolutely not," Gheric snapped, looking at her coldly.

"It would keep you and the rest of Caldor safe," she argued.

"Do you really think so?" Gheric questioned. "Malhallow is a killer, plain and simple. He cares nothing for the people of Caldor, so long as they do as they are told and make him money. Why do you think he wanted your farm so badly? With it and everyone else's, he would have complete control of the village. These people, these families, would live out their lives scraping by. They would endure a lifetime of indentured servitude, with no hope of freedom."

Gheric paused and looked closely at Aurelia. "This is why I came here. This is what we are fighting for. I will not let you sacrifice everything you have fought for now, no matter how you feel about me."

Aurelia blinked at him in astonishment, nearly forgetting herself.

"Do you truly love me so much?" she asked.

"You know I do," he answered, his voice softening. "Now, let there be no more talk of joining Malhallow. As I said, today, you will leave the fighting to me."

"Gladly," Jorrell managed to say, breaking the tension as he sank into his seat. "Bother this wound," he griped. "Sabra, I hate to be a nuisance, but could I trouble you for some healing?"

Aurelia felt a slip of fear trickle down her back. "I . . ." She hesitated, not knowing what to say.

"I'm sorry," Jorrell said, seeing her discomfort. "You are probably still recovering. Might I request something to drink?"

"Of course," Aurelia answered in relief, striding purposefully into the house.

"An interesting woman," Jorrell said, looking up at Gheric after she'd left. "Are you going to marry her?"

"Let's try to get through today before we start planning any nuptials," the dark-eyed warrior answered sarcastically.

Jorrell grunted with laughter. "I must apologize for any presumption. After my drink, I need to get back to the keep and make sure everything is ready."

"I will go," Gheric stated. "You stay here and rest for a bit. Gyles has been sent out to summon the villagers. You sit awhile and make your way to the keep on the wagon with Sabra and her wards."

Jorrell nodded and gave the man across from him a long look.

"What?" the warrior-mage asked, frowning back at Jorrell.

"I wanted to tell you . . ." His voice trailed off, and he

glanced through the window to see a pair of blue eyes staring back at him.

"Tell me what?" Gheric asked, looking perplexed.

The woman inside shook her head, halting Jorrell's words.

"If it comes to a duel today," the baron said, changing what he was going to say. "That big Shar will not fight fairly. He was a renowned gladiator only a few years ago, mad it all the way up to Gladiator Three. He fought in eleven death bouts and won them all."

"I have seen him fight," Gheric replied with a nod. "But I thank you for your warning."

The door opened behind them, and Aurelia returned bearing a mug of cool cider.

"Here you are," she said, handing the mug to Jorrell, looking at him anxiously.

"Thank you," he answered, drinking deeply from it.

Gheric took Aurelia's hand in his. "I have to go to the keep and ready its defenses," he explained. "I'm entrusting the baron's safety to you, Sabra. Keep him from harm. Do not linger here long. If either of you are taken, we are lost."

Aurelia nodded, hating that she had not told him the truth of who she was.

"I will see you soon," the handsome warrior said, leaping atop the baron's horse.

"Gheric!" Aurelia shouted, moving toward him. "No matter what happens today, I want you to know—I . . . I love you. Last night, it meant everything to me. You are the best of men."

He looked down upon her beautiful face and smiled. "I do my best," he said with a wink. "I'll see you soon."

The powerful warrior reared the horse back on its hind legs and galloped off, racing toward Caldor.

She watched him go, the amber rays of a new day shining on her face.

"Aurelia?" she heard Jorrell ask from his place behind her.

Her heart froze, and she dropped her eyes to the ground. With a sigh, the eldest daughter of Rathstone turned around and looked at Duke May's son.

"How did you know?" she asked.

"No Druid I've heard of needs more than twelve hours to recover their strength," he answered. "I should have guessed it yesterday, but I was in too much pain to give it any thought. The Sabra I know would have healed me the moment I stepped off my horse."

"Do you think Gheric suspects?" she asked.

Jorrell shook his head. "He's fallen so deeply for Sabra, but, no, I don't think he suspects anything."

"I'm sorry." She sighed, moving closer to him. "My sister and I agreed this would be the best course for us all . . . Gheric included."

"By deceiving him?" Jorrell questioned, his tone harsh.

"This gives us the best chance to keep him safe," she answered. "Sabra insisted upon it."

"Did he bed you last night?" Jorrell asked.

Aurelia said nothing, her silence speaking volumes.

Jorrell stared at her and shook his head, easing himself to his feet. "I knew it. Ah well, you won't be here for long… and it's not like you fall in love with…"

Jorrell trailed off, seeing the worldly Aurelia begin to blush.

"I'll be damned," he muttered in surprise.

"What?" she asked defensively.

"I did not think I'd live to see the day," he said with a

grin. "The hardest heart in the barony has met its match. You *have* fallen in love with him, haven't you?"

"I . . . " she started before shaking her head. "It does not matter. I will go north with my father, and Sabra will stay here with Gheric. I'll not rob either of them of that happiness, no matter how fleeting it may be."

Jorrell said nothing at first. He just looked at her with his cool dark eyes. "Help me to the wagon." He grunted, raising his hand toward her.

"Are you going to tell him?" she asked.

"No," he answered. "I will let you decide the time and place. However, now that I know . . . I have the length of a wagon ride to tell you what we have planned for today's defense in case I fall. I'm naming you as my successor here in Caldor."

"Me?" she gasped.

"Yes, Aurelia, you," he answered. "I know of the plight you have suffered through the years. While you are a beautiful woman, you are capable of much more responsibility. I would use you to rule here in Caldor, if you think you can manage it?"

"I . . . thank you," she breathed, still in shock.

"Now," he said with a grunt, standing once more, "let us see if we cannot find a way out of this debacle with your father."

CHAPTER 26

The column of three hundred soldiers moved steadily forward, the sound of their hard-soled leather boots thrumming along the dirt road. To the east lay open fields of golden grass and the fertile grounds of dark earth lying fallow, awaiting the dawn of a new spring. Sprinkled above the haze of the morning mist were a melody of trees, their remaining tenants fluttering in remnants of yellow, red, and orange leaves that signified the coming onset of winter. To the west stretched the still waters of the Lesser Rhone, a lake that stretched nearly fifteen leagues from north to south. Turning a blind eye to it all, Malhallow's army of regulars entered the outskirts of Caldor.

Sabra had seen the borders of her homeland hundreds of times. Now, at the cusp of losing it, she noted its rustic beauty with fresh eyes. Sabra felt as though she was bound to this land. She would not see it fall into the callous hands of her father, not while she drew breath in her lungs.

Malhallow rode ahead of Sabra, carefully positioned in the middle of the column. Dressed in his house colors of green and gold, he sat upon the back of a beautiful white mare, and he was deep in conversation with Captain Harmon, the two discussing the possibilities of the upcoming day.

As the column reached the northernmost fringe of her farm, a rider galloped out of Caldor, galloping along the road until he reined in next to the baron.

"What news? Malhallow asked, sounding supremely confident.

"No one was on the streets," the scout answered. "From what little I saw, I believe everyone has gathered inside the keep."

"I trust neither Jorrell nor Gheric," Harmon commented. "They are not fools. There might be men hiding in the buildings near the center of town. That's what happened when Niles tried to cow them into a surrender."

"I heard your report last night, Captain," the scout objected. "I took care to search the buildings as closely as I could. There was no movement inside or out. If the people of Caldor are hiding somewhere, they are a damn sight better at it than I am."

"Hmmpt," the captain snorted, unwilling to concede his point.

"So, they wish for a siege?" Malhallow mused, shaking his head. "To what end? With almost no fighting force, we can take the keep by early this afternoon."

"Shall I have men cut down a tree to construct a ram?" the scout asked.

Malhallow shook his head. "No, let us see how they are arrayed before we waste time with that. What of the other matter? Did you find him?"

"Yes, my lord, though he put up a bit of resistance," the scout answered. "He is being brought to the Billerton Farm now."

"You are dismissed," Malhallow said with a wave.

"As you command," the scout replied, bowing his head in acquiescence.

The scout rode off, and Sabra heard Harmon snort in derision. "He thinks it best to batter down the gate before we know what we are up against? Where do you find these men?"

"Corporal Luthias is a decent man, if a tad overzealous," the baron sniffed.

"The only decent soldier you have is Lieutenant Locke," Harmon snorted. "He hasn't returned?"

Malhallow shook his head. "No, more's the pity. We will have to go with what intelligence Luthias has given us."

The baron tugged lightly on his reins and led his mare to the left of the column.

"Come, let's have our reluctant guest perform his magic in the unlikely event it comes to a duel."

"What are you talking about?" groused Harmon. "What guest?"

"The one Luthias just spoke about," the baron answered. "On the off chance this does result in a one to one combat, our guest will assure you of victory."

Harmon straightened in his seat. "I can win without any assistance from you!"

Malhallow's eyes flashed in anger. "You said Gheric has magic, did you not?"

"I did," the captain answered.

"This will negate that advantage."

"As you command," Harmon said with a shrug. "We will do this your way."

The baron nodded. "Very well, push forward. I want to have my breakfast inside the keep within the hour."

"Column!" Sabra heard Harmon bellow. "Ready line, march!"

The sound of trumpets blared up and down the column signaling the soldiers to pick up the pace and begin advancing on the village with purpose.

Sabra took a deep breath and kicked at the sides of her mount, preparing to move forward with her father's troops, but the sight near the entrance of her farm stopped her. Blinking her eyes in surprise, she felt her blood run cold. Standing at the entrance of her farm, blood dripping from his mouth, was Temper, the Druid. Behind him were three men, each holding bared steel.

The baron and Harmon reined their horses in front of the wizened old man, kicking up tufts of dust into the air. "Time to decide if you want to live or die," Malhallow threatened.

Temper flared his eyes upward, looking upon the baron with unveiled loathing. "What wrong have I done to you that I should be treated like this?" he asked, his eyes burning with anger.

Harmon dismounted and walked forward, while Malhallow sniffed with indifference. "None directly," he said, answering with a wave. "Though I wanted to ask, why did you not save my nephew yesterday? Surely his wounds were not beyond your ability."

"I cannot infuse the dead with new life," Temper snapped. "Jorrell's blade cleaved your nephew's heart before cutting his head clean off. The Forestmother herself could not mend such violence."

"You invoke the name of the Seraph of Healing as a defense against your failings, yet you would refuse me now?" Malhallow questioned.

Temper shot the baron with a look of malevolence. "I am old beyond my years, my lord, not long for this world. I do not fear death," he stated.

"How about pain?" Harmon asked, his voice cold. "Do you fear crushed bones and a broken skull?"

"You are afraid," Temper guessed, shifting his gaze from the baron to Harmon. "Afraid Gheric will wipe the floor with you."

"I will tear his limbs from his body!" Harmon shouted, raising his hand to strike the Druid.

"Wait!" Sabra shouted, unwilling to see the old man bloodied.

All eyes shifted to her.

"What is this?" the baron asked with a frown. "I don't remember you being so squeamish, child."

"Let me speak with him," she said, dismounting. "I am sure I can get him to see reason."

Malhallow turned and looked to his army still marching past. "You have until my standard-bearer reaches me," he said, nodding at the green-and-gold sigil that was moving closer by the second.

Sabra nodded and moved toward Temper. The three guards behind the Druid did not move.

"Call off your dogs," she snapped, looking at Harmon. "I cannot convince him with your men breathing down my neck."

The captain glowered at her but waved his men away. "You should show more respect," he warned.

"Your words have been noted," she replied, moving Temper away from the group.

The pair made their way to the side of the farmhouse where they could speak without being overheard.

"What nonsense is this?" Temper snorted. "Why are you riding with Malhallow, Sabra? Where is your sister?"

"You recognize me?" Sabra asked with a start.

"Of course I do." The Druid snickered. "I have looked

after you since your birth. You think I would not recognize my own kin?"

"We are kin?" Sabra whispered, stunned.

"Aye, I am your great-uncle on your mother's side," he sniffed. "Fiora was my grandniece. The two of you made a beautiful family."

"You are my great-uncle?" She gasped, shaken to the core.

"Of course," he answered. "Where did you think you got your magic from? It runs in our family, you know."

Sabra glanced over at her father, as a multitude of questions filled her mind. Knowing her time was running short she suppressed them all.

"Listen, they want you to cast some kind of spell on Harmon. Do it or they will kill you."

"I'll do no such thing," Temper said, shaking his head. "I will not lift a finger to help another soulless Turner. I've seen enough from his despotic nephew. The both of them can rot in hell."

"It will be all right," she assuaged, seeing the green-and-gold standard-bearer less than a few yards away.

"No," he insisted. "I'll not compromise Gheric in that way. He is a good man, better than I would have thought to find for you."

"Please," she begged. "Aurelia and I have a plan where no one will have to fight. Casting your spell will not matter in the least."

Temper studied Sabra's face before letting out a pent-up breath.

"I don't know what you are playing at girl, but whatever plans you've made with Aurelia won't work."

"Please," Sabra pleaded seeing the standard bearer drawing close. "You have to trust me."

Temper glanced from Sabra to the baron and shook his head. "All right," he agreed reluctantly. "I'll do it for you and your sister. I owe Aurelia that much. I tried for years to get her out from under her father's yoke and failed miserably."

Sabra breathed a sigh of relief. "Thank you," she said, squeezing his hand.

"Let's get this unpleasantness over with," Temper snarled, looking sourly at the guard captain.

The pair began to walk back to the farm entrance.

"I hope you are right," Temper murmured, quietly enough that only Sabra could hear. "If it does come to a fight, this spell will render Harmon nearly invulnerable."

At his words, Sabra felt an icy finger of uncertainty slip down her spine.

"Horval is in place?" Gheric asked Gyles, who was standing next to him, his glaive held at the ready.

"Yes, yes, everyone is where they are supposed to be," the innkeeper answered, nodding to where Aurelia stood next to Jorrell. "Your lady love was the last to come in. The gate to the keep has been barred from the inside, as requested—whatever good that will do us."

Despite the butterflies in his stomach, Gheric nudged his old friend. "Is this not how you thought things would transpire when you penned me the missive weeks ago?"

"Pshht." Gyles grunted and shook his head. "I thought you would give Niles Turner a little rap on the head and we'd drink in celebration. I hadn't the faintest idea we'd all be thrust into a pitched battle against three hundred of Malhallow's finest. Hell, I'm ready to piss myself in fear, and his soldiers haven't even shown up yet!"

Gheric clapped him on the back. "That's war for you. For those of us that fight it's always, 'Hurry up and wait for something to happen,' all the while dealing with the discomfort of a full bladder."

"Here they come!" shouted Jorrell, who was standing on top of the wall next to the mayor and Aurelia. Tamalin's color was a sickly green, and he looked like he'd rather be anywhere else in the world than on these battlements. Aurelia's eyes were fixed in the distance as they all watched hundreds of soldiers pouring in from the outskirts of Caldor.

"Give the signal," Jorrell commanded, looking over his shoulder. "Now, while they cannot see."

On the northeastern corner of the keep, a tall farmer raised a long wooden pole with a red cloth tied to the end of it from his place on top of the wall. The farmer waved it back and forth several times, the banner billowing through the air. Before Malhallow's men were in sight, he dropped the pole and laid it against the battlements next to him.

"The die is cast," Gheric muttered, hoping their plan would work.

"I meant to ask you . . ." the innkeeper said. "Why did you ride Jorrell's horse in from Sabra's farm? Where is Kat?"

Gheric gave his friend a long look but did not answer.

"Tell me you didn't," Gyles said.

"I did," Gheric muttered.

"You left her with the bandits?" the innkeeper gaped.

"I wanted at least one ally I trust with them," the powerful warrior answered.

"As good a reason as any," Gyles agreed.

"I guess."

The innkeeper gave Gheric a suspicious frown. "Who is he with?"

"Othar."

"By the beard of the All Father," Gyles swore. "*Him?*"

"I know," Gheric said with a shrug. "I didn't have too many options."

"I'll tell you this . . ." Gyles grunted from next to him, shaking his head. "When I wrote to you, I never thought our well-being would rely on a bunch of lawless ragamuffins that live on the borders of Caldor's Forest."

Gheric did not reply. He glanced to the north, muttering a prayer to the gods that Yetter was a man of his word.

"I'M TELLING YOU, IT CAN'T BE DONE!" A RED-FACED BANDIT shouted, shoving a man with an eye patch away.

"That's bollocks!" the one-eyed man retorted, pushing him back.

"Goddamn it!" Othar thundered, stepping between the two. "What in the name of the gods are you two arguing about?"

Both men looked at the lanky farmhand, anger etched on their faces.

"Rufus says it ain't possible to yawn with your mouth closed," the red-faced man said. "But I know for a fact it *is*, because I have done it."

"That's goat shit, Crain!" the bandit with the eye patch roared. "It's impossible!"

"Suck my ass, Reece! No one calls me a liar!" Crain bellowed back.

Both men surged forward, ready to continue their fight.

Othar grabbed them by their ears, twisting the fleshy cartilage painfully with his fingers. "If you two sods don't shut the hell up, I'm going to thrash you both until your dicks fall off! You are scaring the horses, and I'll not lose out on ten silvers because of you! Now, keep your gaps shut and get back in position! If we somehow survive the day, I'll preside over a yawning contest myself to see which one of you nit wits is right. Until then, get your asses back in line!"

Othar released the bandits, who both shot him with murderous looks before doing as he ordered.

"Well handled," Yetter remarked, glancing at the taller man from his place at the front of the group.

"Bunch of idiots," the stocky farmhand muttered, shooting a look of disgust over his shoulder.

The two farmhands waited in silence, standing in front of the fifty-six bandits who had agreed to join them. Between each pair of bandits stood a horse. Most were work animals used to plow the fields in and around Caldor.

"You know we can just steal these horses and leave the villagers to their fate," Othar murmured.

Yetter's face soured as he flicked a contemptuous glance at his compatriot.

"Don't give me that look," Othar spat. "All the others are thinking it . . . I'd wager my left nut you are too."

"Not me," Yetter replied. "I'll not abandon Sabra nor Gheric."

"Why not?" Othar asked. "What the hell did they ever do for you?"

Yetter gave his companion a sidelong look. "She gave me a home. Gave one to Marn, Grada, little Drei, even you."

"She lives in that huge farmhouse while *we* make do in the farmhands' quarters," Othar complained bitterly.

"Bitch all you want," Yetter scoffed. "But I live in a real building with a roof and four walls. Better than I thought I'd get . . . but that is not why I stay."

"For shit's sake, then why?" Othar demanded. "Because of the coin?"

Yetter turned to look at the taller man, his eyes filled with pity. "Because in Caldor, we are men. Gheric gave us that. Gheric never threatened me, never offered something he couldn't give. He didn't look down on us, not once—even when we tried to rob him that first day. The man gave me a respect I don't deserve. He's entrusted me with this task. I'll not let him down now."

Yetter hocked and spat off to the side. "The truth is, out in the woods, I was a nobody. We all were. He and Sabra have given us a chance to be human again. Providence doesn't come along for evil sods like me often. When it does, well, I figure I need to rise to the occasion."

He turned and gave Othar a hard look. "You do what you want with your own hide, lad, but I don't think either of us will get a better chance to regain our respect."

Othar looked stunned. For a long moment, there was silence between them, Othar measuring the weight of Yetter's words.

"The hell with this," Crain said from behind them, grabbing the horse he held by the reins. "I'm not sticking around to—"

"Get your ass back in line!" Othar thundered, whirling around.

"Why should I?" Crain barked back.

Othar glanced at Yetter, who gave him a crisp nod. "Because we are men of Caldor now. Should Gheric and the rest succeed, we will be welcomed back into their society. You want to keep scraping out a living here in the woods? Go ahead, I won't stop you. But me? I plan on making more of my life than stealing for a living."

Crain halted in his tracks, wrestling with the same decision Othar had moments ago.

"Well, shit," Crain swore, trudging back to his place in line.

At that moment, they saw a long stick with a red flag move across the horizon no more than half a league away.

"That's it!" Yetter shouted. "That's the signal!"

"I hope this works," Othar muttered, moving back to Gheric's fiery mount.

"Kick up as much dust as you can!" Yetter yelled. "And raise those banners! We are supposed to be an army!"

Fifty-eight men and half as many horses began walking along the dirt road that ran from Kath to Caldor, trying for all the world to look like a force ten times as large.

SABRA RODE INTO TOWN, ITS FAMILIAR SETTING FAR FROM what she was used to. Instead of an active market and the sounds of commerce, there was not a single soul to be seen. The baron's forces came to a halt outside the keep's gate, making sure to stay at a safe distance from any bowman stationed atop the walls.

Standing at the base of the gate were four people. She recognized each but only had eyes for one.

"Come with me," Malhallow commanded, flicking his hand toward his daughter. "You too, Captain," he said, nodding at Harmon.

"Keep ready, Vars" Harmon rasped to a black-bearded sergeant who commanded the infantry.

"Yes sir," the sergeant answered, giving a crisp salute.

Malhallow dismounted and moved forward with Sabra and Harmon in his wake.

"That's far enough," Gheric warned once the baron had come within thirty paces of the gate.

Sabra felt a thrill run through her at the sound of his voice. She noted he was dressed for battle, but his face was obscured by the black hood of his cloak.

"This village is under my jurisdiction," Baron Turner snapped, continuing forward. "I go where I choose here."

"That's fine with me," Gheric hissed. The broad-shouldered warrior stepped forward and raised his hand, ready to order an attack.

"Wait," Jorrell commanded from his place behind Gheric.

The baron slowed, looking at Jorrell. "So, you are Aldin's whelp," he sniffed. "I hear you killed my nephew."

The proud-eyed former lieutenant did not let the insult pass.

"You must be referring to my father, *Duke* Mays," Jorrell corrected, his voice sharp. "And to answer your query, yes, I relieved your nephew of his head, just as he relieved my sister of her virtue."

The two men glared at one another as Malhallow came to a stop not twenty paces from the gate. Harmon drew up alongside the baron and loomed in the background, his eyes boring a hole into Gheric, trying to see the man's face underneath the hood. Sabra stood to the left of her father, her eyes searching what she could see of her lover's countenance.

"Why have you brought this army into my domain?" Jorrell asked.

"*Your* domain?" Malhallow scoffed. "I am the ruling lord in the absence of its rightful sovereign."

"The last lord was defeated in a duel by me, leaving me as the highest-ranking nobleman in Caldor," Jorrell replied. "Thus, I am his successor, as the law dictates."

Sabra watched as Malhallow shifted his focus to the mayor. "Tamalin, is this true?"

The red-faced mayor glanced furtively at both parties

from his position next to Aurelia, clearly uncomfortable addressing the situation.

"Well, from a legal standpoint, the law states—"

"Yes or no?" snarled the baron, his eyes blazing with impatience.

"Yes," Tamalin answered, the word dragging from his mouth.

The baron's icy-blue eyes flashed in irritation.

"So, I ask again," Jorrell stated. "Why have you brought this army into my domain?"

Malhallow spoke aloud, his eyes fixed on Jorrell. "Captain, prepare the men for an assault. We will put down this rebellion inside the hour."

"With pleasure," Harmon growled as Sabra looked imploringly at Aurelia.

Now, sister, she thought, silently willing her twin to enact their plan.

"You might want to rethink that decision," Jorrell stated, his voice calm, "before it ends up killing you and everyone under your command."

Harmon snorted. "You think the rabble behind those walls can stop us?" he sneered.

"No, Captain," Jorrell answered. "Your force is bigger, stronger, better equipped. I think the keep would fall within the hour."

"Then why bother delaying the inevitable?" Malhallow asked. "Stand down. If you do, I will take my youngest daughter, place Aurelia in command of the village, and be on my way."

He paused, giving Jorrell a disgusted smirk. "I'll even let you slink back to your father, so long as you agree to stay out of my demesne."

"You will not be taking Sabra anywhere," Gheric interjected, his voice as cold as a winter's frost.

Sabra felt her heart hammer against her chest as she heard Gheric speak her name. She wanted nothing more than to keep him safe. That was the entire reason she had chosen to switch places with Aurelia.

"My father speaks wisely," she found herself saying, stepping forward with a glance at her twin. "Let my sister and I change places, and we can all leave here in peace."

"Says the woman who betrayed us," Gheric spat, his voice flat and filled with revulsion.

Sabra's words froze in her mouth, her blood running cold at the harshness of his tone.

"I wasn't speaking to you, peasant," Malhallow said distastefully. "Still your tongue or I will have it removed."

The broad-shouldered warrior jutted his chin forward enough where Sabra could make out a leering smile. "Come and try, you little bitch," he taunted. "Put an end to this farce and agree to let your pet gorilla fight me. I am Baron Jorrell's champion. Let this feud be settled in the old way. We can avoid shedding the blood of the good people of Caldor *and* the men under your command."

Malhallow gave Gheric a look of pure malevolence. "Do not think to bait me," he sneered in answer. "Unlike my nephew, *I* would not gamble such stakes on the desperate hope of one to one combat."

Malhallow focused his attention back to Jorrell. "Unless you have more to say, pup, I'd suggest you and this mercenary scamper behind your walls. It may delay your death for an hour or two, but eventually, you will fall."

"You will follow me into the afterlife before the day is done," Jorrell stated.

The baron snorted in laughter. "How is that, boy? Will the gods strike me down from on high?" he derided.

The baron's army echoed their leader's sentiment, as the laughter of hundreds of soldiers filled the market square.

"Not the gods," Jorrell stated, his voice firm. "Rather, it will be at the hands of the troops my father has sent to Caldor. They will be here within the hour."

Jorrell raised his arm, pointing it at the northeastern road that led toward Kath. "A week ago, I penned a letter to the duke telling him of the corruption I found here in Caldor. I implored him to send aid."

Jorrell took out a folded piece of parchment from underneath his tunic and tossed it to Malhallow.

"My father responded three days ago. As you can see, he is not happy with the developments here or in Rathstone. His forces draw near. Tell me, old man, can you see the dust his cavalry is kicking up with that failing eyesight of yours? If so, you will see five hundred of my father's best marching on Caldor. Kill me if you will, but your death will surely follow mine, as will the word of your treachery."

Malhallow's eyes lifted in surprise, peering into the distance.

Sabra could plainly see a large force moving steadily down the road, though they were somewhat obscured by bits of flying dust. She suspected they were the absent bandits, working some trickery at Gheric's behest. At the front of the column, Sabra could make out the blue-and-white banners of Kath raised overhead.

"That's not possible," Malhallow gasped, his eyes growing wide.

Sabra felt sick. If her father thought a greater force was on its way, he *would* likely have Harmon fight Gheric.

Now, Aurelia, before it is too late, she thought, looking at her twin standing across the sands of the marketplace.

"Not only is it possible," Gheric rattled in anger, "that army is descending upon your forces like an ocean wave ready to break your men against these walls."

Damn his noble heart, Sabra thought. *He's trying to save me by forcing the issue.*

Angry mutterings could be heard from the baron's men, as each could plainly see the approaching force.

"There is another way," said a voice from behind Jorrell.

"What are you doing?" Gheric whispered, looking at the blue-eyed woman behind him.

"I will go with my father," Aurelia said with a nod to her sister.

Sabra felt a wave of relief flood through her.

"No, you will not!" thundered Gheric, his eyes flashing dangerously.

"Please," Aurelia voiced. "There is no need for anyone to die today. I beg you, Gheric, let me do this for you . . . and for my sister."

A pang of guilt ran through Sabra, knowing she might be condemning Aurelia to death.

Gheric wet his lips and looked over at the woman across the way. Sabra felt her heart skip, knowing he was at the cusp of agreeing.

Sabra's breathing froze as she saw Gheric lean forward and whisper something into her twin's ear. She saw Aurelia's eyes widen, completely awestruck.

"That cannot be," Sabra heard her say.

"It is," Gheric stated, his tone deadly serious.

Aurelia looked across the sands of the market, staring in wonder at her twin.

"I . . . I withdraw my offer," Aurelia said at last, her eyes dropping to the ground. "I cannot go to Rathstone."

Sabra looked imploringly at her sister, knowing something Gheric said had changed the plan they had discussed the previous day.

Aurelia looked up, giving Sabra the barest shake of her head.

"So, what will it be, my lord?" Jorrell asked. "Die fast or die slow? Should you agree to our duel, the worst thing that could happen is that you will lose. Afterward, I'll even allow you to—how did you put it?—slink home empty handed."

Baron Turner licked his lips nervously, the irony of Jorrell's insult not lost on him. He looked up at the massive figure of Harmon.

"Give me a moment," he said to Jorrell, turning around to address his captain.

"Take your time," Jorrell answered. "My father's forces grow ever closer."

Sabra leaned in, straining to hear the two men's whispered conversation.

"What do you know of this approaching army?" Malhallow asked his captain.

"I see what you see," Harmon answered, his eyes locked on the dust kicking up in the distance. "Those are Kath's colors, along with the kingfisher sigil. Jorrell, damn his house, may well have sent a message to the duke."

"How long will it take us to get inside the keep if we attack now?" the baron asked.

Harmon shrugged. "The door is solid oak, at least six inches thick. The crossbar is reinforced with black iron on the inside . . ." He hesitated and glanced at the scout who had delivered the earlier report. "And . . . it will take time to procure a battering ram."

Malhallow stared at Harmon, his mind whirling.

"Can you beat this . . . Gheric?" the baron asked.

Harmon snorted. "Even if I had had to go without Temper's ministrations, I would have still been able to kill him quickly."

"Then it is decided—you will be my champion," Malhallow said, seeing no other recourse.

The captain gave the baron an evil smile. "Should I carry out this task successfully . . . I will rule here in Caldor and take Aurelia as my wife."

"As we agreed last night." The baron nodded. "You have my word."

"Your word isn't enough," Harmon said, pulling out a scroll from under his armor. "You will sign here, now, or there is no deal."

Malhallow looked at him with annoyance and snapped his fingers. "You, scribe! A quill and ink, now."

The ruddy-faced scribe nearly sprinted over, handing the baron a feathered quill from his satchel.

Sabra stood helplessly, racking her brain for a way to get her father to change his mind. She knew only earth magic, which was used mainly to culture growth and healing. Attacking the captain was foolhardy, as she knew he would kill her instantly.

"One last thing," the captain growled as he pocketed the scroll once more. "That arrogant swine Jorrell belongs to me. He killed several of my men. There will be no peaceful ride home for him. He is mine to torture until I tire of his screams."

"He is a noble of House Mays," Malhallow reminded Harmon.

The captain glowered down at the smaller man. "Agree to my terms, or you can fight Gheric yourself."

The baron's eyes flashed dangerously. "Careful, Captain," Malhallow warned. "My patience is already frayed. Caldor and Aurelia will be yours, that is my offer."

Harmon stood, implacable, his face set like stone.

"Fine," the baron muttered darkly. "You may keep Jorrell for your . . . voracious appetites."

"It seems you have your champion," Harmon said, looking across the way at Gheric. "It will be my pleasure. I've wanted to kill this arrogant shit since he first came to Caldor."

Sabra felt a jolt of nerves swirl at the bottom of her stomach at the end of their exchange. Despite her best efforts, Gheric was going to have to fight the enormous captain after all. She wanted to scream out in protest, her frustration mounting. Sabra's eyes shifted across the marketplace to stare daggers at her twin. Sabra was going to lose Gheric, all because Aurelia had gone back on her promise.

"I accept your challenge," Malhallow stated darkly, turning back to Jorrell. "It seems we have a deal."

"If Gheric wins, you will withdraw your force, and Sabra stays in Caldor," Jorrell said. "You and your army will return to Rathstone and await my father's pleasure."

"If your champion falls?" the baron queried.

Jorrell glanced at the woman next to him, who gave Jorrell a faint nod. "Then you will take Sabra with you in exchange for her twin," he agreed.

"What of you?" Malhallow pressed.

"I will withdraw from Caldor, and you may appoint a new baron," Jorrell growled.

"Then we have a deal," the baron said, moving back toward his own forces.

"Clear the front of the gate!" Jorrell shouted as he, the

mayor, and Aurelia moved inside the keep and to the top walls to watch the fight.

Sabra shuffled back out of range, keeping close to her father and helplessly staring at Gheric, knowing there was nothing she could do to help him.

Captain Harmon stood; his arms crossed in front of him. Standing only a few feet away was Gheric, his eyes smoldering with fury underneath the depths of his hood.

Sabra barely heard the mayor, who was reading the rules of the challenge. Across the market, she watched as her twin appeared atop the battlements and stared down at her.

If he dies, sister, you will not see the dawning of a new day, she promised herself.

"Begin!" shouted the mayor.

Sabra's eyes moved to the sands in front of the gate, hoping Gheric could somehow win the day against the colossal former gladiator standing in front of him.

CHAPTER 27

"Oi! How long we gotta do this?" shouted an exasperated bandit from somewhere in the middle of the column.

"Shut your clack and keep going!" Othar snarled over his shoulder. "We're done when I say we're done!"

The fifty-eight bandits had been marching slowly for the last ten minutes. Every one of them was covered in a sheen of dust.

"It's not like they have something better to do," Yetter muttered, wiping the sweat from his brow. "Why, I'd wager—"

From behind them came the faint sound of the men shouting in outrage.

"Goddamn it, what is it now?" Othar shouted, spinning around.

Underneath the cries of surprise, he could hear the dull thrumming of a horse in full gallop.

"That can't be good," Othar muttered as Yetter turned around. The rider, dressed in the black-and-gold colors of

Rathstone, was tearing along the coastline on the back of a dun-colored stallion.

"By the Sons of Dourn, who is that?!" Othar yelled as the rider barreled past the head of the column.

"A scout maybe?" Yetter guessed.

"He was wearing the colors of Rathstone," Othar growled.

"And he saw we are *not* an army," Yetter added grimly.

"Well, tits on a stick," Othar cursed. "What do we do?"

Yetter looked at the keep in the distance, knowing Gheric and Sabra were there fighting for him. He straightened his posture and twirled around to address the men behind him. Gazing at the sour faces in the column, the Billerton farmhand shouted to them at the top of his lungs. "Any man who doesn't want to freeze his ass off this winter, mount up and ride for Caldor!"

Yetter leaped atop Kat and helped Othar scramble on behind him.

"By the gods, you need to bathe," the taller bandit complained.

"You think I smell now? Wait till I break wind with you behind me!" Yetter grunted, kicking his heels into the sides of his horse.

Kat whinnied in excitement and bolted forward.

"Did any of the others bother to follow us?" the elder farmhand shouted against the noise of iron-shod hooves pounding along the ground.

Othar chanced a look behind him and gaped in amazement. "Damn me!" he shouted in surprise.

"We all alone?!" Yetter howled.

"See for yourself!" replied Othar.

Yetter craned his neck behind him to see every bandit had mounted up and was following their lead.

"This must be what it feels like to lead men into battle!" Yetter whooped in genuine excitement. "It is incredible!"

"It might feel good," Othar howled from his place behind Yetter, "but it smells like fresh ass!"

AURELIA NEEDED TO INTERCEDE ON GHERIC'S BEHALF. THE elder daughter had seen Harmon in battle. She knew Gheric, despite his experience, had little chance of defeating the monstrous captain of Caldor's guard.

"Not only is it possible," she heard Gheric rattled in anger, "that army is descending upon your forces like an ocean wave ready to break your men against these walls."

Aurelia understood the oncoming army was a ruse. It was only a matter of time before her father discovered the truth. If she did not act quickly, Malhallow may well accept Gheric's challenge, and she'd be forced to watch the only man she'd ever cared for be killed in front of her.

Aurelia flicked her gaze across the marketplace and saw that Sabra was staring at her. The elder sibling knew her sister was willing Aurelia to enact their plan.

"There is another way," she interjected from her place behind Jorrell, knowing it was time.

"What are you doing?" Gheric whispered, staring at Aurelia as though she had lost her mind.

"I will go with my father," Aurelia offered, nodding at her twin.

"No, you will not!" thundered Gheric, his eyes flashing dangerously.

"Please," Aurelia voiced. "There is no need for anyone to die today. I beg you, Gheric, let me do this for you . . . and for my sister."

"The hell with your sister," he hissed softly enough that only Aurelia could hear. "She left us to rot!"

"It is not your decision," Aurelia whispered firmly, ignoring the sting of his words. "I must do what I think is best."

She saw him wet his lips and look across the market at her twin. He was about to agree, she knew. Aurelia could feel the words of affirmation coming.

It was then that Gheric leaned forward and spoke softly into Aurelia's ear.

"I did not think it fair to speak of this matter until after the events of today unfolded, but . . . Temper told me something about you yesterday morning."

He leaned in closer, his lips right next to her ear.

"You are with child," he whispered. "Our baby is at stake, Sabra. I'll not risk losing you or our unborn child to these monsters. Let me carry out a father's first responsibility. Let me fight this son of a bitch! Let me protect my child."

Aurelia's eyes widened, completely awestruck by the news.

"That cannot be," she whispered, her mind whirling.

"It is," Gheric stated, his tone deadly serious.

Aurelia looked across the sands of the market, staring in wonder at her twin.

Sabra was pregnant with Gheric's child! And the poor girl had no idea. A sudden panic filled Aurelia. For the briefest of moments, she did not know what to do as a feeling of terror threatened to overcome her senses. She took a deep breath to calm herself, seeing into the heart of the matter. It was then Aurelia saw with absolute clarity the two choices set in front of her.

In her mind's eyes, Aurelia's youth flashed before her. She glimpsed the unborn child's future. If she chose to stay with Gheric, the child would be born in Rathstone. It would be taken from Sabra and raised from infancy to a life in Malhallow's power-hungry court. Aurelia knew better than anyone the child would live its life without a single moment of happiness. The thought made her heart cry out in anguish.

The other choice was to follow through with their plan, to trade places with Sabra. However, it would not be long before Malhallow would see he'd been played for a fool. He would come to Caldor for an already pregnant Sabra. The child would be killed outright, tainted with Gheric's peasant blood.

Both terrible choices flashed through Aurelia's mind inside the length of a heartbeat. She realized the unborn child's fate now rested in her hands. In an eyeblink, she knew what she had to do.

A feeling of guilt knotted inside Aurelia's stomach.

Knowing it went against her word to her sister, Aurelia braced herself and made the decision she believed was in the best interests of the unborn child.

"I . . . I withdraw my offer," Aurelia said, her eyes dropping to the ground. "I cannot go to Rathstone."

Sabra looked across the open space between them, silently imploring her twin to make the switch and spare Gheric the duel.

Forgive me, sister, Aurelia thought, raising her eyes upward and shaking her head ever so slightly in warning.

"So, what will it be, my lord?" Aurelia heard Jorrell ask. "Die fast or die slow? Should you agree to our duel, the worst thing that could happen is that you will lose. Afterward, I'll even allow you to—how did you put it?—slink home empty handed."

Aurelia's mind was racing, hoping she'd done what was right. The eldest daughter of Malhallow waited with bated breath as she watched her father speaking quietly with Harmon.

"I accept your challenge," she heard her father say darkly, turning back to Jorrell. "It seems we have a deal."

"May the gods forgive me," she whispered, searching Sabra's face.

"If Gheric wins, you will withdraw your force, and Sabra stays in Caldor," Jorrell was saying. "You and your army will return to Rathstone and await my father's pleasure."

"If your champion falls?" Malhallow queried.

Jorrell glanced to Aurelia, who gave him a faint nod. "Then you will take Sabra with you in exchange for her twin," he agreed.

"What of you?" Malhallow pressed.

"I will withdraw from Caldor, and you may appoint a new baron," Jorrell growled.

"Then we have a deal," the baron said, moving back toward his own forces.

Jorrell turned around and entered the keep, and Aurelia absently followed, her legs unsteady as she struggled to climb to the top of the walls to watch the fight that was to come.

As she looked down upon her twin, Aurelia could see the malice in Sabra's eyes.

"I am sorry, sister," she whispered.

"Are you all right, lass?" came a voice from next to her.

Aurelia glanced over and saw Gyles looking at her with concern.

"I . . . I've fallen in love with him—with them both," she admitted, her fear getting the better of her.

"Both?" Gyles questioned. "You mean Gheric and Aurelia?"

"Yes . . . " She faltered as a single word sounded in the crisp morning air. It froze Aurelia's heart in her chest.

"Begin!"

Aurelia's eyes widened in horror. She watched helplessly from atop the battlements as the man she loved came face-to-face with the most powerful warrior Aurelia had ever seen.

"Win, Gheric," she whispered to herself. "Win, or everything you love will die."

GHERIC SEETHED UNDERNEATH HIS HOOD, TRYING TO KEEP HIS mind calm. The butterflies he had felt earlier were gone. Now was not the time for fiery rage. He was fighting to protect the woman who he loved and their unborn child.

As the mayor read off the details of the challenge, the broad-shouldered warrior thought back to the last time he'd seen the former gladiator in action.

Harmon came to the ancient city of Gallanse looking for employment. It was early spring, and the mercenary companies were replenishing their numbers. Gheric was sitting inside the Box and Rum, a gaming house famous throughout the Crystalline Sea. His employer, Khaine Forrester of the Battle Mage, was speaking to the massive gladiator, shaking his head politely.

"I'm sorry, but I only take on new folk if they have the proper references from people I trust," Khaine was saying.

"I was Gladiator Three on the sands of Tal-Mur this past year," Harmon argued.

"It is not your martial skills that are suspect," Khaine admitted. "Rather, it is your temperament."

Harmon furrowed his brow in anger. "I've yet to meet a fighting man who needed to stay calm in the arena."

"We do not fight inside arenas," Khaine explained. "I'm sorry, but we cannot offer you employment at this time. I'm sure there are other companies in Gallanse that will be happy to sign you on."

The massive Harmon stalked from the common room, fuming with rage.

"What do you think?" Khaine asked Gheric, who had been standing quietly behind him.

"I think he's going to cause an uproar," his second-in-command replied.

No sooner had those words been spoken did the sounds of battle ring in the streets outside the Box and Rum.

"I hate it when I'm right," Gheric mumbled dryly.

"You'd best get out there and make sure he doesn't kill anyone," Khaine suggested mildly.

Gheric went outside and looked on as Harmon laid out every fighting man within range. Three mercenaries were down, bleeding, or senseless. Four others were locked in a desperate fight with the former gladiator. Gheric saw Harmon kick sand in the face of a large man in front of him. The now half-blind warrior threw a wild haymaker, desperately trying to defend himself. Harmon batted aside the swing with ease, lifted the man off his feet, and threw him into a pair of mercenaries in front of him, sending them all to the ground in a heap. The last man in front of Harmon was young, willowy thin. His mouth was agape, full of fear. Panicked, he sank to his knees.

"Mercy!" the youth cried, holding his arms in front of his face.

"I don't give mercy!" Harmon barked, stalking forward.

"Enough!" Gheric shouted, bounding down the stairs. "He is just a boy!"

Harmon ignored him and swung his broadsword with all this strength, intent on cutting the young man in half.

"Tergio!" Gheric shouted, extending his hand in front of him.

A knot of magical force struck Harmon, knocking the huge man off-balance.

"I said that is enough!" the warrior-mage shouted, standing protectively in front of the youth.

Harmon shrugged off the magical strike and loomed over the stocky warrior in front of him. "You and your master had your chance to hire me," he snarled, raising his sword. "Now, sod off! There are plenty here who will take me in after this display."

"No one will hire an undisciplined wretch like you!" Gheric shot back.

"The hell they won't!" Harmon roared, launching a new attack.

Gheric, expecting the strike, drew his sword and parried the blow. He lashed out with his fist and smashed Harmon's jaw. The big gladiator grunted and shrugged it off, raising his sword once more.

"Don't do this," Gheric warned.

"I'll do whatever I want!" Harmon roared, lunging forward.

Gheric raised his hand and sent another burst of magic, this time with enough strength to knock Harmon to the ground. In the blink of an eye, the mercenary was kneeling on the cobblestoned surface next to him, a knife at Harmon's throat.

"You will leave Gallanse, never to return," Gheric hissed. "Do you understand?"

"You'll die for this, you son of a bitch!" Harmon roared, defiant in the face of his defeat.

"We will take it from here," said a stern voice from among the onlookers. A guard, dressed in the blue-and-white colors of Gallanse, stepped out into the street. With him were a dozen men.

"You are lucky I don't know your name," Harmon fumed as the guard placed shackles on his wrists. "You best pray to the gods I never see you again. If I do, I'll cut out your heart!"

"Don't threaten me, you worthless shit," Gheric warned, his ire flaring.

"I'll gut you *and* that bitch Khaine," Harmon promised.

Gheric remembered very clearly the rage he felt coursing through his veins as the huge man threatened the life of the man he served. It unleashed a fury in him he had not experienced since.

"Until that day, here's something to remember me by," Gheric retorted, boiling blood flowing through him. He stepped forward and slashed his knife across the huge man's face, drenching Harmon's neck with blood.

"Think of that scar when you think of me, you black hearted bastard!" Gheric bellowed.

"You whoreson!" thundered Harmon, straining under the weight of a dozen guards. "When I hunt you down, I'll rip your goddamn head off and send you to hell!"

"I'll be waiting!" Gheric had roared in a towering anger.

Even now, years later, the memory caused Gheric's blood to boil.

Blinking back to the present, the dark-eyed warrior heard his name being called by Tamalin.

"Gheric," the mayor said a second time. "Do you have any questions?"

"No," he answered, looking into the dead eyes of his opponent.

"Captain Harmon," Tamalin said, "do you have any questions before we commence?"

"Yes," the huge captain snarled, his eyes boring holes into the figure standing across from him. "Why don't you take off that hood? I want to look into the eyes of the man I'm going to kill."

Gheric did not move.

"What's wrong, Gheric?" Harmon continued, saying his name for the first time. "Worried the others might see your fear?"

In response, Gheric undid the clasp that held his cloak in place and threw it to the ground. He stared back at Harmon, finally revealing himself to his enemy.

"You," the captain said, his eyes filling with malice.

"Nice scar," Gheric taunted.

Harmon drew his blade, taking a few practice swings and loosening his shoulders. "I told you once I would cut out your heart."

"You also said you'd rip my head off," Gheric sniffed. "Yet here I stand, unbowed and unbroken."

"Until now," Harmon snarled.

"I heard you escaped in Gallanse . . . " Gheric said. "Killed three guards and fled. We wondered where you'd been hiding."

The warrior-mage flicked his gaze toward Malhallow. "I should have guessed you would serve a man whose soul is as dark as yours."

The baron's gaze turned to Tamalin. "Shall we begin? I'd like to see this arrogant cock dead before my breakfast cools."

"Indeed," the mayor acquiesced, bowing in supplication. Tamalin backed away and stood with his back to the keep wall before he shouted a single word.

"Begin!"

CHAPTER 28

Gheric did not hesitate to use his greatest advantage.
Pugnu ignis!
A torrent of flame shot from the warrior-mage's extended hand to engulf the huge man in front of him.

For a moment, the figure of Harmon was bathed in fire, his huge form unmoving. A heartbeat later, the captain ran forward, his broadsword leading the way.

"No," Sabra gasped under her breath as she watched Gheric desperately parry the attack. It did not stop the smaller man from being shoulder slammed to the ground by the massive captain.

"Your magic is useless!" Harmon roared, raining blows downward.

Gheric managed to block the first two attacks with his sword before casting a second, desperate spell.

"Tergio!"

A knot of air blasted into Harmon. It did no damage, but it managed to disrupt the captain's attacks long enough for Gheric to scramble to his feet.

"You've no bag of tricks to turn to this time," Harmon hissed. "It's just you against me."

Gheric did not respond. Instead, he raised his sword in a ready position.

Sabra watched the fight, caught somewhere between horror and amazement. For all his size and strength, Harmon moved with incredible speed. His footwork was exceptional, always in balance, whether he was on the defensive or moving to attack. Despite her fear concerning the former gladiator's martial prowess, her dark-eyed lover seemed up to the task. Gheric was nothing short of magnificent. He fought coolly, countering every strike, launching attacks of his own when the opportunity arose.

Sabra gasped again as she saw Harmon's sword slice across the top of Gheric's shoulder. Blood sprayed into the air. The swarthy warrior accepted the wound, doling out one of his own as his sword ripped open a cut above Harmon's hip. Both men moved backward, more wary now, each seeking a weakness in the other.

Gheric's blood was running down his arm, dripping onto the dirt under his feet, and Harmon's side was drenched in red, his hip bleeding freely.

Harmon tried a feint to the left, followed by a murderous lunge to the right. Gheric parried the blow and lashed out, striking the larger man on the triceps. Harmon withdrew his sword, and a line of red streaked across his arm.

Sabra saw Harmon's eyes narrow. The huge man launched himself forward in an all-out attack borne of frustration. Gheric defended, both men hacking and slashing at one another in furious assaults.

Harmon overextended his attack a fraction, and Gheric lashed with his fist, striking his adversary on the temple. The larger man tried to roll with the punch but moved too slowly.

He was left off-balance, and Gheric took advantage. The smaller man kicked out with his right foot and swept Harmon's leg out from under him. The captain of Malhallow's guard went down in a heap, his sword flying from his grasp.

Gheric charged in, determined to finish the fight once and for all.

Desperate, Harmon rolled left and grabbed a fistful of dirt in his right hand. With a frantic heave, the former gladiator threw the dirt upward, showering Gheric across the face. Sabra's heart leaped to her throat as she saw the man she loved blinded by the cowardly ploy.

"No," she whispered, as Gheric tried unsuccessfully to wipe the dirt from his eyes.

Wasting no time, Harmon rose to his feet, ran to his left, and picked up his sword.

"Father," Sabra said, her voice filled with panic. "Stop the fight. You . . . your honor will be stained. The captain broke the rules."

"What rules?" he sniffed, drinking from his wineskin. "This is a duel to the death. The better man will win."

On top of the keep wall, Sabra's sentiment was shared.

"Hold your attack!" Jorrell roared. "The captain has broken the rules of engagement."

Harmon glanced at the baron, who nodded for him to continue.

"If that blow falls, so too does our agreement!" Jorrell shouted.

"Then we will capture the keep and take my daughter by force," Malhallow answered, his face determined.

"Father, no!" Sabra cried, moving forward.

"Restrain her," Malhallow said to his men, giving his daughter a look of disapproval.

Sabra felt hands grab her, keeping her from running to Gheric's aid.

She watched in horror at Harmon's approach, his massive sword in hand.

GHERIC WAS AWARE OF WORDS BEING EXCHANGED, BUT HE was too busy trying to clear his vision to focus on what was being said. Blinking rapidly, he could feel tears running down both sides of his face. His right eye was completely blind. However, he could make out the fuzzy shape of Harmon advancing toward him with the blurred vision in his left. The captain was close, his sword already moving backward for a killing blow.

"I told you," Gheric heard Harmon hiss.

Barely able to see, the warrior-mage raised his blade in an attempt to block Harmon's attack. With a steely clang the two swords met, and Gheric's broke in two. Following through, Harmon smashed the flat of his blade into the smaller man, throwing Gheric to the ground.

Pain exploded along Gheric's torso as the broadsword hammered through his armor and snapped the ribs on the left side of his body. Looking up, he saw Harmon draw his sword back, readying a thrust to the heart. Unbowed, Gheric let his broken sword fall to the ground and drew his knife.

Instead of trying to avoid the attack, Gheric leaped off the ground moving forward. He grunted in pain as the big Shar's sword impaled him through the chest. Determined, the warrior grabbed Harmon's forearm with his left hand. He lashed out, thrusting his knife through the neck of his opponent. The steel blade sliced through Harmon's jugular, spraying his lifeblood on both fighters.

Taken by surprise, the huge man threw himself backward, but it was too late. Blood fountained from the wound, as Harmon managed a choking, half turn toward Malhallow before pitching forward onto his face.

Still on his feet, Gheric withdrew the sword from his chest and let it fall to the ground.

"I win," Gheric gasped at the stunned face of Baron Turner, blood bubbling from his mouth. "Take Aurelia and go, as we agreed."

Gheric turned and looked atop the battlements toward Aurelia and spoke with the last of his remaining strength. "Sabra!" he called out. "You are safe, my love . . ."

His lifeblood streaming out of him, Gheric collapsed to the ground.

He did not move again.

CHAPTER 29

"No!" Sabra screamed, trying unsuccessfully to wrest her arms from the guards holding her.

"What is the matter with you?" Malhallow asked, his eyes flashing with disappointment.

Hot tears streaked down Sabra's face as she looked on, helpless to do anything.

"Orders, my lord?" the sergeant closest to the baron asked.

Malhallow looked again toward the northern road, seeing the riders approaching at speed. "There is something strange about that cavalry," Sabra heard her father mutter. "Stand at the ready, Sergeant, I suspect something is afoot."

The gate to the keep ground open, and Sabra's twin stepped outside. Moving quickly, she knelt at Gheric's side, pressing her ear to his chest.

"Is he breathing?!" Sabra heard Jorrell shout from atop the battlements.

"Barely!" Aurelia answered, fixing her gaze upon Malhallow. The elder daughter of the baron rose to her feet and stood to address both Sabra and her father.

"I wish for no more bloodshed," Aurelia said. "I . . ." She licked her lips nervously. "I will come with you, Father. In exchange, you will keep your word and let my sister stay here to rule in Caldor. I will come north with you and stay for as long as you wish."

In the distance, there was a rumble of hooves pounding down the road.

"I agree," Malhallow said, giving a wave of his hand. Turning to his guards, he looked down upon Sabra.

"Go," he ordered. "Your use to me has run its course. Perhaps your twin will provide me with what I need. Goodbye, Aurelia. May we never meet again."

The guards released their hold upon Sabra, and she ran across the market square. She slowed only long enough to hear her twin's passing words.

"Save him."

Sabra nodded once and ran past the still form of Harmon without a glance. She sank to her knees and placed both hands upon Gheric's chest, focusing her power.

"*Magna mater, sana haec vulnera,*" she whispered, feeling her healing magic flow through her.

Gheric did not show any signs of change.

"*Magna mater, sana haec vulnera,*" she said again, this time loud enough to garner the attention of her father.

"What is this?" she heard him ask from behind her.

Still, Gheric did not move. Looking deep inside her, words spoken by her mother long ago sprang to her mind.

"*Quad confractum est fiet unum!*" she shouted, her hands glowing white. Underneath her palms, she felt the rise and fall of Gheric drawing a deep breath. The terrible wound on his chest closed, and his eyes fluttered open. He sat up on his own, very much alive.

"By the gods, who are you?!" thundered the voice of Malhallow toward Sabra, for the first time sounding angry.

"Sabra?" Gheric questioned, looking first at the woman in front of him and then at Aurelia.

"I am sorry for the subterfuge, my love, but . . ." She turned around and looked at her twin. "Aurelia and I thought it best to switch places in order to keep you alive."

For the first time in many years, the baron of Rathstone was rendered speechless. He moved his gaze from Aurelia to Sabra and back again.

"Apologies, Father," Aurelia said, her tone mocking. "But you always said 'keep your enemies guessing.'"

Malhallow's face turned red, ready to explode.

"Careful, old man," Aurelia warned. "The duke's men are close. If I were you, I'd ride away now, while you still can."

The baron could see the riders on the North Road approaching, the blue-and-white banners proudly displayed before them.

"Sound a retreat," he said to his sergeant, looking murderously at his eldest.

"My lord?" the sergeant asked hesitantly.

"I said sound the—"

Baron Turner was interrupted by a single rider who galloped into the market square. His mount, a great dun-colored stallion, was lathered in sweat. Breathing heavily, the rider reined in next to Malhallow, his voice coming in deep gasps.

"Lieutenant Locke," the baron said, surprised to see him. "What news from the North Road?"

"It's a trick, my lord," the lieutenant breathed, pointing behind him. "They are bandits, made to look like a larger force."

"How many?" Malhallow asked, his face turning to stone.

"No more than three scores, my lord," Locke reported. "With not a single fighting man among them."

The baron fixed his eyes upon the battlements, eyeing Jorrell in contempt.

"Sergeant!" he bellowed. "My youngest is not to be harmed. Kill the rest!"

"You lost the duel!" Jorrell barked. "Have you no honor?"

"Not for a lying dog like you!" Malhallow roared, his face flush with anger.

"No!" Aurelia shouted, raising her hand. Her blue eyes flashed white, glowing with power.

"*Furorem deducere caelos!*" she shouted.

There was a crackling of power in the air around Aurelia, loud enough to shake the ground. A bolt of lightning shot from her hand, smashing into her father with a burst of energy.

She slowly dropped her appendage and looked at the results of her attack, her mouth agape.

"It's not possible," she murmured.

Sitting atop his white mare was Malhallow, alive and well.

"Pathetic," he rasped, looking down upon his eldest. "You are not the only one to keep your enemies guessing."

He glanced up to Jorrell, who was looking on in surprise. "Any last words before we raze this village to the ground?"

"Yes," Gheric said, looking at Sabra.

"What is it?" Malhallow derided, his face twisted in loathing. "A last cry for mercy? Some pitiful attempt to delay the inevitable?"

Gheric shook his head.

"Then what is it?" demanded the baron. "What is it you want to say?"

Gheric looked up at the sky and closed his eyes, whispering something under his breath.

"What was that?" the baron asked, moving his horse closer.

Again, Gheric said something just beyond the hearing of the baron.

"Speak up!" Malhallow snarled, edging a bit closer.

"I said I want Silence!" Gheric thundered at the top of his lungs.

The baron began to laugh. "Silence?" he scoffed, turning to his army. "Did you hear that, men?"

The three hundred soldiers under Malhallow's command laughed along with their lord.

The baron waved his hand forward. "Give them what they want!" he shouted. "Give them an eternity of silen—"

His voice was cut off as a steel tipped arrow was buried in his throat.

Malhallow jolted backward on his horse, with an incredulous look on his face. Sitting up straight, he lifted his hands to his throat, shocked to feel an arrow protruding from his neck. With a look of absolute disbelief, he toppled from his horse and fell dead upon the ground.

At that moment, Yetter, Othar, and the fifty-six other bandits following them rode into the village and crowded the market square.

"Did it work?" Yetter asked, completely out of breath.

"It better have," Othar complained. "I just inhaled half your noxious fumes for the last quarter of an hour!"

"Aye, it worked," Gheric answered, looking up to the highest spire of the keep.

Every eye, from those in the marketplace to the battlements, turned to see a lone figure standing on the top of the tower.

There stood a single man, Lieutenant Horval, affectionately known as Silence. He looked on in satisfaction, his arrow having found its mark.

"The Willet Farm sends its regards, you traitorous son of a bitch!" Silence shouted, raising his bow overhead.

Caldor had been saved.

CHAPTER 30

After the fall of Malhallow, Lieutenant Locke was left as the ranking commander of Rathstone's forces. The lieutenant saw no reason to follow his predecessor's treasonous ways. He ordered the men of Rathstone to stand down on the outskirts of Caldor and await orders from Jorrell.

A day later, a force of five hundred soldiers arrived from Kath, the steely eyed Duke Mays at the head of the column. He sat and listened as his son detailed the events of the past week. Afterward, the Duke of Kath issued a number of orders.

First was to Gyles. The innkeeper of the Bad Apple Inn was awarded with an honorary knighthood to show his service to the duke. He was cited for both valor and bravery under duress.

Next was Horval. The former lieutenant was praised for his service. Even after he'd been afflicted with a spell of silence, he chose to stay the course. Horval was made the captain of the guard in Caldor, placed in charge of keeping the duke's peace. He was also awarded with a recurve bow from the Seven Provinces—a powerful weapon fashioned far from the shores of the Crystalline Sea.

Jorrell was slated to travel north with his father, where, after much debate, he would be named the new baron of Rathstone. With them would go the three hundred men previously under the rule of Malhallow. Most swore an oath and pledged to serve faithfully under Jorrell's command.

The select few who refused were stripped of arms and armor and summarily executed for treason.

Before the duke and his son retired north, there was one order of business that remained.

After hearing testimony from Jorrell, Gheric, Sabra, and Horval, Duke Mays called Aurelia to court. He sat upon the baron's chair, looking sternly down upon the elder of Malhallow's daughters.

"Tell me," the duke began, his voice cold and stern. "Before I issue my decision regarding your actions here in Caldor, is there anything you have to say for yourself?"

Aurelia looked up at the duke, her blue eyes clear and bright. "I have much to say to my sister and Gheric," she began. "However, I doubt that is what you are asking."

She smoothed the front of her dress and plunged forward. "It is true that I was sent here to capture my sister and keep the truth of my father's plans of rebellion hidden. I also used my magic to curse Lieutenant Horval and keep the truths he carried a secret. I made many missteps along the way, all under the orders of my father, though I know now that is not an excuse."

She paused in her oration and lifted her chin proudly. "I am not an evil woman, though I deem from your perspective that you may see it otherwise. For what it is worth, I am sorry for much of what happened while I was here in Caldor. I take full responsibility for my actions and will accept whatever punishment you wish to mete out."

The room fell silent while the duke considered her words.

"If I may, your grace?" Sabra said, looking to the duke.

"Of course," Mays replied, nodding his head.

Sabra stepped forward, standing in front of her twin and facing the duke. "I know not what Aurelia's life was like in Rathstone, though from what little she's told me, it was far from pleasant. Having spent less than a single day in my father's presence, I can see why she acted as she did upon her arrival in Caldor."

Sabra turned around and looked at her twin. "My sister, it seems, has much to atone for, but I would be remiss if I didn't point out some of her actions from these past days to help our cause."

Aurelia gave Sabra a slight shake of her head. "Sister, you don't need to do this," she said softly.

"It was Aurelia who brought to us the idea of eliminating Niles and Harmon," Sabra continued. "She did so at great risk to herself. It's true she cursed Lieutenant Horval, just as it is true she reversed the spell on her own discourse."

"Sabra, please," Aurelia tried again, looking imploringly at her sister. "I am not in the right, and you know it."

"It was also her idea to switch places with me," her twin added, ignoring Aurelia's protests. "She did so knowing full well if all went to plan, she would be sent north with our father, sparing me that horrible fate."

Sabra turned back to the duke. "If my opinion has any weight with you, I ask that you take into account all of her actions, both the good and the bad."

"Aurelia saved me as well," Gheric put in. "I was dying at the time, but your son told me how she ran outside after my duel with Harmon and immediately brokered a deal to switch places with Sabra. She did it so her twin could heal me."

Gheric looked at her, his eyes sympathetic. "I would not be here today if it weren't for her quick thinking and sacrifice. She had nothing to gain from trading places with Sabra at that time. She did it to save me, plain and simple."

"Thank you," the duke said simply, glancing at his son. "Anything to add?"

"She was instrumental in keeping Caldor safe," Jorrell said. "It was her idea to use the bandits as decoys to try and fool Malhallow. In all, I'd say Aurelia has earned some kind of punishment, tempered by the weight of her good deeds."

"Very well," Mays said, looking at Aurelia. "I believe I have come to a decision that fits your crimes against me and the people of Caldor."

The duke stood and bade Aurelia forward.

"Aurelia Turner," Mays began. "For your crimes of treason against me and the good people of the duchy, I sentence you to a lifetime of servitude atoning for your mistakes."

He reached to his side and drew forth his sword. "I name you Aurelia Hastings, Baroness of Caldor."

"My lord?" Aurelia faltered, not quite certain what she was hearing.

"From this point forward, you will be placed in charge of the village and the lands therein," Mays continued. "Do you accept this responsibility?"

Aurelia was speechless. She looked to Sabra, who gave her a helpful nod.

"I do," Aurelia said in wonder.

The duke smiled. "Good. Now, let us have a drink to commemorate the moment. Jorrell and I will leave at first light tomorrow, and I hear Sabra still has a crop to bring in."

THE NEXT DAY, JORRELL LEFT ALONGSIDE HIS FATHER, WITH Gheric and Sabra present to see him off.

"We did well, you and I," Jorrell said, taking hold of Gheric's forearm in the warrior's handshake.

"Aye, though I'd just as soon hope that we never have to do it again," the mercenary quipped with a grin.

"I wanted to thank you," Sabra said, kissing Jorrell lightly on the cheek. "Without you, none of this would have been possible."

Jorrell gave her a smile. "I think we all played a part in it, you as much as anyone. I hope to see you both in the spring. My barony is only a two-day journey away, and I hear the woods are exceedingly low on bandits."

"Speaking of my new subjects," Aurelia said, walking up to them. "How are they settling in?"

"Yetter and Othar seem to have things under control," Gheric answered. "No skulls cracked yet."

"It's been one day," Sabra said dryly. "Let's see how they fare when the cold weather hits."

Jorrell turned to Aurelia. "As the new baroness, I look forward to communicating with you for the betterment of our people."

"As do I," Aurelia replied, bowing her head.

"I best be off," Jorrell said, climbing onto his horse. "I'll see you in the spring."

"Be lucky, my friend," Gheric said, clapping Jorrell on the shoulder. "Keep those sword skills sharp."

"You too," Jorrell replied, leaving them all with a smile.

With a last wave Jorrell rode off, joining his father's forces as they rode out of Caldor.

Aurelia turned and forced herself to look at her twin.

"I . . . I have much to do today in the keep, but . . . I think the three of us need to speak in private."

"I agree," Gheric said, frowning at them both. "Like why neither of you deemed it prudent to tell me you'd switched places."

A tinge of red flushed in Sabra's cheeks. "I, too, have much to do today. Perhaps we can discuss everything that happened later tonight," Sabra said, turning to Aurelia. "Meet me and Gheric at my farm at dusk."

As Sabra spoke, she reached out and clasped Gheric's hand in her own.

"I will see you there," Aurelia answered, feeling her heart sink in her chest.

GHERIC SPENT MOST OF HIS DAY AT THE BAD APPLE INN. HE was kept busy doling out silver to the bandits who had come to collect their wages. Afterward, he stayed on to help Gyles keep both the bandits and the townsfolk in line. It had been four days since the inn had last been open, and the folk of Caldor were in the mood to celebrate. A few of the bandits in particular were rowdy with food and drink, but a swift word from Gheric was enough to keep things from getting out of hand.

An hour until dusk, the barrel-chested warrior managed a private word with Gyles in the back room. Something had been eating at him all day. The innkeeper was his oldest friend in the village and someone Gheric knew he could trust.

"What's wrong with you?" Gyles asked, his face turned in confusion. "You haven't been yourself all day."

Gheric ran a hand through his hair and sat down on a stool of pine.

"Is it the money?" Gyles guessed. "Hell, those bandits will spend it all in my inn by tonight. Never seen anyone feast like they are. The missus and I are likely to run out of food and ale by sunset!"

"It's not that," Gheric answered with a wave. "I have copious amounts of coin in my account back in Adian, ten times what I brought here."

The innkeeper draped an arm over his friend's shoulder. "I thought as much. With the face you've been sporting all day, it can only be trouble with a woman."

"*Two* women!" Gheric said harshly. "Why couldn't they rely on me to keep their secret? I trusted them both, and they failed to do the same."

Gyles cleared his throat. "I want to ask you something, lad, and I suggest you answer as honestly as you can. Do you love the girl?"

"Which one?" Gheric answered, exasperated. "I thought I loved Sabra, but the last two days, it was Aurelia I was with. I loved her too, at least I thought so. At least as much as I did her twin."

"Did you . . .?" Gyles left his unasked question hovering in the air.

"Yes, I slept with them both," Gheric answered, more defiantly than he wanted. "Go ahead and say it. I'm a lecher, through and through."

Gyles let out a deep laugh, rich with genuine humor. "Oh, Gheric, you *are* in a bind. You are in love with them both and, gods help you, you cannot decide what to do."

"There will be no afterlife for me," Gheric said miserably. "I'll probably be stoned to death when the villagers find out I've bedded them both."

Gyles laughed even harder, clapping his friend on the back. "Stop being so melodramatic," the innkeeper said once he got his laughter under control. "Women are a wonderfully horrible mixture of simple and complicated all rolled into one."

"This isn't making me feel any better," Gheric muttered.

"Then let me tell you something that will," the innkeeper stated. "You won't have to decide. They will do it for you."

Gheric's face twisted in confusion. "What?"

"I have known Sabra for a while now. Let me tell you something . . . she is not a woman who will be forced into anything. Believe me when I say this: she will decide what is best for her."

"But she's carrying my child," Gheric protested.

"What?" Gyles gasped, completely stunned.

"You didn't know?"

"Did anyone?" Gyles asked. "Oh, my friend, that makes things even easier for you."

"What the hell is that supposed to mean?"

The innkeeper gave Gheric a look of fatherly patience. "It means she won't even be deciding what's best for herself. She will decide what is best for the child."

"Yes, well, there is a problem," Gheric admitted.

"Another one?"

"Shut up, you are supposed to be helping me."

The innkeeper chuckled again. "All right, what's the problem?"

Gheric shook his head and placed his temples on the fingertips of both hands. "I told Aurelia that she was pregnant with our child. Of course, I thought it was Sabra I was talking to at the time. I did not know the two of them had switched places."

"So, Aurelia knows Sabra is with child, and Sabra has no idea?" Gyles guffawed.

"Correct," Gheric confirmed.

"Does Sabra know you slept with Aurelia?" the innkeeper asked.

Gheric threw his arms in the air. "I haven't the faintest idea who knows what!" he announced, clearly frustrated. "I'm ready to take my vows and join the men of the cloth after this debacle."

Gyles could not help himself. He tried mightily to suppress his laughter and failed.

"This is not funny," Gheric grumbled, shaking his head.

That just made the innkeeper laugh harder.

"I think I need a drink," Gheric announced bitterly, slipping off the stool.

"*A* drink?" Gyles roared, tears of mirth streaming down his face. "You need an entire casket of my finest, at the very least!"

Gheric glowered at his friend. "You are no help at all."

THE WARRIOR CLASPED HIS CLOAK AROUND HIM TIGHTLY AS the evening air began to drop in temperature. It was cooler than it had been, as the last full moon of autumn soared overhead. Gheric arrived moments before sunset to see Yetter and the other farmhands leaving with heavy-laden wagons.

"I did not think to see you working today," Gheric said, waving at the lanky former bandit.

"Mrs. Billerton wanted to see the crop in, and by heaven, that's what you hired us to do," Yetter replied, mopping his forehead with his sleeve. "This is the last of it."

"You did well yesterday," Gheric said, glancing down the line. "You all did."

"Thank you," Yetter replied, giving the swarthy warrior a nod. "If you'll excuse us, we need to get this hauled into town. Pyle said he'd stay open for us, and I'd just as soon get Drei to bed before it's too late."

"Don't let me stop you," Gheric said, impressed with Yetter's leadership.

"See you tomorrow," the stocky farmhand waved, rattling the reins. The oxen began to walk east, heading into town.

The last wagon slowed, and the driver, Grada, turned to Gheric and pursed her lips. "She's out in the western fields."

"Thank you," the dark-eyed warrior replied with a nod.

Grada looked as though she was going to keep her wagon moving, but thought better of it and ground to a complete stop. "I know it is not my place to say, but," Grada began, "a woman can endure much if she believes she is loved."

"Are you speaking of Sabra or Aurelia?" Gheric asked, his voice sour.

"You are upset that they lied to you," Grada acknowledged. "I understand that . . . but matters of the heart are rarely so simple."

"Do you think so?" he asked, a well of bitterness rising inside him. "It seems quite simple to me."

Grada shook her head in disappointment. "You are a good man, Gheric, one of the best I have ever known. You treated the bandits of our group with respect, even before you knew their hearts."

"Give me an honest battle every time over the wiles of a woman," he said with a growl. "Men, at least, I can understand."

Grada leaned forward from her perch in the wagon, her dark eyes searching his. "My request is a simple one: Before you lash out in anger and say something you will regret, I ask that you hear what the women who have captured your heart have to say. Listen to their reasoning with an open mind."

Gheric looked at her, his face softening, knowing what she said made sense.

"I had no idea bandit women could offer such sage advice," he replied, giving her a half smile.

"The benefit of living with next to nothing," Grada sniffed, her eyes sad. "I have had plenty of time for empty reflection. I am happy to say that is no longer the case. Before I go, I offer you one last nugget of wisdom."

Grada straightened herself in the wagon and pulled tight on the reins.

"After you hear what the twins have to say, ask yourself this—does it matter in the end how you got where you are?"

Grada shook the reins and clicked at the horses. Her wagon began to move, heading east on the old village road.

Grada's question lingered in Gheric's ear. He stared after her, the wheels in his mind turning.

"I was beginning to think you weren't going to show," said a voice from behind him.

Gheric turned around and saw Sabra standing near the fence that separated the fields from her farmhouse. His breath caught in his throat.

Garbed in a yellow dress of spun cotton, the owner of the Billerton Farm was radiant. The dress was cut short in the front, showing a tantalizing amount of her legs. Gheric felt any remaining bitterness recede as he took in her magnificent form.

"Which one are you?" he asked, giving Sabra a wry grin.

"A fair question," came a voice identical to the first. Riding atop a chestnut bay was Aurelia. She leaped down from her mount and led the horse next to where her sister was standing with Gheric. She was wearing a blue dress; one cut to accentuate the curve of her hips and bosom. While the dress was made from a higher quality material, Gheric found the women next to him equally beautiful.

"I apologize for my tardiness," Aurelia said. "Our uncle Temper insisted on seeing me off."

"Quite all right, sister," Sabra replied.

"Uncle?" Gheric gasped in surprise.

"Great-uncle, actually," Sabra stated mildly.

"Might I stable my horse in your barn?" Aurelia asked politely.

"Of course," her twin answered.

Gheric took the reins from Aurelia. "Allow me," he said, frowning at them both. "Are there any other secrets you wish to spring on me?"

"Not at the moment. Come with me, sister," Sabra said, reaching out and taking her sister's hand. "Meet us at the edge of the field when you finish," she instructed Gheric, leading Aurelia away.

"I should have my head examined for thinking this is going to work out in my favor," he muttered, leading the horse into the barn.

Minutes later, Gheric made his way past the fence, seeing the twins comfortably sitting next to a pit made of stone. Inside was a roaring fire, its orange and yellow flames licking upward into the night.

"Sit here," Sabra offered, patting a cushioned chair between the two sisters.

Gheric nodded and took a seat. He glanced upward and felt a smile crease his face. Overhead was the brightest moon he had ever seen.

"Beautiful," he whispered, gazing skyward.

"The last full moon of autumn," Sabra agreed, casting her gaze to the heavens.

"The beginning of a new season," Aurelia added, looking at the faces of the pair next to her.

For a moment, all three sat quietly under the light of the Harvest Moon.

"We were just discussing our situation when you walked up," Aurelia began. "Neither Sabra nor I know where to begin. We decided it might be best if we let you ask any questions you have for us. We did, after all, keep you in the dark."

Gheric looked at both women and nodded thoughtfully. "I have several questions to ask you both, but I will start with my initial one. Why did neither of you tell me you switched places? Did you deem me unworthy of such trust? I feel as though I had a right to know what you were planning."

Sabra glanced at her twin, and Aurelia bowed her head. "The decision not to tell you was mine," the younger sibling confessed. "It had nothing to do with not trusting you. Quite the opposite. Of all the people I know in this world, you, Gheric, are the one I trust the most. Everything good that happened here in Caldor is because you decided to help me."

"That doesn't explain why you didn't tell me," he insisted.

"We needed your reactions to be authentic," Aurelia put in. "Think about it, Gheric. If you had known who I was, would you have acted in the same way?"

The handsome warrior made to speak but decided to hold his tongue.

"You do not love me . . . I know that," Aurelia went on to say. "Had you known it was me at your side those last two days, you would have done many things differently."

"That is true, I suppose," he agreed, feeling sheepish. "But, two nights ago . . . I . . . We . . . "

Sabra placed an understanding hand upon his knee.

"Aurelia and I knew that might happen," she said. "I did not let it concern me then, nor will I let it bother me now. It was a risk I was willing to take because I did not want you endangering your life in an effort to save me. Aurelia and I were supposed to switch places with our father never knowing what we had done."

"Sadly, that's not what happened," Aurelia said dryly. "You ended up having to fight Harmon anyway, despite our efforts to keep you safe."

Gheric looked at both women and gave each a slow nod. "I still don't agree with what happened, but, under the circumstances, I understand."

"I have a question," Sabra said, looking at her twin. "Why didn't you go through with our plan? What did Gheric say to you that made you change your mind?"

Aurelia flashed a quick look at Gheric and licked her lips.

"You have not told her?" the elder sister asked.

"Tell me what?" Sabra asked.

Gheric let out a deep breath. "I have not had the chance," he answered sheepishly. "I'm sorry I didn't tell you earlier, Sabra, but . . . you are with child," he said simply. "We conceived a baby on our first night together. I . . . could not risk our child falling into your father's hands. My words convinced Aurelia not to make the switch."

"I'm pregnant?" Sabra gasped, touching her belly with her right hand.

"I could not let your unborn child be raised in Rathstone with our father," Aurelia added. "I have lived that life. I would not see my niece or nephew grow up as I did. I'm sorry, sister, but I had to consider your baby's life before Gheric's. Win or lose, the child would have stayed here in Caldor, away from the clutches of Malhallow."

Sabra did not speak. Instead, she stood up and wrapped

her arms around Aurelia. "I'm so sorry, sister," she said, with tears in her eyes. "I thought . . . I thought you . . ."

"You thought I would abandon our plan?" Aurelia said archly. "That is understandable, especially because no one could have guessed your condition."

"That was incredibly brave of you," Sabra whispered, holding Aurelia's arms tightly. "Why did you do it?"

Aurelia looked deep into her sister's eyes. Gheric could tell she was fighting back tears of her own.

"The only family I have ever known is my father," she answered. "He was, to say it plainly, a terrible man. You and this unborn child are the only family I have left."

"And Temper, apparently," Gheric chimed in.

"Yes," Aurelia laughed, "and Temper."

She halted her speech a moment before pressing on.

"I . . . I love you, Sabra," Aurelia blurted nervously. "Though we don't know one another well, I will not let anyone stand between us ever again."

Sabra let out a sob of joy, and the two embraced once more.

"Should I leave you two alone for a while?" Gheric offered, causing the sisters to laugh and quit their embrace.

"I'm sorry," Aurelia said, wiping tears from her eyes. "It has been an emotional week."

"What's been so emotional?" Gheric deadpanned. "You tried to kill your sister, then saved her. You lost your sadistic rapist of a cousin to the new baron of Rathstone. Your abusive and repugnant father was slain in battle after sullying the family name, and you had a sexual encounter with the father of your sister's baby. What's there to be emotional about?"

Both Sabra and Aurelia burst out laughing, just now realizing how hazardous their week had been.

"There is still one mystery that I have yet to fathom," Gheric stated, poking a stick at the fire.

"What is that?" Sabra asked.

Gheric threw the stick into the pit. "I spoke with Jorrell after the duel. He told me that you, Aurelia, volunteered to switch places with Sabra *after* Harmon was killed."

"That is true," she answered, her voice tinged with fear.

"Why?" he asked. "Malhallow did not yet know the forces riding toward Caldor were a ruse, and I had already won the duel. Why switch places with Sabra when you did not have to?"

Aurelia looked closely at Sabra and back again at Gheric.

"I told you," she began. "The baby—"

"The baby was fine," Sabra cut in. "Your father was already going to leave me—you—in Caldor to rule."

"No . . . I—" Aurelia tried again, but Gheric cut her off.

"No lies," he said softly. "We are all friends here, bound to one another. Let us have the truth."

Aurelia's shoulders sagged in defeat.

"I knew it was the only way Sabra could heal you," she admitted. "Time was critical. I knew you were near to death. If I hadn't acted then, she would not have been able to save you in time."

"Save him," Sabra quoted, looking sharply at her sister. "That's what you said to me."

"Yes," Aurelia nodded, casting her gaze downward.

"Why would you risk . . ." Sabra began, before the answer dawned on her. "You're in love with him!" she exclaimed. "You've fallen in love with Gheric!"

"No!" Aurelia shouted, her face white with fear.

"You are," Sabra insisted, seeing the truth flash in Aurelia's eyes.

"Are you?" Gheric asked, looking at Aurelia in surprise.

Aurelia's hands began to shake. "Yes," she finally admitted, looking up at them both with tears streaking down her face. "I am sorry to you both . . . to you most of all, sister."

"How did this happen?" Gheric asked, completely stunned.

"It . . . I did not want this," Aurelia confessed, shaking her head. "It just happened, and for the most foolish reason I've ever heard of."

"What was that?" Sabra asked kindly, looking at her twin with empathy.

"It was after Sabra left to go with Harmon," Aurelia explained. "Gheric asked for my council. He wanted to hear my thoughts on what our best course of action was."

She paused, looking at Gheric, a longing in her eyes. "You were so kind to me," she continued. "It is the first time in my life a man asked for my opinion."

"What else?" Sabra asked, suspecting there was more.

"That night," Aurelia continued, "Gheric kissed me, thinking I was you."

Aurelia's face took on a moment of pure happiness. "The way he kissed me . . . I'm sorry, sister, I tried to resist. I wanted to tell him, but . . ."

Again, tears began to streak down her face. "I have known the touch of many men in my life," she explained. "A few were kind and gentle, while others were brutes who cared only about themselves."

She paused, sighing with disappointment. "Most were indifferent toward me. They used me as a broodmare is used in mating season."

Aurelia looked up at Gheric and stretched out her hand toward his face. "But you, you were the first person who ever touched me with true affection. I could feel it, in every breath you took, in every beat of your heart. I have never known such a feeling from any of the men I have been with."

She let her hand fall in front of her.

"I envy you, sister," Aurelia said. "Gheric is the best of men. He loves you more than anyone I have ever known."

Aurelia stood and made to depart.

"I should leave," she said, casting her eyes downward. "I think it best if I give you two some time alone. Thank you for inviting me—"

"So, this is where you got off to," came a voice from the darkness.

"Temper?" Aurelia guessed, peering into the night.

"Yes, child," the old Druid said, coming into the light of the fire.

"What are you doing out here?" Gheric asked, frowning at the man.

"Searching for bluebells," the Druid snapped. "What do you think?"

"Uncle is here to make sure Sabra gets the proper foods she will need since she's feeding for two now," Aurelia explained.

"That's right," Temper snapped, tapping Gheric on the chest with his staff. "So, mind your business and let me do my work."

"I will go," Aurelia said, making to leave once more.

"You'll sit back down and listen," Temper snapped, frowning at the new baroness. "Saves me from having to go over all this again."

"What's he talking about?" Gheric muttered.

"Fah, I didn't get a chance to tell you because you ran off," the Druid groused.

"Tell me what?" Aurelia asked.

"You're with child," Temper announced. "You need to stay and learn everything I'm about to tell your sister."

"*Aurelia's* with child?" Gheric asked, shocked.

"Are you stupid or something?" the old Druid asked, tapping Gheric on the top of the head with his staff. "Yes, Aurelia is going to have a baby."

"But . . . I thought you were barren?" Sabra asked, her voice as shocked as Gheric's.

"I . . . I am," her twin stammered in answer. "At least, I thought I was."

Temper took in the trio with a look of irritation. "I have been delivering children in this village for more than twenty years. I know what to look for, and I know what my magic tells me. You, Aurelia, had an affliction that repressed your reproductive organs. I slipped you that elixir days ago, and it cleared up the problem. You two are going to have babies next summer. I'm assuming the oaf making calf eyes at the both of you is the father."

"What . . . how is that possible?" Gheric stammered.

"By the gods, do you really need me to go over with you?" Temper fumed.

"That's not what I—"

"Here," Temper said, throwing a piece of parchment at Gheric. "I wrote it all down in case you simpletons couldn't remember what I had to tell you. It's clear to me now that you won't. I'll be checking in on you ladies every week. Until then, eat, eat, and eat some more."

Temper stood up and made his way into the darkness of the night. "To think I, Alabaster Hastings, would live to see these young idiots try and . . ."

His voice faded off into the night.

The trio left by the fire stared at one another in wonder.

"It was meant to be," Sabra said, breaking the silence.

"What do you mean?" Aurelia asked.

"The three of us," Sabra explained. "We all needed one another in each other's lives."

"What are you saying?" Gheric asked.

In answer, Sabra took his hand in hers and placed Aurelia's on top of theirs. "I love you both," Sabra said simply. "I want us all to stay together."

"You do?" Aurelia asked, a faint light of hope crossing her face.

"Yes," Sabra answered with a smile. She looked at the handsome warrior next to her. "What about you, Gheric? Are you able to love two women?"

Gheric looked from one to the other and cocked an eyebrow at them both.

"I have a question," he said.

"What's that?" Sabra asked.

Gheric's face broke into a smile.

"Will I be in charge of the sleeping arrangements?"

ABOUT THE AUTHOR

Michael K. Falciani was born in upstate New York. An avid reader, Michael finally turned his hand to writing. On April 22 he published his first book in the fantasy series, The Raven and the Crow. It is titled, Dark Storm Rising and is the first in a planned six book series. Michael currently lives in the southwestern United States. He has currently finished the 2nd book in his series. It is titled, "The Raven and the Crow: The Gray Throne," along with a steampunk epic fantasy that revolves around dwarves called, "The Dwarves of Rahm: Omens of War." Michael continues to write and is working on the 3rd book in his, The Raven and the Crow, series.

Printed in the USA
CPSIA information can be obtained
at www.ICGtesting.com
JSHW010249220324
59633JS00004B/13